HOW TO FALL IN LOVE AT AN ENGAGEMENT PARTY
by Hannah Farley

1) While congratulating the happy couple, notice a surly—but sexy—stranger who has just burst into the party and is causing a scene.

2) Get into a sparring match with Mister Tall, Dark and Gorgeous that makes you hot in more places than just under the collar!

3) Determine to find out just who this hunk is and what he's up to.

4) Uncover some *very* incriminating evidence.

5) Share a slow—and intimate—dance with the stranger that has you hungering for much, much more!

Dear Reader,

LET'S CELEBRATE FIFTEEN YEARS OF
SILHOUETTE DESIRE®...

...with some of your favourite authors and new stars of tomorrow. May's MAN OF THE MONTH is the simply irresistible Ramon Cortero, in an eagerly awaited **Diana Palmer** story, *The Patient Nurse*. Next month's MAN OF THE MONTH title is from Ann Major, so don't miss that, either!

This month also sees the start of an exciting new miniseries ALWAYS A BRIDESMAID!—where five couples say 'I do' with a little help from their friends. The first book is *The Engagement Party* by Barbara Boswell; we're sure you'll love all of them. *The Bridal Shower* by Elizabeth August is in Desire™ next month, and then there's one a month in every other Silhouette® series.

Next, sexy Joe Camden gets a surprise mail-order family in Raye Morgan's fantastic *Wife by Contract*, and then for a really sexy story, meet wild Jed Ryder in *The Midnight Rider Takes a Bride* by Christine Rimmer. And Amy Fetzer brings us her first romance, *Anybody's Dad*; it's a story concerning parenthood—with a twist. Finally, if you're looking for fun and frolics—and a high dose of sensuality—don't miss Patty Salier's latest, *The Honeymoon House*.

Enjoy these celebration books and may we have many more years of happy reading together!

The Editors

BARBARA BOSWELL

The Engagement Party

*Silhouette, Silhouette Desire and Colophon
are registered trademarks of Harlequin Books S.A.,
used under licence.*

*First published in Great Britain 1998
Silhouette Books, Eton House, 18-24 Paradise Road,
Richmond, Surrey TW9 1SR*

© Harlequin Enterprises, B.V. 1995

ISBN 0 373 05932 9

22-9805

*Printed and bound in Great Britain
by Mackays of Chatham PLC, Chatham*

BARBARA BOSWELL

loves writing about families. 'I guess family has been a big influence on my writing,' she says. 'I particularly enjoy writing about how my characters' family relationships affect them.'

When Barbara isn't writing or reading, she's spending time with her *own* family—her husband, three daughters and three cats, whom she concedes are the true bosses of their home! She has lived in Europe, but now makes her home in Pennsylvania. She collects miniatures and holiday ornaments, tries to avoid exercise and has somehow found the time to write over twenty wonderful romance novels.

Other novels by Barbara Boswell

Silhouette Desire®

Rule Breaker
Another Whirlwind Courtship
The Bridal Price
The Baby Track
Licence To Love
Double Trouble
Triple Treat
The Best Revenge
Family Feud
The Wilde Bunch
Who's the Boss?

CAST OF CHARACTERS

The Women:

Hannah Farley: Blue-blooded bad girl.

Emma Wynn: Once burned, twice shy.

Sophie Reynolds: Single mum with secrets.

Lucy Maguire: Not left at the altar for long.

Katie Jones: Always a bridesmaid...

The Men:

Matthew Granger: Stranger in a small town.

Michael Flint: Mr Wrong has never been so right.

Ford Maguire: Lucy's lawman brother falls for a shady lady?

Max Ryder: Mystery man appears in the nick of time.

Luke Cassidy: Single dad makes impassioned plea.

Why is Matthew *really* in Clover? Will Hannah *ever* walk down the aisle? Can Emma forget the man she let get away?

One

─────

"The party is great, Katie. And Abby and Ben look so happy."

Hannah Farley smiled with satisfaction as she gazed at Abby Long and her fiancé, Ben Harper, who were standing in the middle of the large living room of Katie's Clover Street boardinghouse. The newly engaged couple were surrounded by a noisy, laughing group of family and friends who'd gathered for the surprise engagement party.

"I didn't think we'd be able to keep the party a surprise, but we pulled it off, didn't we?" Hannah, a longtime friend of Abby's and one of her bridesmaids, was helping fellow bridesmaid, Katie Jones, replenish the snack dishes on the long, linen-covered table that had been set up to hold the refreshments. "Abby and Ben didn't suspect a thing."

"They both did a credible job of *acting* surprised," Katie said dryly. "But yesterday at the Beauty Boutique, I overheard Jeannie Potts talking about the party to every customer who sat down to be shampooed. You have to assume if Jeannie knew..." Her voice trailed off, and Katie shrugged, not bothering to state the obvious.

"How did Jeannie find out about the party?" demanded Hannah. "It was supposed to be a secret. Who told?"

"Who knows? When it comes to gossip, Jeannie Potts has more sources than any tabloid or wire service."

"You're right. Jeannie doesn't hear things *through* the grapevine. She *is* the grapevine of Clover, South Carolina."

Katie grinned. "So if Abby and Ben didn't know about this party, I'll take a swim in the punch bowl. But who cares if it was a surprise or not? We're all here celebrating their engagement and they really do look happy."

Both the bridesmaids-to-be watched Ben reach over to lovingly tuck a loose strand of hair behind Abby's small diamond-studded ear. Abby smiled at him, her eyes radiating an almost tangible tenderness.

"They're really in love, aren't they?" Hannah sighed wistfully. "I wonder what it feels like. To love someone enough to want to spend your whole life with them."

Katie gave her a measuring look. "*You* don't know?"

Hannah laughed, her slate gray eyes suddenly lighting with humor. "You really are tactful, Katie. And so diplomatic! It's very kind of you not to refer to my three engagements, my three *broken* engagements. My family certainly does often enough. And to answer your question, no, I never have really been in love."

"I guess it wouldn't be tactful or diplomatic of me to ask why you got engaged three times when you weren't in love," Katie murmured. It was a question she never would've asked anyone else, but Hannah was so frank and open it was easy to respond in kind.

"Ah, The Question. Don't think I haven't asked it myself a few thousand times." Hannah tossed her head and her thick, dark hair fell luxuriantly over her shoulders—a feminine, seductive gesture that she'd perfected back in her early teens. Now she was twenty-six, and her practiced gestures had become so natural they were an integral part of the alluring Hannah Farley charm.

"I was eighteen the first time I got engaged," she continued, smiling ruefully in reminiscence. "Some of my sorority sisters were getting pinned to Brent's fraternity brothers, and Brent and I thought it would be cool to get engaged instead. Imagine our shock when his family and mine began making wedding plans! We ended that engagement on a note of mutual panic."

Her smile dimmed a little. "My second fiancé came along the year both of us were graduating from university. Neither of us knew what we wanted to do with our lives. Getting engaged seemed like a good idea at the time."

"Until faced with those wedding plans again?" Katie guessed.

Hannah nodded, growing pensive. "My third engagement was shortly before my grandmother got sick three years ago. You remember, I was living and working in Charleston back then. So was Carter Moore, who was a virtual clone of my brother and brothers-in-law. He convinced me that it would 'serve both our interests to get married.'"

"That's how he proposed?" Katie arched her brows. "Not quite the romantic type, was he?"

"Not quite. Instead of an engagement ring, he presented me with some stock certificates, which he considered far more sensible than a frivolous piece of jewelry." Even three years later, Hannah's gray eyes flashed with indignation at that spectacularly unromantic gesture.

Katie couldn't suppress her amused smile. "And you ended the engagement then and there?"

"I should have, but I didn't. My family was so thrilled with Carter, I sort of felt I owed it to them to make him an official member of the clan. I swear they liked him better than they liked me. When we got engaged, all the Farleys were ecstatic. I'd finally done something that pleased them, something they understood! It was a heady feeling, for a while." Hannah rolled her eyes. "But then my grandmother got sick and nearly died and I moved back here. Carter couldn't understand why I'd give up my job and life in the city to be with what he called 'a dying old woman whose days are numbered anyway.' *That's* when I told Carter to take back his stock certificates, we were history."

Katie winced. "Sounds like you had a lucky escape from Bachelor Number Three, Hannah."

"I agree. And everything worked out for the best. Grandmother recovered, and I have my antique shop here in Clover. I'm very happy," she added resolutely. The firm line of her jaw was set with a determination underestimated by those who saw only her striking beauty. "In fact, I've never been happier. At this point in my life, I'm dedicating myself to buying antiques and collectibles to resell at outrageous prices to tourists and Clover matrons who like to redecorate their houses every other year." Hannah smiled mischievously. "So who needs men? Who needs a social life? We're businesswomen, Katie—the backbone of Clover's economy. Someday we might actually get elected to the *board* of the chamber of commerce and then look out—we'll rule this town!"

Katie laughed along with her. Hannah's exuberance was contagious. "There's just one thing I have to dispute," Katie said, her green eyes twinkling. "Your *alleged* lack of a social life. You haven't spent a Saturday night dateless since you turned thirteen, Hannah."

Hannah didn't deny it. "That doesn't mean I don't find dating an insane concept. I've had some unsuccessful dates—I specialize in them, actually." She cast another glance at Abby and Ben. "And even though I am definitely *not* looking for another fiancé, when I see those two together, I can't help but wish—"

"Hannah!" Tall, lanky Sean Fitzgerald came up behind her. "You're looking beautiful as always. Have I ever told you that you're the unrequited love of my life?"

"You've mentioned it on occasion." Hannah smiled languidly, knowing he was posturing. Sean, whose grandfather had founded the ever-popular Fitzgerald's Bar and Grill on Clover Street, and Hannah had been friends for years. They playfully flirted with each other without a single thought of deepening their relationship.

"And here is the lovely Lady Kate!" Sean turned his megawatt smile on Katie. "Well, the surprise was probably the worst-kept secret in Clover history but this party is terrific. Even the weather cooperated, huh? A beautiful June evening made to order for the happy couple."

He laughed as another violent crack of thunder seemed to shake the house to its very foundation. The summer thunderstorm intensified, and the rain, which had been steadily drizzling all day, suddenly began to teem. The heavy drops pelted the windows so hard, the glass rattled.

"When your conversation sinks to bad jokes about the weather, it's time to move on, Sean." Hannah gave him a friendly shove, her gray eyes gleaming. "Go chase Ben's cousin, the blonde in from Charleston. I saw you drooling over her earlier."

"As always, your wish is my command, Dream Girl." Sean winked at Hannah as he moved toward the perky blonde dressed in pastel pink from head to toe.

"Heaven help the woman who takes Sean seriously. He breaks new ground in superficiality every day," Hannah said wryly as she and Katie watched him approach the giggling pink blonde.

Katie nodded, amused. She agreed with Hannah's assessment, though she never would've voiced it aloud. Hannah had no such inhibitions; she said exactly what she thought. Katie, who was reserved by nature and tended to keep her private thoughts just that, found Hannah's company entertaining, albeit occasionally unnerving.

Undoubtedly the difference in their stations in life affected them as much as their contrasting introvert-extrovert personality types. Though both young people were Clover businesswomen—Katie owning and operating the Clover Street Boardinghouse, Hannah the proprietor of Yesterdays, which featured an eclectic assortment of antiques and collectibles—the two sprang from very different roots.

Katie had been raised by her aunt Peg, the warm, hardworking owner of Peg's Diner, a Clover Street institution, the past and present town hot spot for down-home cooking, people-watching and good-natured gossip. Despite her own busy schedule at the boardinghouse, Katie still helped out her aging aunt at the diner, dividing her time between the two places.

Hannah was the youngest daughter of Clover's old-moneyed, blue-blooded Farley family, who traced their genealogy back to the aristocratic antebellum South. Hannah, a cheerful flirt, lively, laughing and teasing, with a gift for mixing with all types and putting anyone at ease, was an enigma to her very proper relatives. With the exception of her beloved grandmother, who doted on her, the rest of the Farleys were still trying to adjust to having "a shop girl" numbered among their kin. They did not understand or wholly approve of her friendships with "tradespersons" such as Katie and her aunt Peg, the Fitzgeralds and Emma Wynn, who managed the bookstore on Clover Street.

At her own insistence, Hannah was the first and only Farley ever to attend the Clover public schools and the state university, and she'd graduated with a degree in marketing despite her relatives' dire predictions concerning her fate.

Hannah knew nothing would please her family more than for her to marry well, although they lived in horror of yet another disrupted engagement. The thought of a fourth broken engagement alarmed Hannah, as well, one of the very few things she had in common with her kin.

A brilliant bolt of lightning reflected through the rain-streaked windowpanes. It was almost simultaneously accompanied by a boom of thunder. The lights flickered, went out, then almost immediately flashed back on. There were groans and squeals among the party guests, followed by a rowdy burst of cheering when the electricity held its own against the storm.

"Miss Jones!" The voice, deep and peremptory, very annoyed and very male, caused nearly every head to turn to the foot of the stairs, where a very annoyed man stood on the landing, his arms folded across his chest, his dark eyes glowering. He projected the air of an infuriated marine drill sergeant, looking over a group of unsatisfactory recruits, and for a moment, the entire crowd shifted uneasily, as if feeling the apprehension of a hapless young corps.

But the group was too jolly to sustain any mood but a festive one for very long. They quickly resumed their partying, ignoring the imperious intruder. Not Hannah, though. She bristled. The nerve of this stranger. *No one* used that tone with her, nor would she permit her friends to be verbally accosted in such a manner. Why, poor Katie looked positively stricken!

Hannah started toward the stairs, determined to cut the obnoxious intruder down to size. When she was through, he would be miniaturized, so small that the antique dollhouse featured in her shop window would be too big for him.

Her eyes met the stranger's when she was only a few feet away from him.

Hannah stopped cold in her tracks. The man's smoldering dark eyes, so dark they appeared as black as onyx, were making a leisurely perusal, moving over her from head to toe and then back again. Males had been giving Hannah the admiring, assessing once-over since she'd donned her first training bra at age twelve. She knew how to deal with it, knew when to be flattered or insulted, knew how to respond playfully or forbiddingly.

But she wasn't sure how to respond to this man. For after taking careful, minute inventory of her every feature, her every curve, he merely blinked and dispassionately looked away, totally dismissing her.

Hannah followed his gaze, saw those dark eyes of his fix on Katie, who was crossing the room to him, looking worried and nervous and apologetic. Hannah's eyes widened. She silently willed the dark stranger to look over at her. She intended to devastate him with her most sultry stare, then reduce him to a quivering pool of nerves with an ego-shriveling insult.

But the man never looked her way again. She might as well have been invisible. It was as if he was unaware she existed, hadn't seen her at all during those few charged seconds when she'd watched him devour her with his eyes.

"Mr. Granger, is there something wrong?" Katie asked breathlessly.

Hannah was standing near enough to overhear the conversation, and she moved closer, listening shamelessly.

"Yes, Miss Jones, you could say that," Mr. Granger growled. "I want you to come upstairs to my room immediately." He turned and headed up the stairs, not looking back, expecting Katie to follow him without question, without protest.

And she did exactly that! Hannah's jaw dropped as she watched Katie trail after the man, up the steps and away from the party.

"*I want you to come upstairs to my room immediately.*" The deep, commanding voice seemed to echo in Hannah's head while her mind's eye kept flashing his image as visual accompaniment.

She pictured him so clearly he could still be standing in front of her, dressed all in black, his T-shirt, jeans and sneakers nearly the same dark shade as his hair. His complexion was swarthy, his teeth very white. It was as if Dracula had appeared at the summer-night party, a dark, menacing presence among the colorful floral and pastel dresses of the ladies and the light ice-cream suits of the men.

Hannah shivered. She felt edgy. Worst of all, she felt ridiculous! Her imagination, always active—why had she been the only Farley ever to possess one?—had clearly gone into overdrive. Dracula, indeed! The man was obviously a tenant here, seeking out the proprietor, and most rudely, too!

His bare arms flashed to mind, unnerving her further. He was muscular, his forearms covered with a sprinkling of hair, his shoulders broad. His hands were big, his fingers long. He was probably very strong.

Hannah was disconcerted by her detailed observation of the man. After all, she'd only seen him for a few moments. And then he had summoned Katie to his room. The party no longer held Hannah's interest. Impulsively she climbed the stairs to the second floor of the three-storied house, hurrying through the halls, listening.

"...I've been in dumps and dives all over the world, but this place has to be the worst! I have never experienced..."

The irate male voice was coming from the end of the hall, and Hannah rushed into the room. Katie was standing beside the window, looking mortified as the man she called Mr. Granger lambasted the Clover Street Boardinghouse, comparing it unfavorably to accommodations found anywhere in an inner-city slum.

Hannah glanced around and understood why. It looked like it was raining inside the room. Water didn't simply trickle or drip; it was pouring through several places in the ceiling, as if there were shower heads embedded in the roof directing the water down into this bedroom.

"The roof is leaking," Hannah blurted out.

"Did you figure that out all by yourself?" The stranger turned from Katie to Hannah, his dark eyes mocking. "You're a real genius, aren't you, little girl?"

"I am not a *little girl!*" Hannah snapped, instantly incensed. "Of all the sexist remarks to make, that one—"

The man's eyes swept over her. "I was referring to your height. You're short. Little. Can't a man make a truthful observation without being called sexist?"

Hannah was indignant. Her height—or the lack of it—was a sore point with her. She was barely five foot three and considered herself too short. She had never stopped wishing that she were tall and willowy like her two older sisters.

Tonight, the nearly four-inch heels she wore gave her a sense of height and power. "You're not much taller than I am. Does that make you a little boy?" She squared her shoulders and held her head high. Her power shoes did bring her somewhat closer to his height, which was an inch or two under six feet.

"You're on stilts and you're still shorter, honey," he observed ungallantly.

"Mr. Granger, I am sorry." Katie jumped into the decidedly confrontational conversation. "I was aware that the roof had a-a couple of small leaky spots but I didn't realize . . . I never dreamed . . . this has never happened before—"

Granger turned back to Katie. "Look at this!" He had been momentarily diverted, but was not ready to be appeased. With a sweep of his hand, he indicated a stream of water splashing onto a case. "That is my laptop computer. If it hadn't been in its case, it would've been soaked." He picked up the case, moving it out from under the cascade. "Do you have any idea what damage water causes to electronic equipment, Miss Jones? And this—" He pointed to the bed where the indoor deluge was in the process of drenching the pillow. "If I'd been asleep, I would have been shocked awake by a blast of rain on my head!"

"Well, you weren't asleep so you weren't shocked awake by a blast of rain on your head," Hannah said coolly. "And your precious computer was in its case so it wasn't damaged by water. As far as I can see, there's no harm done, certainly nothing to warrant this tantrum you're throwing. What's a little water anyway? Are you a complainer by nature, Mr. Granger? Would you like some cheese to go along with your whine?"

She had the immense satisfaction of watching his face redden. She knew how very much men hated to be accused of whining! It was the antithesis of the ideal of strong, silent male fortitude.

Katie, however, was aghast. "Oh, no, Hannah!" She gripped her throat, gulping for breath. "Mr. Granger has every reason to be infuriated. I agree with him. These conditions are inexcusable and totally unacceptable! Mr. Granger, I hope you'll give the boardinghouse another chance to make this up to you. I'll move you to a new room immediately, and of course, you won't be charged for today or tonight—or—or tomorrow, either. I am so terribly, terribly sorry."

"Katie, there is no need to grovel to this man." Hannah was speaking to Katie, but her eyes were focused on the darkly rugged Mr. Granger. He was staring back at her, his black gaze piercing and intense. "I think he owes *you* an apology," Hannah continued gleefully. "He's behaved rudely, summoning you up here as if he's some sort of feudal lord taking the servant girl to task."

Katie choked. "Mr. Granger," she began placatingly, "please don't—"

"Who is she and why is she here?" Granger asked Katie, his eyes never leaving Hannah. "If she turns out to be the demented co-owner of this place, I'm checking out immediately."

Katie ran her hand through her hair in an agitated manner that left it tousled. "Mr. Granger, this is Hannah Kaye Farley who—who owns a shop here in Clover. Hannah, my guest is Matthew Granger. He checked in this morning. And, Hannah, I would greatly appreciate it if you would go back downstairs and make sure the party is running smoothly while I move Mr. Granger to another room."

Hannah and Matthew Granger continued to stare at each other.

"Since Miss Farley made it a point to stick her elegant little nose into your business, I think it's only fair that she stay and help you make the room switch." Matthew arched his dark brows, his expression challenging. Before either Hannah or Katie could say another word, he dumped the wet case containing the laptop computer into Hannah's arms. "Here, you can carry this."

Hannah was so startled she nearly dropped it. "It's all wet!" She felt the bodice of her silver minidress absorb the moisture and knew it would leave a visible damp spot.

"What's a little water?" Matthew drawled. "Are you a complainer by nature, Miss Farley? Perhaps you'd like some cheese to go with your whine?"

Katie froze, bracing herself for Hannah's response while mentally reviewing the coverage in her insurance policy.

But instead of flinging the laptop to the floor or on Matthew's head, Hannah flashed a sudden smile. "Touché, Mr. Granger."

Matthew was completely disarmed. He studied the sensual perfection of her mouth and had to remind himself to breathe. His heart began to pump faster, making heat surge through him. Her face was exquisite, her complexion smooth and milky white, an intriguing contrast to her raven black hair. Her gray eyes, wide set and framed by dark lashes and brows, shone with intelligence and fire.

He'd been attracted to her the moment he laid eyes on her, when he'd come downstairs to rail at Katie. He'd been *too* attracted to her. Sensing trouble, he'd looked away, not daring even to glance at her one more time.

But it was happening all over again. The darkly gorgeous Hannah Farley had totally unhinged him. This time he couldn't tear his eyes away from her. Her well-shaped, scarlet red lips were made for kissing. For passion. Matthew's body began to tighten with need.

As a man who prided himself on never losing his head over a woman, on always maintaining control over his emotions in his dealings with the opposite sex, he found it more than a little disturbing that she could command his attention so easily and so completely.

Every primitive male instinct within him urged him toward the shapely, petite raven haired beauty in the eye-popping silver minidress and provocative spike-heeled sandals.

It was the sudden splash of cold water on the top of his head—yet another leak!—that jolted him out of the powerful sensual grip she had on him.

Hannah Farley was dangerous, Matthew decided. She used that smile of hers as a weapon. One flash, and bam! The unsuspecting recipient was disoriented, a willing captive to her sultry Southern charms.

Well, not him. Matthew flicked the raindrops from his hair. The smile she'd almost coaxed out of him rapidly turned into a defiant scowl. He was not here to lust after a teasing little flirt who was oh-so-confident of her appeal. He couldn't allow anything or anyone to divert him, even temporarily, from the vital mission that had brought him to Clover.

He suspected that Hannah Farley could be far more than a temporary distraction. Becoming absorbed in her might easily become a full-time preoccupation. Matthew steeled himself against her allure. She was tempting but not irresistible. He could and *would* resist.

"Save it, sweetie," he growled. "What you're selling, I'm not buying."

Hannah heaved an exasperated groan. "Are you one of those vain, tiresome men who thinks that any time a woman smiles at him, she's coming on to him? Well, let me assure you that I am not, Mr. Granger."

Matthew watched the warmth fade from her gray eyes as they narrowed to slits under her dark brows, watched her smile turn into a frown as fierce as his own. He was appalled that he felt regret, that he wanted to recall his insult and make her smile at him again. Her spell was potent indeed!

That feminine power of hers refueled his determination to send her on her way. Safely out of his way. She'd made it plain that she resented male condescension; therefore it became his weapon of choice.

"I guess it's time for me to tell you that you're beautiful when you're angry." He taunted her with his tone, with his expression. "The way you toss your hair, the way your eyes flash—baby, you project the image of glamorous anger as well as any soap-opera queen."

Only his eyes, hot and intent, belied his cocky attitude.

Katie was right there to catch the laptop case before it hit the ground. She had rightly anticipated Hannah's next move. "Hannah, please, the party," she prompted under her breath. "It would be so helpful to me if you would go down and—"

"Throw the unruly mob out into the rain?" Matthew suggested. "I'm surprised none of the other tenants has complained about the noise. When I checked into this place, I thought it would provide the quiet I was seeking. Instead, there is a rowdy party going on downstairs with the Hit Parade from Hell playing in the background. Is this a nightly occurrence, Miss Jones? If so—"

"If you wanted a dark, quiet place, why didn't you check into the city morgue?" Hannah said crossly. "The accommodations there would be ideal for an icy stiff like you."

Matthew actually laughed. "Touché to you, too, Miss Farley."

It was Hannah's turn to be rendered speechless. Matthew Granger was attractive in a severely masculine way when he was angry and upset but he was absolutely charismatic when his dark eyes sparkled with humor and his face was lit with laughter.

Hannah slid a sidelong glance in Katie's direction. If Katie had been equally floored by Matthew's charisma, she was covering her reaction well. Katie appeared more concerned with balancing the dripping-wet computer case than gaping breathlessly at the mercurial Matthew Granger.

Which Hannah found herself doing, much to her own disconcertment. She took inventory of his face—and his body. He was not a classically handsome man but he had interesting features. The sharp blade of a nose and hard slash of a mouth were as compelling as his black eyes, arched by black brows. He was lean and muscular and almost vibrating with a restless energy that she instantly understood because she possessed it herself. A need to make things happen. An edginess combined with a daring need for something that hadn't been found because it had yet to be identified.

"Mr. Granger, if I may, I'll set the computer down here." Katie laid it safely down in a dry spot and wiped her hands on the skirt of her light summer dress. "And I'll get the key to room 206. I'll be back in a minute."

"Don't forget to take your sidekick with you," Matthew called after her, as Katie fled down the hall.

Hannah folded her arms across her chest. She decided then and there not to do anything to accommodate him. If he wanted her gone, she would stay put. "I won't conveniently go away, giving you free rein to bully and disparage poor Katie. She obviously needs your business and you're taking full advantage of that fact."

"What about you?" taunted Matthew. "According to Katie, you're a shop owner. Shouldn't you be patronizing me as a potential customer for your wares—whatever they might be?"

Hannah gave him a dismissive laugh. "I certainly don't need to cultivate the likes of you."

"Because you're a rich girl whose shop is just a diversion until a suitable candidate for your privileged little hand shows up?"

"My shop holds its own, not that it's any business of yours. And I am definitely not in a rush to marry anyone," she added, a little too fervently.

"Why not? Every woman I've ever known has been burning to find a husband and take that long walk down the aisle, all decked out in white lace and sequins."

"Good heavens, what kind of women have you been spending time with?"

"Ones with bad taste in wedding attire?"

"Not to mention bad taste in men, if they're burning to take that long walk down the aisle with *you!*"

He grinned. "I didn't say they all wanted to marry me. I said they all wanted to get married. Just like you do, honey. Let me guess. You want some tall, elegant Southern aristocrat who'll keep you in the grand style you've always been accustomed to. Or maybe a good-looking, fun-loving socialite who glides along on his connections and his boyish charm."

"Been there. Done that." Hannah feigned boredom, but she was far from bored. There was a current of sexual tension sizzling between them, which energized her, challenged her, too.

"So you're a lady with a past? I'm intrigued."

"Don't be. You're not my type."

"You're saying I don't stand a chance with you?" He sounded amused, not insulted.

"Not a chance," Hannah affirmed. She sashayed by him, deeper into the room, taking care to avoid the water dripping steadily from the various leaks in the ceiling.

On top of the bureau lay a big canvas bag, which was half open and crammed full of notebooks, folders and books, both paperback and hardcover. She peered inside, but before she could glimpse any of the titles, Matthew stalked across the room to stand between her and the bureau, blocking both her view and her access to the bag.

"Do you make a habit of barging into people's rooms and snooping through their things?" His tone was light but his dark eyes were hard and forbidding.

"What do you have in there that you don't want me to see?" Hannah asked curiously. When she took a step closer, he sidestepped her, continuing to block her view of the bag and its contents.

"Why do you feel the need to know?" he countered.

"I don't." Hannah shrugged. "But you're awfully defensive about it. Are you one of those creepy perverts who travels with his own personal stash of hard-core pornography?"

"You do have an interesting imagination." Matthew tried but failed to suppress a grin. "But the answer is no. Sorry if I've disappointed you."

Her body reacted to his smile, her heartbeat accelerating as hot little quivers pierced her abdomen. Hannah tried to will them away. "Why are you here in Clover, Mr. Granger?" she demanded sharply.

"I'm a writer." His eyes held hers. "This bag holds research and reference materials. I'm here to... gather information for the book I plan to write."

"I checked room 206 and it's fine." Katie rushed into the room, panting from exertion. "Shall we get you moved in there, Mr. Granger?"

"I would appreciate that. And please call me Matthew." He zipped up his canvas tote and grabbed its straps. "Lead the way, Miss Jones."

"If we've moved to a first-name basis, you must use Katie, please." Katie was relieved that his fury seemed to have abated and that he was willing to be placated. "May I carry something for you, Matthew?"

"The laptop." Matthew pointed, and Katie scooped it up.

"Katie, did you know he's a writer?" Hannah eyed him dubiously. "At least he claims he is. He says he's here to do research for his book."

"A writer here in Clover?" Katie paused at the threshold. "Are you going to write a book about the town?" she asked him eagerly. "I read a wonderful novel about Savannah a few months ago and—"

"I know the book," Matthew cut in. "Mine won't be anything like it. I'm going to describe the insect life of a small Southern coastal town. Clover seemed a likely setting."

"You're writing a book about insects in Clover?" Hannah was incredulous.

"I'm sure it will be very interesting," Katie said diplomatically.

"Will it be like a textbook?" pressed Hannah.

"Like, yes." Matthew's eyes mocked her. "I promise to send you both an autographed copy."

"I don't believe for one minute that you're here to write an insect textbook," Hannah declared boldly. The gleam in his dark eyes was all the proof she needed to know that he was putting them on. Katie was too polite to call him on it, but Hannah had nothing to lose. He wasn't *her* tenant. "And I don't—"

"As long as you're determined to stick around, you may as well make yourself useful, angel face. Take my shirts from the closet and bring them to 206," Matthew directed Hannah.

He didn't wait around to see if she followed his orders. Obviously he expected to be obeyed, just as he had assumed that

Katie would follow him upstairs after he'd issued his earlier command. Matthew strode from the room, Katie at his heels.

"Yes, sir. Whatever you say, sir." Hannah gave a mock salute. The man barked out orders like a general on the battlefield. But it was her curiosity, not any sense of obedience, that drove her to open the closet door.

An assortment of shirts was hung neatly on hangers on the rod, and Hannah draped them over her arm. From the number of them, it appeared that Matthew Granger planned to stick around for a while. There were also two lightweight summer suits hanging there. Hannah decided she could carry them, too.

She felt the hard lump in the inside pocket of the jacket as she added the suits to her load. The same innate curiosity that had prompted her to examine the books inside his canvas bag caused her to investigate the bulge in the pocket.

Hannah's eyes widened in shocked alarm when she pulled out a small, gleamingly polished handgun.

Two

Hannah dropped the gun back into the pocket as if scalded by its touch. Her heart thumped wildly against her ribs. She hadn't believed Matthew's lame assertion about being here to research and write about insect life in Clover, and the sight of this gun confirmed her doubts.

Why would he carry a gun? Was he a police officer? She knew Ford Maguire, sheriff of Clover; just yesterday she'd had coffee with him at the diner, and he hadn't mentioned anything about a new officer coming to town. And it seemed logical that Katie would've mentioned that her new tenant was a cop when she'd introduced him.

Unless Katie didn't know. Perhaps Matthew Granger was doing some sort of undercover investigation that required total secrecy. But what? Clover was not exactly a hotbed of crime. Oh, there were the occasional domestic disputes, petty larceny and disorderly-conduct arrests, but the downtrodden Polk clan usually figured in most of those. Certainly, no secret agent was necessary to deal with the Polks!

That left the other side of the law.

Was Matthew Granger a criminal who'd chosen to hide out here at the boardinghouse? Laying low until the heat is off, as a movie gangster would say. It occurred to Hannah that the only things she knew about gangsters were from the movies because she had never met a bona fide mobster in her life.

But here was Matthew Granger, dressed all in black, projecting an aura of danger, demanding and insolent and *secretive.* He definitely had not wanted her to see what was in that canvas bag of his, although why a criminal would take pains to hide his reading material escaped her. Unless the titles offered some sort of clues or evidence against him? Perhaps the books were simply decoys, hiding the real secrets in the bottom of the crammed satchel? Drugs?

Hannah shivered. What else did racketeers do? Laundering money, bookmaking, loan-sharking. Murder-for-hire? She flinched. She did not want Matthew Granger to be a criminal! A telling insight that unnerved her as much as the possibility that he was one.

Nervously, Hannah hung the suits back in the closet. She didn't want Matthew Granger—if that was his real name—to know that she knew he had a gun. She heard his voice and Katie's outside the room and quickly slammed the closet door.

"I have your shirts," she sang out, hurrying into the hall, where she came face-to-face with Matthew. "They go to 206, right?"

"You have amazing recall, little girl," he growled.

She met his eyes—they were dark and hot and challenging—and a sharp thrill tore through her. What she should be feeling was fear, Hannah admonished herself as she fairly ran down the hall to room 206. *She would not be attracted to a gangster!* Not even Grandmother, the soul of patience and understanding, would condone such lunacy.

She hung his shirts inside the closet in his new room and turned to see the canvas bay lying on the floor beside the bed. A quick peek assured her that there was no one in the hall, so Hannah succumbed to temptation, pulled the zipper half open and reached into the bag.

She examined the hardcover titles first. *Inside the Criminal Mind,* a textbook written by a psychiatrist. Three other books on the personalities of serial killers by three different criminologists. Was Matthew Granger a criminologist or psychologist himself, taking a vacation in Clover? If he was accustomed to the crime-infested urban scene, Clover would be a welcome change of pace for him. Her anxiety began to dissolve; she preferred this new, favorable theory.

She next turned her attention to the paperbacks, which were all bestselling thrillers. Hannah recognized the names of the authors but hadn't read any of the books. She preferred historical novels with plenty of romance. There were none of those in the bag.

Delving deeper, she pulled out a beat-up copy of *The First Families of South Carolina,* a privately published book that also graced the shelves of the Farley family library, although that particular copy was in mint condition. There was a thick piece of folded paper in Matthew's tattered copy, perhaps marking a page?

Hannah turned to it. The heading at the top of the page read "The Wyndhams." That family, who was so important, wealthy and influential within the state that they rated two entire chapters in the book, had a major branch in Clover. The collective Wyndham tribe boasted judges and senators, past and present, along with the usual assortment of attorneys and financiers. All the Wyndhams were well educated and cultured, sophisticated and socially prominent, a credit to their glorious name and history.

Hannah knew them, of course. While the Farley family did not possess the enormous wealth and political power of the Wyndham family, the Farleys were well-bred and well connected and therefore considered worthy to socialize with the grand Wyndhams. Hannah's oldest sister, Sarah, had gone to school with Esme Wyndham Chase; now *their* young daughters were friends.

The closed and clannish upper-class social scene had never appealed to Hannah. She stared at the book and wondered why on earth Matthew Granger was reading about it.

Her eyes flicked over the thrillers and the behavioral studies of real-life criminals. One thing was certain; he had wildly divergent tastes in books. And there wasn't a thing in the bag having to do with insects, either. He had been kidding her and Katie, though he teased so seriously, it was difficult to tell.

And then she saw the map. It had been there all along, although it hadn't registered until right now that the thick folded paper, marking the chapter on the Wyndhams, was a map. She unfolded it. A map of Clover.

Her eyes immediately focused on the red circle drawn near the outskirts of town. Beside it, handwritten in the same red ink were the words "Wyndham estate."

Hannah drew a sharp breath. Why would he mark the Wyndham estate on this map? It wasn't as if it was a tourist attraction! Her imagination began to conjure up yet another scenario, supplanting her comfortable criminologist-on-holiday theory.

What if Matthew Granger was a cat burglar who'd come to Clover to rob the Wyndhams? She had been to the family mansion and knew it was a virtual treasure trove filled with priceless antiques and paintings and objets d'art, which had been collected by generations of Wyndhams. It was an antiques dealer's dream, though Hannah had never, ever approached any Wyndham about selling anything. They would've considered any commercial interest crass and ill-bred, and Hannah knew it.

But suppose Matthew Granger had been hired by some fanatical dealer or collector determined to possess what the Wyndhams would never sell? Or perhaps he was acting on his own, hoping to make a killing in the black market, which thrived on stolen treasures? Every cat burglar she'd ever seen in the movies dressed in black, just like Matthew, the better to sneak around on rooftops in the dark, she presumed.

And then there were the Wyndham jewels, a fabulous collection that had graced the throats and wrists and fingers of generations of Wyndham women. Just last month at a charity ball, Hannah had seen the stunning heirloom emerald necklace and matching earrings worn by the incomparable Alexandra Wyndham, that genteel paragon of beauty and class.

She swallowed. That necklace alone could secure a jewel thief a luxurious retirement—if he could remove it from the Wyndham estate. Was Matthew Granger here to try?

Hannah closed her eyes and tried to still the wild pounding of her heart. What should she do? Alert Sheriff Maguire to warn the Wyndhams? But she had no evidence of any wrongdoing or even potential wrongdoing, only her own anxious speculations. She could almost hear Ford Maguire tell her so. It didn't help that he still thought of her as a flighty little schoolgirl who'd played with his younger sister, Lucy.

Matthew's and Katie's voices sounded in the hall. Hannah glanced down at the map and the book in her hand. She couldn't let him catch her going through his things!

Just as she slipped the map back into the book, she noticed a name written in ink at the bottom of the chapter's opening page. Alexandra Wyndham. Hannah gasped. She'd envisioned Alexandra in her emeralds, and now her name had turned up in Matthew Granger's book. As his primary target? The coincidence was creepy enough to make her hair stand on end!

Matthew and Katie were very near, practically outside the door. Hannah had just enough time to rezip the bag and plop down on the edge of the bed. She crossed her legs, affecting a languorous pose while studying her crimson-painted fingernails.

Matthew's eyes brushed over her, lingering on her lips before lowering to the fullness of her breasts straining against the silver bodice of her dress. Her short shirt had ridden high, exposing her well-shaped silken legs.

Katie glanced uneasily from Hannah's seductive pose to Matthew's fixed stare.

"My nail polish is chipped," Hannah said with a vexed sigh. She hoped she sounded sufficiently insipid, like a self-absorbed idiot who would never bother with a follow-up of that suspicious bag.

Unfortunately, Matthew saw right through her act. "If it really is chipped, which I doubt, you probably did it trying to break into my bag," he drawled.

Hannah's head shot up and she met his cool, assessing gaze. He was carrying his suits, and the sight of the light gray coat— the one with the gun in its pocket—shattered her studied composure. "I did not!" she snapped, automatically hiding her hands with ten unchipped nails behind her back. "I don't care what's in your stupid bag!"

"What do you think, Katie?" Matthew turned to her. "Doth the lady protest too much?"

Katie opened her mouth to speak, then closed it, choosing not to take sides between her paying guest and her fellow bridesmaid.

Hannah recrossed her legs. Matthew was watching her very closely, reading every nuance in her expression, taking in her edgy, agitated behavior. She was not well skilled when it came to deception, Hannah thought glumly. She would make a terrible criminal and an even worse sleuth.

Katie, who had been pulling on Matthew's wheeled suitcase by its strap, hoisted the case onto the bed beside Hannah. "Well, we'll get out of your way and let you get settled here in your new room, Matthew," Katie said heartily. "Thank you so much for your understanding and your cooperation. I hope the rest of your stay in Clover will be—"

"How long do you intend to stay in Clover, Matthew?" Hannah cut in. She forced herself to rise slowly to her feet and then sauntered toward the door, deliberately making her every movement graceful and sensual. Matthew's dark gaze never wavered from her. It was as if she was putting on a performance for a private audience of one man only.

"My stay is open-ended. I'll be here as long as it takes to get the job done."

"The job being your insect research, of course," Hannah baited him.

"Of course." He shot her an arrogant grin, his eyes gleaming with challenge.

He knows I know he's up to no good, Hannah thought, her nerves tingling. She pictured him casing the Wyndham estate. Pulling off the heist. The scene unfolded in her mind like a movie, with a black-clad Matthew Granger playing the lead. Her own role was more nebulous. Was she the gullible girl seduced into thinking the villain was really some sort of redeemable antihero? Or the sharp lady who set the trap and brought the felon to justice?

There was a loud whoop from the party downstairs. Katie, remembering her tenant's expressed irritation over the noise level, caught her lower lip between her teeth and took a bolstering breath. "Matthew, I want to invite you downstairs to join the party. If you're going to be in Clover for a while, you might enjoy meeting some—"

"Why would he need to meet people when he's here to study bugs?" Hannah interjected scornfully.

"We have plenty of food and drinks. Maybe you would like some refreshments, Matthew?" Katie grated through her teeth. It was difficult playing the gracious hostess when Hannah kept lobbing verbal grenades at her guest. "You're very welcome to join us if you wish," she added cordially.

"Thanks for your kind invitation." Matthew's smile was genuine when he addressed Katie, but transformed into a sardonic smirk when he turned to Hannah. "But I'm not feeling particularly social. I'll stay up here and unpack."

"Maybe you'll get lucky and find a spider whose web is chock-full of flies," said Hannah. "That should make an exciting opening chapter for your book."

Katie winced, caught Hannah's arm and firmly hustled her out of the room. "If you should change your mind, please feel free to join us downstairs, Matthew," Katie called over her shoulder. She half dragged Hannah down the hall. "I realize that manhandling a Farley defies social convention, and for that, I apologize," muttered Katie. "But, Hannah, I'm desperate. I couldn't let you start in on him again! Matthew Granger is a paying customer. He could probably sue me for that leaky roof fiasco, and last but far from least, I need his business. I have the roof to repair and plenty of vacancies until next month when I'm finally fully booked for the rest of the summer. Please try not to alienate a dependable source of income for this place."

"Katie, surely you don't believe that ridiculous story about his being here to write about insect life in Clover?"

"I don't know. Maybe he is. I've never seen an—an insectologist, or whatever they're called, have you? Why couldn't he be one?"

"Why would an insectologist have a bag filled with crime books, a map of Clover and a copy of *The First Families of South Carolina?*"

"Oh, Hannah, you did go snooping in his bag!" Katie was aghast.

"I didn't have time to get to his notebooks," Hannah lamented. "Or those files. I wonder what was in them?"

"Hannah, the man is my guest!" Katie cried. "It's bad enough that the first room I put him in was like being lodged under Niagara Falls, but then you insult him and search his things! I wouldn't blame him if he checked out—oh, I hope he won't!"

"Because you consider him a dependable source of income?" Hannah paused on the stairs to scrutinize Katie's flushed face. "Or because you think he's—he's . . ." Her voice trailed off and she actually blushed.

"Oh, yes, he definitely *is,* isn't he?" Katie laughed. An incoherent Hannah was a rare an amusing sight. "And he is obviously attracted to you, Hannah. I thought he was going to pounce when he saw you stretched out on his bed."

"I didn't want him to know that I'd looked into his bag. I was trying to distract him. Do you think it worked?"

"I think the contents of his bag were the last thing on his mind when he was looking at you, Hannah. But if you're so certain he isn't what he says, why is he here? And why the need for subterfuge?"

"I don't know. But I'm going to find out," Hannah asserted resolutely.

"Hannah, from what I've seen of Matthew Granger so far, I wouldn't recommend, uh, getting on his bad side." Katie looked concerned. "We already know he's quick to anger, and he's aggressive and demanding, too. He is *not* the most agreeable guest I've ever had, but with the leaky roof to fix and the sump pump in the basement on the verge of giving out, I can't be choosy. Whoever can pay, stays. But I intend to keep well out of his way, and I'd advise you to do the same."

"Because you think he's dangerous?" Hannah whispered, suddenly breathless.

The reckless glitter in her eyes disturbed Katie. "I don't think he's threatening in a physically harmful way. But I do detect a sense of danger about him, Hannah."

"So do I." Hannah's face was aglow. "He makes me nervous, Katie. Me! That's never happened to me before. When I'm around him, I feel jittery, both afraid and excited at the same time. Does that make any sense?"

"Yes." Katie looked grim. "And those kinds of feelings and the kind of man who inspires them can be very dangerous, Hannah." She had a haunted, faraway look in her eyes. "Emotionally dangerous," she added bleakly.

Hannah stared at her, intrigued. Katie was three years her senior, slender and pretty with long, light brown hair and green eyes. Though she was warm and friendly and smiled often, during unguarded moments—like this one—there was a certain sadness about her. Was it inspired by an emotionally dangerous man?

Hannah remembered that some years ago Katie had seriously dated a man named Luke Cassidy, but he'd left town and never came back. Though Katie had never revealed what happened with Luke, the general consensus in Clover was that she'd had her heart broken. But nobody had any real facts, and Katie's firmly quiet reserve did not invite intimate questions. Not even gossip maven Jeannie Potts dared to pry. This was the most personal conversation Hannah had ever had with Katie and she was tempted to take it further.

But before she could ask any questions about men in general or Luke in particular, Abby Long joined them on the steps. Slightly tipsy, she took Katie and Hannah by their hands. "I was looking for you two," Abby exclaimed effusively. "Ben and Sean want to have a shag dance contest. Katie, do you still have those old records?"

"As if I would ever get rid of such nostalgic treasures!" Katie grinned, her somber mood evaporating. "I have *Carolina Beach Classics*, volumes one and two, and all four volumes of *Shagger's Delight*. Why, those records are icons of the glorious past, handed down to me for safekeeping."

"Maybe I should think about carrying them in my shop, along with the Victorian lady's writing desk and the French Egyptian Empire chest and the Kestner baby dolls," kidded Hannah.

"Katie, go get the records," Abby ordered. "Sean, Tommy Clarke and Zack Abernathy are all demanding to have you as a partner, Hannah. You can either choose one or enter the contest with each guy."

"Suppose I choose none of the above?" Hannah's eyes danced. "I think I'd rather have that adorable hunk, Ben Harper, as my partner in the contest. Do you think his fiancée will mind?"

"That jealous witch?" Abby grinned, playing along with Hannah's joke. "Keep away from her. She'll get revenge by making you wear a hideous bridesmaid's dress, say, something in puce with three hoopskirts and lots of ruffles."

"Anything but that!" Hannah feigned a horrified gasp. "I swear I won't go near the man!"

Laughing, the bride-to-be and her bridesmaids rejoined the party.

It took Matthew less than ten minutes to unpack, then he unzipped his canvas bag and pulled out his copy of *The First Families of South Carolina*. He turned to the index, found the name Farley and smiled slightly. It didn't surprise him that the dark-haired beauty was a member of an affluent, highborn clan. She not only possessed the natural confidence of one blessed by money, brains and looks but also that intangible aura of class and privilege.

But Hannah Farley added sexual magnetism to the package; she had a provocative sparkle that other high-society types he'd met had lacked. That silver dress of hers with its halter top and short, tight skirt and those wickedly high-heeled sandals were unlikely to be seen at any proper country-club affair or society ball.

The jolt of pure desire that hit him caught him off guard, and he had to steel himself against it. He had not come to Clover to have a fling with the sultry little Southern belle with skin as soft and white as the magnolia blossoms that seemed to bloom in every yard in town. He was here to discover who he really was....

Matthew opened the top bureau drawer and removed the framed photograph he'd put there. The photo had been one of his mother's favorites, always displayed on a small mahogany end table in the living room wherever they had lived. It was a five-by-seven color portrait of Galen and Eden Granger and their dark-haired, dark-eyed five-year-old son, Matthew, who gazed solemnly into the camera lens.

He had always been a serious child, intense and focused from an early age, and had grown into a responsible, hardworking student and athlete who'd made his proud parents even prouder. Matthew thought of the milestones—his graduations from high school, college and law school. His father, a camera buff, had been there to photograph the events, his mother smiling adoringly at her son. They had been there for the smaller everyday things, too—school programs, Little League games, helping with homework, a game of catch in the back-yard. No son could have had a more loving, devoted set of parents. Matthew had been the center of their lives, and he knew it.

He had a shelf filled with albums of photos chronicling his life, from the day he'd been carried home from the hospital as a newborn to the family shots beside the gaily decorated Christmas tree snapped six months ago. It was the last Christmas he would ever spend with his mother and father. They had been killed in a car accident just two weeks later.

A spasm of grief, physical in its intensity, radiated through him. He remembered that devastating phone call from Albert Retton, his father's best friend and fellow retired navy captain, the call that had shattered his life. And then the second shock, which had come only days after the funeral...

"You were adopted, Matthew," Al Retton had told him. "Your parents knew you should have been told earlier but they couldn't bring themselves to do it. They wanted you to believe you'd been born to them. I think they came to believe it themselves. But I was instructed to give you this letter if anything ever happened to them."

The letter confirmed the adoption story and reassured Matthew of their great love for him. There were no references to the woman who had given birth to him or the man who'd fathered him, no mention of where he'd come from.

The news sent him reeling. He hadn't had a clue. According to the letter, Galen and Eden had tried for years to have a child of their own before considering adoption. Matthew had been three days old when he'd left the hospital maternity ward with his adoptive parents, who had considered him their own from the moment they'd held him in their arms.

And from that moment on, adoption was never mentioned. Since the family had lived on naval bases all over the world and were without close relatives, the fiction had been easy to maintain.

Matthew placed the picture back in the drawer and reached inside his canvas bag. Inside were paperback editions of the books he'd written—page-turning thrillers with lawyers as the protagonists and the villains. He had used the pseudonym Galen Eden, a combination of his parents' first names, and they had been thrilled with his success. He'd written the first book as a lark in his spare time, because he found the corporate law he was practicing both boring and unfulfilling. When the book turned out to be an unexpected blockbuster with the movie rights optioned, he decided to try again. After all, the first book might've been a fluke. It wasn't. Two bestselling books later, he found himself retired from the corporation to write full-time.

But he hadn't written a word since he'd learned that his whole life had been based on a lie. Six months later, he was still angry, bitter and disconnected, deeply grieving for his late parents yet hungry for the truth about his identity. A rather shady private investigator in Tampa, who demanded an out-rageously expensive per diem, had promised him satisfaction, and finally, weeks later, had delivered his clandestinely obtained original birth certificate.

Carefully, Matthew removed it from the file at the bottom of the canvas bag.

He held it, not needing to read it because he'd studied it so long and so often that he knew it by heart. On the document, his name was listed as Baby Boy. No first name, no surname. Galen and Eden Granger were the ones who had named him Matthew John Granger, which appeared on a subsequent birth certificate, the familiar one he had always believed to be true.

Matthew's eyes lingered on his birth mother's name—Alexandra Wyndham, who had been just sixteen years old when her son was born. His father was listed as Jesse Polk, aged eighteen. There was no other information available. According to the detective, the maternity home for unwed mothers in central Florida where his mother had spent her pregnancy no longer existed.

But just last month, more information had turned up. The P.I. had tracked Alexandra Wyndham's and Jesse Polk's origins to a small, quiet and quaint city in South Carolina, situated very close to the ocean. Clover.

At first, Matthew had been dead set against coming to Clover. He'd tried to convince himself that the information he now possessed, the names of his birth parents, was enough. But the turmoil that had become his life continued unabated.

He couldn't write; his concentration and his imagination seemed to have been suspended. He still lay awake night after night, troubled by grief and anger, grappling with the lifelong deception and all that was unknown to him. When he went to the library to research his latest book, he found himself researching South Carolina. Especially the coastal area. And finally, inevitably, Clover itself.

And so here he was, in the town where two lusty teenagers had taken no precautions and conceived him. He wondered if they were still here, although they certainly were not teenagers now. His mother would be forty-eight, his father, fifty. Still, they seemed startlingly young to him because his adoptive parents had been forty years old when he was born. And adopted.

Matthew stared at the battered copy of *The First Families of South Carolina*. His maternal relations were the upper-class

Wyndhams. Their social position, wealth and prestige had come as a shock to him. Of his father, Jesse Polk, he knew nothing. The Polk family was not in the book, which meant they weren't one of the first families of South Carolina.

But the Farleys were. Matthew turned back to the section on them. They rated only a few pages, as compared to the Wyndhams' two full chapters. Both families had been given royal land grants in the latter half of the seventeenth century, but the Wyndhams, while keeping their land holdings, had soon moved up into the great wealth of the shipping business, with branches of the family based in Charleston. Through the centuries, the Farleys had remained socially prominent and well-to-do while the Wyndhams had achieved superstatus.

And he was part Wyndham. Part of their illustrious history. Matthew closed the book as confusion enveloped him like a heavy cloud. Matthew Wyndham. Matthew Polk. Matthew Granger. Who was he? It was a shattering blow to reach the age of thirty-two, only to find out that the life you'd been living and the identity you claimed as your own was a lie.

The sounds of music and laughter drifted up to his room, breaking the silence that enshrouded him. He was filled with a terrible loneliness. Since his parents' death, he had distanced himself from everybody—his friends, his agent, his editor at the publishing house. His love life had been nonexistent. He had no energy or desire to pursue any of the women who wanted him.

Even before the tragedy, he had always been in control, remaining slightly aloof with his lovers because he wasn't looking for emotional intimacy with all its accompanying entanglements. He'd enjoyed women and sex but steered clear of involvement. That dreaded phrase "serious relationship," when uttered by a dewy-eyed woman, made him want to run in the opposite direction. He'd had his writing, his parents' adoration, his friends and his woman of the moment. Who needed anything more?

Now his life seemed singularly empty, without focus, without love.

"Hannah Kaye Farley, you're not allowed to invent new steps! You have to follow the rules!" A female voice, so loud and shrill that it sounded as if it were in the same room with him, startled him from his gloomy reverie.

Matthew looked around, discerned that the earsplitting voice came from downstairs and felt a flash of sympathy for those in close proximity. It seemed that somebody was scolding Hannah Kaye Farley for breaking the rules.

He smiled grimly. He'd bet that little Miss Farley was a rule breaker extraordinaire whenever it suited her purposes. From their brief acquaintance, he'd pegged her as a headstrong, spoiled beauty who said and did as she pleased. The kind of woman he avoided because he preferred quiet, compliant, worshipful types who let him call all the shots from beginning to end.

But thoughts of Hannah continued to haunt him as he sat on the bed listening to the rain pound on the roof. He had never met a woman who affected him as viscerally as Hannah Kaye Farley. She was vibrant and sexy, provocative and elegant, her face alight with laughter one minute, then stormy with anger the next. It occurred to him that she was the first woman since the accident to capture his interest, to make his body tauten and rise with desire.

He visualized her on his bed, but carried the image a step further, stripping her of that eye-catching silver minidress, picturing her silky, naked body lying open and ready for him. He thought of her mouth, not laughing or pouting, but swollen from his kisses, her gray eyes dreamy with passion.

Matthew stood, sensual heat and urgency coursing through him. Hannah stirred his senses, and while it was a relief to know that he was still a virile, functioning male, an affair with her was out of the question. She was already suspicious of him and with good reason. His imagination must still be in limbo if he couldn't come up with a better cover story than that insect textbook nonsense. Katie was too tactful—and too interested in keeping him as a paying guest—to question the story, but Hannah had no such reticence.

And why should she? As the beautiful daughter of one of the first families in the state, she undoubtedly played by her own set of rules. And he was accustomed to making and breaking his own. An affair with her would be a disaster. She would expect things of him and from him, *demand* them even. The last thing he needed right now was a demanding woman who wouldn't respect his need for boundaries and control.

No, he wasn't willing or ready to get mixed up with the beautiful Miss Farley, however hot and hard she made him. He had to focus all his thoughts and energy on his secret mission, learning as much as he could about his birth parents. Only then could he make an informed, intelligent decision about whether or not to meet them and, possibly, introduce himself to them.

The surge of sexual energy made him restless, eager to turn the pulsating tension into action. Why not begin his investigation tonight?

It was as good a time as any to start, he decided, placing the canvas bag in the closet and pocketing his room key. He had an invitation from Miss Katie Jones herself to join the party of Clover citizens downstairs. He could ask some subtle questions, perhaps pick up some information about Alexandra and Jesse, as he'd come to think of them. Never mother and father. He preferred to view them distantly, like characters in a novel: interesting to contemplate but having nothing to do with him or his life.

He assured himself that the fact that Hannah Kaye Farley was there had nothing at all to do with his decision to join the party.

The music and the laughter grew louder as he walked downstairs. He stood at the threshold of the crowded living room and watched the couples dancing to some old rhythm-and-blues classics. He recognized some of the songs but not the fast, rather intricate dance steps they were doing. Hannah was one of the best dancers, animated and lithe and vibrant as she moved with her partners, and she seemed to have several.

Matthew tried to turn his eyes to others in the crowd. Invariably his gaze returned to Hannah.

"She's a knockout, isn't she?" A smiling blond preppy type joined Matthew and handed him a drink.

Matthew accepted the glass. "Who?" he asked, and the other man laughed.

"Hey, it's nothing to hide. Every guy in town has been slavering over Hannah Farley for years. Unfortunately, she never slavers back. She likes to play things strictly as friends."

"Is that so?" Matthew took a gulp of the drink, which was straight bourbon on ice. The liquid burned a fiery path down his throat and seemed to ignite sparks deep within him.

"I'm Blaine Spencer, a friend of Ben Harper's." The toothsome preppy introduced himself. "And I know you're Matthew Granger. I understand you'll be staying at the boardinghouse while you do some scientific research here in Clover?''

"News travels fast," murmured Matthew. He found his new acquaintance overbearing and presumptuous. *He had not been slavering over Hannah Farley like some slack-jawed dolt!*

"Katie filled me in when she sent this drink over to you," Blaine replied amiably. "She said you seemed more the bourbon on the rocks than the wine-punch type."

"Wine punch?" Matthew grimaced at the concept.

"I believe the ladies are partial to it." Blain winked. "So, Matt, I guess Hannah wins your vote as the best shagger here tonight. Am I right, my friend?''

"I have no idea what you're talking about," Matthew said testily.

Blaine took no offense. "The dance is called the shag. We're in the midst of a highly competitive contest here tonight. My partner and I have already been eliminated. The shag was a classic fixture in the beach towns during the sixties and we like to keep the spirit alive. Every kid in Clover learns the shag and passes the steps along to future generations."

Matthew finished his drink in one gulp. "This is a very strange town."

"We Clover natives like to think of ourselves as colorful. Originals." Blaine grinned, seemingly impervious to insult. "Clover is a timeless place, where the past is intermingled with today and tomorrow will—"

"Are you a real-estate agent?" Matthew demanded. "You might as well save your spiel because I'm not planning on buying any property here."

Blaine laughed. "I'm a dentist, Matt. My office is a few blocks farther down on Clover Street, near the Beauty Boutique."

"I'll keep that in mind if I lose a filling," Matthew muttered. Since his new friend seemed disinclined to leave—had Katie asked him to baby-sit her new tenant?—he decided to use Blaine's affable presence to his own ends. "So you're a Clover native, huh?"

"Born and raised here, like my daddy and his daddy before him," Blaine said proudly.

"I guess you know the, uh—" Matthew paused. His pulses were pounding in his ears, so loudly they almost drowned out the blare of the shag dance tunes. "The Wyndhams." For the first time, he dared to use the name of his birth mother's family—*his* family—in conversation.

"The Wyndhams!" Blaine looked pleased. "Well, I don't know them personally, of course. I mean, I'm not in their social orbit. They're in the stratosphere of society and my family and friends are earthbound, if you get my drift. But occasionally I see members of the Wyndham family when they come into town to shop. Good-looking people. Classy. *Upper* classy."

Mention Alexandra Wyndham, Matthew silently urged himself. *Say her name.* He felt almost sick with anticipation, desperate to hear even the slightest bit of information about the woman who had given birth to him. And had given him up. His mouth was dry. He couldn't get the words out.

"Hannah knows the Wyndhams," Blaine continued. "Her family socializes with them. The Farleys are up there, too, you know."

Matthew scowled at his frustration. He was not here to discuss the Farleys!

"You wouldn't catch the Wyndhams or the Farleys at a party at the Clover Street Boardinghouse. Of course, Hannah is nothing like the rest of the Farleys."

"Because she chooses to socialize with you earthbound peasants?"

Blaine laughed good-naturedly. "Hannah can mix with anyone. Say, would you like me to introduce you to her? She'll probably dance with you if you ask. She's very gracious."

"Just a little Carolina belle brimming with Southern hospitality?" Matthew remembered their contentious meeting upstairs when she'd been far from gracious or hospitable. He watched her now, flirting with every guy at the party, and his face hardened. "I think I'll pass on the privilege of doing the shag with Hannah Farley, but thanks for offering, Biff."

"Blaine."

Matthew took a deep breath. "Whatever."

Three

_____

From the corner of her eye, Hannah watched Matthew Granger talking to Blaine Spencer as the two men stood together watching the dancers. She had known the exact moment that Matthew had set foot in the living room, as if she possessed some kind of psychic radar that attuned her to his presence. She was acutely aware of him every second, knowing when he was watching her—which was almost constantly, except for those moments when he'd turned his eyes on the others.

She'd known the instant he looked at Maureen Fitzgerald, Sean's cousin, a striking, sexy redhead whom Hannah had always liked. Until she'd watched Matthew Granger smile slightly at Maureen. Then she'd felt a disgraceful urge to dunk the other woman's head in the punch bowl!

Hannah continued to dance and laugh and flirt, her nerves tingly and taut. She realized that she was overdoing it; her dancing, her flirting, her laughter had an almost desperate edge.

Matthew disapproved of her behavior, Hannah was certain of that. Cold fire burned in his onyx eyes. She pretended to ignore him, taking care not to glance in his direction except very covertly. He would never know that she had seen his every move, gauged his every response. His reaction to the compulsively genial Blaine Spencer almost made her laugh out loud. Matthew stood there, dark and surly and brooding, while Blaine nattered on, his smile never wavering.

"I think it's time to announce the winners of the contest," Katie said, lifting the needle from the record player, thus ending the music. "The best shaggers in Clover are—"

"Abby Long and Ben Harper, of course," Hannah cried, grabbing Abby's left arm and Ben's right and holding them high in the air.

Everybody clapped and cheered.

"Well, hey, if you can't win the shag contest at your own engagement party, when can you?" Blaine exclaimed happily.

He turned to Matthew, who was surveying the scene, his arms folded across his chest, the only person in the room who wasn't clapping or laughing or even smiling.

"It was generous of Hannah to name Abby and Ben the winners," Blaine murmured confidentially to Matthew. "Of course, we all know Hannah is really the best dancer of them all."

"So does she," Matthew growled. "She is fully aware that she is the most fascinating woman in this room."

Blaine raised his brows but made no comment.

"As the official contest winners, we'd like our prize to be a slow dance," Ben announced, pulling Abby close.

"Aren't you even going to wait for the music?" Hannah teased.

Matthew glowered. The little flirt was irrepressible. She was even batting those long lashes at the prospective groom! And if the pretty bride-to-be didn't seem to mind, well, Matthew minded for her!

"Hannah!" Blaine called and waved. "Come over here. There's someone I'd like you to meet. A newcomer to our fair city."

Blaine kept waving and calling and would not be ignored. Reluctantly, Hannah responded to the summons and joined him and Matthew, who had retreated to a dark corner of the living room. In his black clothes, he blended into the dim recess like some kind of otherworldly shadow prince. Or perhaps a gun-toting cat burglar who read about serial killers for entertainment.

To Matthew and Hannah's mutual dismay, Blaine proceeded to introduce them to each other.

"I hope I'm not telling tales out of school but Matt was riveted by your shagging talent, Hannah," Blaine exclaimed merrily. "You didn't learn to dance that way at Miss Perkins's ballroom dancing cotillion classes, did you?" he teased.

Hannah smiled weakly. Matthew scowled.

"Now I'm going to make a suggestion." Blaine forged ahead, clearly enjoying his role as matchmaker. "Hannah, why don't you do Matt the honor of welcoming him to Clover with a dance?"

At that moment, music sounded through the speakers, this time a romantic ballad, another classic from an earlier era. Couples began to pair up. Abby and Ben were already clinging and swaying in the middle of the floor.

Hannah and Matthew stood facing each other.

"Go on, you two, dance with each other! Don't be shy!" Blaine insisted jovially.

Matthew caught Hannah's hand. "Let's get this over with." He pulled her against him, close, very close.

Too close. Hannah gasped as he fastened his arms around her, linking them tightly around her waist. She had no choice but to raise her arms and rest them on his shoulders. "You're holding me too tight!" she grated.

"You mean this isn't the way you learned to dance at Miss Pennypacker's Ballroom Academy for Proper Young Ladies and Gentlemen?" He didn't loosen his hold.

Hannah's lips curved into a reluctant smile. "No, we didn't dance like this in Miss *Perkins's* cotillion classes. Poor old Miss Perkins would've burst an aneurysm."

Matthew made no response. He was not in the mood for light banter.

Hannah gulped, her every nerve wired and tingling with sensual electricity. She hadn't felt this nervous slow dancing with a male since her days at Miss Perkins's cotillion classes. And not even then, not really. Even as a young girl, she had been socially confident, self-assured in her dealings with the opposite sex.

But being in Matthew Granger's arms, pressed tightly against his hard body evoked a vulnerability she never dreamed she possessed. She felt intensely feminine in contrast to his unyielding masculinity. She was aware of his superior male strength in a way she'd never been before.

She had never met a man she couldn't manage; she could charm, cajole, guide or boss every male she'd ever known. But she wasn't sure how well she'd be able to handle Matthew Granger. He seemed to be the one doing all the handling—of her!

"Relax," he growled against her ear. "You're wound tight as a spring."

"That's because you're holding me so close you're practically suffocating me." Hannah was flushed and breathless and resented him for it.

He was so close that his heartbeat seemed to echo in her own chest. Against the burgeoning pressure of his thighs, her legs felt supple and boneless, her knees weakening so quickly she wondered if they would support her. Her breasts swelled and her nipples hardened into taut buds. They were excruciatingly sensitive and she knew a wild, wanton urge to rub them against the muscular wall of his chest to seek relief. And to heighten the stimulation.

She could feel his breath against her hair, his big hands moving slowly over her back. His touch was strong and possessive. Her skin felt damp and feverish, and she knew that the warm June night and energetic bout of shagging had nothing to do with it.

Every erogenous zone in her body was on full alert and conspiring against her. As much as she'd protested his too close, too tight hold, she knew that the real problem was that he wasn't close enough.

Her thoughts disturbed her. She drew back her head and lifted her eyes to his. "I don't want to dance anymore," she said in a low, husky voice she scarcely recognized as her own.

"Tough." He held her gaze. "If I don't dance with you, Dr. Smiley will take it upon himself to make me feel welcome again. I can't cope with any more of his unrelenting good cheer. Even your brattiness is preferable to *that*."

In the shadowy dimness, she could see the amused gleam in his dark eyes. Hannah was totally disarmed. In her sexually charged panic, the last thing she'd expected from him was humor.

Of its own volition, her body suddenly relaxed, the tautness draining from her muscles, leaving her soft and pliable. She melted against him, her soft curves flowing seamlessly into the hard, masculine planes of his body. A giddy excitement coursed through her, making her feel daring and reckless. She wanted to tease him, to bait him. To challenge him and win.

"I was a little surprised to see you deeply engrossed in conversation with Blaine." Hannah gazed up at him from under her lashes in tried-and-true vamp style. "You two are an unlikely duo. It was kind of like watching Barney, the jolly purple dinosaur, trying to befriend a carnivorous raptor."

"Is that how you see me? As a ferocious predator?" Matthew smiled, his even white teeth appearing even whiter in the darkness. "Are you afraid of me, little girl?" He lowered his head and took her earlobe between his teeth, biting gently.

Hannah trembled. But not with fear. Excitement ricocheted through her like a piercing bullet. But she tried to halt it, or at least tame it. "Stop calling me little girl," she ordered firmly, seeking the upper hand. "My name is Hannah, although you seem to have trouble remembering it. In the short time we've known each other, you've called me everything *but* my name."

"You don't fit my idea of a Hannah." He was nuzzling her neck now while rubbing his body against hers, his movements slow and subtle and arousing. "I picture a Hannah out on the prairie in her sturdy pioneer clothes, weaving cloth and drawing water from the well and hitching the oxen to the plow. A hardy frontier type."

"My parents thought Biblical names would be proper and appropriate for us," Hannah murmured. "My older sisters are Sarah and Deborah and my brother—"

"Must be Noah?" The tip of his tongue tickled the sensitive skin of her throat.

Hannah shifted against him. "Actually he's Baylor Carleton Farley IV. When it came to their son, Farley tradition was considered even more proper and appropriate than the Bible."

Her head was spinning. His lips felt cool and firm yet soft against her skin. How would they feel against her mouth? Her eyes drifted shut and she stifled a moan.

"Your name should conjure up an image that is sensuous and exotic," Matthew said huskily. "Beautiful, like you are." His caresses were growing bolder. One big hand slid down to audaciously knead the curve of her thigh. The other slipped under the thick curtain of her hair to curl around the nape of her neck. "If you were my creation, I'd call you Vanessa or Jacqueline, maybe Juliet or—"

"What about Alexandra?" Hannah blurted out.

Matthew went still. Then his fingers sank into her hair and he grasped a handful to pull her head back, forcing her to meet his gaze. He was not gentle. Hannah felt the pressure on the roots of her hair, but even more alarming was the hard, angry glitter in his onyx eyes. "What game to you think you're playing, little girl?"

Hannah berated herself as a prattling fool. The name had just slipped out in an unguarded moment, and no wonder. She was still burning with curiosity about why Alexandra Wyndham's name happened to be written in Matthew's copy of *The First Families of South Carolina*. During the shag contest, she'd moved as if on automatic pilot, her footwork independent of her mind, which was focused on Matthew Granger and his probable reason for being in Clover. Alexandra's name seemed to be a major clue.

Hannah stared at Matthew, wide-eyed.

Had she given herself away? Did he now know for sure that she'd been snooping in his things? If he was here for nefarious purposes, he wouldn't want anyone armed with evidence against him. Would he consider her decidedly sketchy knowledge to be evidence? Her pulse raced into overdrive.

"I want an answer from you," Matthew demanded, tightening his grip.

Hannah was alarmed, but she'd never been a meekly passive type who allowed anyone to bully her. She wasn't about to turn into one now, either, not even with Matthew the Possible Mobster holding her by the hair.

"You're the one playing games," she said with a bravado she was far from feeling. "Consigning my perfectly respectable name to pioneer drudgery and renaming me Jacqueline or Vanessa. Well, I happen to have an opinion in the matter, too, and if I were to be renamed, I'm partial to the name Alexandra."

She decided she might as well go for broke. To pretend that she knew nothing of his aspirations concerning the Wyndham estate by initiating the subject of the Wyndhams herself. It was a form of reverse psychology, and at this point she had nothing to lose.

"Alexandra is the name of one of the most attractive, elegant women in town. I think the name exudes class and style, just like she does." Was this working? Hannah wondered nervously. Or was he planning where to stash her body before he pulled the heist. "I think Alexandra Wyndham must be close to fifty years old but she looks years younger," she chatted on. "She has dark hair, and not even Jeannie Potts knows if she dyes it, but she must at her age, right? And of course, she has the Wyndham blue eyes. All the Wyndhams have these deep, vivid blue eyes. I don't think there's every been a brown-eyed Wyndham."

Her words swirled around Matthew's head. She was talking about his mother! A maelstrom of emotion surged through him. His body was already charged and throbbing with unslaked desire for this maddening, enticing woman he held so close, and the unexpected information about the stranger who'd given birth to him unleashed the tight reins of his control. Talking wasn't enough for him. He had to act.

Hannah felt like a wind-up toy that had just wound down. "Well, I guess we've exhausted that subject, haven't we?" She managed a shaky smile.

Her faced burned under his steady stare, and his silence daunted her more than any threats he might have made. She saw sexual intent and something else, something she couldn't identify, flaming in his eyes.

Still holding her hair, he suddenly, firmly, cupped her chin with his other hand and took her mouth with his.

It was a rough, wild kiss, his lips demanding, his tongue rapacious as it invaded her mouth, taking possession. Hannah was too shocked to protest, and then it was too late. She didn't want to protest.

A hot swell of excitement crashed through her, and she trembled from the force of the fast-building urgency. She was only vaguely aware that Matthew's arms folded her deeply in his embrace, that her own arms had wound around his neck as her body surged against his.

The kiss deepened and grew more intimate, more insistent. Pure raw pleasure flooded her. Her senses were filled with Matthew, with the feel and the scent and the taste of him. His hands stroked and caressed, learning the soft, warm curves of her body, smoothing over her back and then gliding around her ribs, where his fingers stopped maddeningly, tantalizingly just below the underside of her aching breasts.

Hannah's mind clouded. The music and the voices of the party guests receded into the hazy distance. She was aware only of Matthew and the strong mastery of his hands and his lips, of the intoxicating combination of hunger and pleasure he evoked in her.

Lost in this delicious world of sensation, she obeyed all the sensuous, unspoken commands. When he finally lifted his mouth from hers to kiss the slender white curve of her neck, she tilted her head to give him greater access. As his hands slid slowly, seductively, over her hips to cup her bottom and lift her higher and harder against him, she settled herself, snuggling into the cradle of his thighs. She wanted to be as close as a woman could be to a man. To have him full and hard, deep inside her.

"Hannah!" he groaned. Suddenly it struck him as having all the sexy, exotic appeal of Vanessa or Jacqueline because it was *her* name.

He opened his mouth over hers again, luring her tongue into an erotic little duel. His whole body was taut and hard with a wild urgency, the force of which he had never before experienced. When was the last time that a flash of sparkling eyes had sent him reeling? When was the last time that a woman's kiss had shattered his iron control?

Never. This was the first time.

The raging need she evoked drove him higher. Her spicy feminine scent drugged him, and the feel of her rounded softness yielding to his frame obliterated all thought but one. To take her. To make her his own.

Hannah felt that virile power within him and sensed that his control was tentative at best. As was her own. She was dizzy with excitement, drunk on a passion she had never before experienced. She ached, she wanted . . .

"Wow! When it comes to *amour,* those two make our guests of honor look like chaste kissin' cousins!" The loud, rather drunken male voice was followed by some wolf whistles and clapping. It was a shocking intrusion into the private, passionate world where Hannah and Matthew had retreated. Confused, slightly disoriented, they broke apart to find themselves in the spotlight. Literally. Sean Fitzgerald was shining a flashlight on them as he kept up a running commentary. "Say, Abby and Ben, you ought to watch these two and take notes. You might pick up some useful tips for the honeymoon."

The crowd was laughing. Matthew blinked at the light. He draped his arm around Hannah's waist and gazed down at her. She looked irresistibly sexy, her cheeks flushed, her raven hair tousled, her lips softly swollen from his kisses.

She also looked mortified, her big gray eyes stricken. Matthew felt possessive and protective and positively enraged that the grinning jokester was embarrassing her.

He lunged toward Sean and snatched the flashlight from his hand. "Unless you want this shoved down your throat, you'll shut up right now, buddy." His tone, as fierce and savage as his expression, left no doubt that he would be only too willing to carry out the threat.

The laughter, whistles and cheers died at once. Sean retreated a few steps. "There's no need to get all bent out of shape," he muttered sulkily. "I was only kidding."

"Well, I'm not." Matthew's eyes glowed like burning black coals. "Leave us alone."

An uneasy silence descended over the room. Nobody moved. Everyone waited to see if Sean would challenge Matthew's ultimatum. Matthew stood glowering, his hand clamped on Hannah's waist, anchoring her to him, his body coiled tight with tension.

Hannah stole a glance at him. He looked like a wild panther, poised to strike. She shivered. Or maybe a wild cat burglar, quite capable of violence if he felt the need to indulge.

Sean shrank back, unwilling to brave Matthew's wrath. "Okay, okay." He turned and walked away, his face sullen. "Jeez, some people have no sense of humor."

Hannah felt a pang of sympathy for her old friend. She watched a few of the other guys cast covert glances at Matthew and then walk over to Sean, presumably to commiserate with him. None dared to approach Matthew. And no wonder! He looked too dark and forbidding for any rational person to tangle with. Except she was not feeling particularly rational right now. Frustrated passion coursed through her, transforming itself into furious anger.

"There was no reason for you to—to bully poor Sean!" Hannah ranted at Matthew.

"*Poor Sean* is a rude, immature jerk who deserved it," Matthew growled. He glanced down at the flashlight in his hand. "I think I let him off lightly. Maybe too lightly."

"Oh, really? You don't think that humiliating him in front of all his friends is a suitable penalty for daring to disrespect the almighty Matthew Granger? Maybe you think he should be put up before a firing squad and—" She thought of the gun upstairs in his room and broke off in midsentence. While she'd been exaggerating for dramatic effect, suppose Matthew Granger took it as a valid suggestion?

I do not belong with this man! she reminded herself. She tried to pry herself loose from Matthew's inexorable grip. He merely tightened his fingers on her waist.

"I was furious because that idiot humiliated *you*." Matthew said through clenched teeth. "You're a lady. You don't deserve that kind of disparagement. I won't put up with it."

"You were being noble?" Hannah was scornful. She refused to be mollified. "I suppose you didn't care at all that Sean was shining that flashlight on *you* and—"

"No, I didn't mind for me. And if you were some cheap, sleazy little tramp, I wouldn't have minded for you, either. I'd have joined in the ribaldry and made some jokes of my own."

Blaine Spencer joined them at that moment, his perennial smile dimmed but not eliminated. "As the matchmaker who got you two together, I feel a certain responsibility for what happened," he said earnestly. "Matt, I hope you'll see fit to forgive Sean. He sometimes get carried away with his pranks and doesn't realize when he's being truly offensive."

"Why are you apologizing for Sean?" Hannah was annoyed by the inexplicable code of machismo. If she was willing to shrug off the embarrassing moment, why must they enshrine it? "The whole incident has been blown way out of proportion. Sean was just being Sean," she added, frowning her impatience.

"No, Hannah." Blaine shook his head. "Sean crossed the line by making you the butt of his joke. I mean, it's not like you're one of the Polks. When it comes to women like that, yes, sexual innuendos and gibes are accepted—even expected."

"I don't think *any* woman deserves to be the butt of sexual innuendos and gibes," scolded Hannah. "You can't excuse it for one woman and approve it for another."

"Hannah, if your family knew you'd taken to defending the Polks, they'd have a collective anxiety attack," Blaine teased playfully.

Others crowded around. Natural curiosity was running high about the newcomer who'd been passionately kissing Hannah Farley and then threatened Sean Fitzgerald. Seeing Blaine Spencer dare to approach the stranger and survive unscathed encouraged other party guests to come forward.

"Who are the Polks?" asked Matthew.

There was a collective roar of laughter.

"Did I say something funny?" Matthew demanded. He was tense and unsmiling. The laughter subsided at once.

"Hmm, how does one describe the Polks?" Blaine pondered the question. "Well, I suppose every town has its own notorious clan of degenerates. In Clover, it happens to be the Polks."

"The Polks are the stereotypical lowlife family-from-the-wrong-side-of-the-tracks," Tommy Clarke exclaimed. "And they actually do live down by the tracks in their ramshackle housing. They're a blight on the town."

Maureen Fitzgerald grinned at Matthew, clearly holding no grudge on her cousin's behalf. "There are so many good things about Clover, don't sour our new visitor on the place by telling them about our town pariahs."

"The Polks are the town pariahs?" Matthew exhaled heavily.

"My family owns the bar and grill here on Clover Street," Maureen continued. "We regularly evict Polks. They're forever getting drunk out of their limited minds and fighting with anyone over anything. My dad and uncles have banned some of the Polks for life from our place. One of these days, they'll all be banned."

"I will never forget when Jonas Polk stole the poor box at St. John's Church," Abby said, frowning her disapproval. "You can't get much lower than that."

"Remember when some of those Polk kids were going up and down the street with cans, pretending they were collecting money for a child in the hospital who needed a heart transplant?" Ben shook his head. "It was all a scam. There wasn't a child who needed a transplant. Those brats just wanted some video-game money. Ford Maguire took them down to the station and read them the riot act!"

"Not that it did much good." Blaine was no longer smiling. "Shortly after that, a gang of young Polks crashed the Strawberry Festival and stole all the strawberries. We've had to hire an off-duty policeman to guard the berries and ice cream every year since.'' He brightened. ''And speaking of the Strawberry Festival, I want to make a pitch for everybody to come. My mother is chairwoman this year.''

''We wouldn't miss it,'' someone assured him, and the talk turned to Clover's traditional June fest.

Matthew didn't join in. He stood stock-still, too stunned by the revelations he'd just heard to move or speak or even breathe. Was Jesse Polk, the man who'd fathered him, one of *those* Polks who were so heartily despised by all? And with good reason, it appeared. The town pariahs. Notorious degenerates. An ornery gang of drunks and thieves reviled by the good citizens of Clover.

Those people were his relatives? He thought of his adoptive mother and father. They were honest and honorable, well respected and loved by everyone who knew them. As their son, he'd been taught their values. His character and his success had been the result of being raised by them. What if he'd been brought up a Polk? Would he have grown up learning how to rip off churches or con generous people into making donations to a phony cause and God only knows what else?

It didn't seem possible that the daughter of the exalted Wyndham family could possibly have had a teenage affair with a Polk, son of the town's lowest clan. Yet here he stood, the living, breathing proof of such a mix.

He glanced down at Hannah to see that she was staring up at him, her expression curious.

''Are you okay?'' she asked. ''You look . . . strange.''

Matthew frowned. She was too observant, too perceptive. Nobody else at the party had taken note of his reaction. They were all laughing and talking among themselves, reminiscing about past Strawberry Festivals, their discussion of the Polks finished, their interest in Matthew Granger fading, as well.

He supposed he did look strange. How could he not? Learning that his paternal relatives were the untouchables in the Clover caste system had been as shocking as finding out that his maternal side ranked high among the elite. A Wyndham and a Polk. Alexandra and Jesse. It was almost a cliché—the rich girl and the bad boy who seduced her. Or was it the other way around, the rebellious young princess slumming with the town outcast?

Whatever the circumstances, *he* was the result, and his birth was far from the idyllic story he'd been told by the Grangers. The knowledge was still new enough to hurt.

"In fact, you look almost catatonic." Hannah surveyed him critically. "I know you have no interest in hearing about the Strawberry Festival, but couldn't you fake a smile and try to look alert, strictly for politeness' sake?"

She'd given him a viable out. Matthew took it. "I'm bored, and I don't believe in faking smiles."

"I guess small-town life must seem tedious to an ultracool, big-city dweller like yourself."

"Is that what you think I am? An ultracool, big-city dweller?"

She nodded. "You have that urban edge about you. That *northern* urban edge."

"Coming from a member of the plantation set, I don't think that's a compliment."

Hannah didn't reply. She was trying to launch another war of words between them but she was having trouble working up the necessary hostility. She was too intensely aware of his nearness, of the strength of his hard body touching hers, of his fingers idly caressing the hollow of her waist. Memories of those hot kisses they'd shared assailed her, and she felt conflicting urges to run away from him and to slip back into his arms.

"I'm ready to leave," Matthew announced. "Do you want to come with me?"

"And go where?"

"I don't know." He shrugged. "My car is parked out back. We could drive around and you could point out all of Clover's landmarks."

"Go sight-seeing?" She arched her dark brows. "At night, in the dark, in the middle of a raging thunderstorm?"

"I take it that means no. Then how about coming upstairs to my room with me? Actually that was my first choice all along but I didn't think you'd go for it, so I came up with the sight-seeing trip."

He spread his hand over the curve of her hip, his fingers making a wide span. He began a slow, sensuous massage.

The sparks kindling inside her roared to full flame. Her belly burned with a pulsating warmth that flared deep in the hot, secret core of her. Hannah gulped, her mouth dry. Had Sean or

Tommy or any other man in the room issued such an invitation, she would've responded with either a quip or a jeer, but both would've resulted in an easy instant rejection.

But Matthew Granger had ignited a conflagration of desire that severely tested her resolve. His taste still lingered on her lips and tongue and she could still feel the hard imprint of his body locked against hers. Just thinking about being in his arms made her feel weak and soft and filled with yearning. She wanted to go upstairs to his room. She wanted more of the heady passion he so effortlessly evoked in her.

Hannah was furious, with herself and with him. She broke away, her skin tingling from his wicked, tempting touch. "You were right the first time. I will not go to your room with you!"

Matthew shrugged lazily. "Not tonight, anyway."

"Not any night!"

He laughed, a husky, sexy sound that sent shivers of excitement chasing along her spine. "Sure you will, sweetheart."

"Hannah," she corrected tersely. "And I have no intention of going to bed with you!"

He shrugged, not at all put off by her ire. "You know what they say about intentions. The road to hell is paved with them."

"And you're certainly a regular traveler on that road, aren't you?" She caught herself before she revealed any more knowledge of his felonious intentions.

She could not trust Matthew, Hannah reminded herself sternly. And though the chemistry between them was potent and exciting, she would have to be crazy to suspend all moral judgment and common sense to get involved with him.

She was not crazy.

Hannah glanced at her watch, a jeweled antique that her grandmother had worn as a girl. "It's time I left. I'm going to say my goodbyes to Katie, Abby and Ben." She walked briskly away, her head held high.

Matthew didn't follow her, but she felt his eyes on her as she flirted her way across the room to bid goodbye to the happy couple.

She found Katie in the small boardinghouse kitchen, filling the coffeemaker with the required amount of water and coffee beans. "Katie, be careful of Matthew Granger." Hannah felt obliged to issue the warning, even though she felt certain Katie wasn't personally at risk.

Katie smiled wryly. "I distinctly remember saying something along those lines to *you* a short while ago. But you seem to be getting along with him very well indeed."

Hannah blushed, remembering how she'd been caught in the spotlight, kissing and clinging to the man. "Th-that was just a momentary lapse. It won't happen again," she vowed.

Katie nodded benignly.

Hannah started out of the kitchen, then rushed back in to whisper, "Katie, if he asks questions about the Wyndhams, don't tell him anything."

"I don't have anything to tell, other than the basic facts known by everybody in Clover. I don't know the Wyndhams," Katie reminded her.

"But *I* do!" Hannah nervously balled her fingers into fists. An awful thought struck. "Do you suppose that's why he—" She blushed to the roots of her hair. "Do you think he's going to try to use *me* to get information about them?"

Katie cleared her throat. "Well, hello there, Matthew!" Her voice grew louder, warning Hannah of his presence. "The coffee will be ready shortly. Would you like a cup?"

"No, thanks." Matthew took Hannah's arm. "I'm seeing the lady home. Ready to go, honey?"

"You—you're not going home with me!" Hannah's voice rose to a squeak. "My parents and my grandmother will still be awake and they'll—"

"You live with your parents and your grandmother?" Matthew was incredulous. "At your age?"

"Age has nothing to do with it." She tried to pull away from him, but he didn't release her. No one had ever been so physical with her, holding her tightly, not letting her go, keeping her in his grasp until she didn't want him to let her go.

"Doesn't it?" His fingers began to lazily caress the soft inner skin of her arm.

"No, it doesn't." Hannah reminded herself to breathe. "My brother is still living at home and he's two years older than I am. Why pay rent for some cramped apartment when there's plenty of room at home?"

It was the same argument her parents gave her whenever she proposed moving out and into a place of her own. They also used her grandmother's presence as a way to emotionally blackmail her into staying. To them, renting an apartment in Charleston was acceptable, but to rent in Clover was disgracefully un-Farley-like. Hannah did not share their views, but she wasn't about to air the Farley familial disagreements, especially not to Matthew Granger.

"Well, I suppose it's perfectly understandable to live at home when home is a mansion," Matthew said, mocking her.

"It's not actually a mansion," Hannah hastened to assure him. Were his cat-burglar instincts on red alert? Suppose he decided to add the Farley house to his wish list? "It's, uh, just an old house. Nothing terribly impressive. I really don't understand why my folks insisted on having two security systems installed. Of course, the Wyndham place is probably armed like a fortress," she added nervously.

It was downright alarming the way Matthew listened so intently when the name Wyndham was mentioned. Perhaps if she were to pass along enough discouraging tips about the estate, he would give up his plans to break into it.

"Katie, didn't we hear that the Wyndhams had some killer guard dogs running around loose on the grounds of the estate?" Hannah had heard no such thing but hoped that the self-preserving instincts of a cat burglar would prevent him from risking an encounter with a pack of homicidal dogs.

"Did we hear that?" Katie murmured blandly. She hid a smile. "Will you two excuse me? I'm going into the other room to ask who wants coffee." She made a hasty exit, leaving the couple alone.

Matthew slid his hand down the length of Hannah's arm, then interlaced his fingers with hers. "Since you aren't allowed to have company at home after midnight, I guess I'll have to settle for walking you to your car," he said smoothly. "Where are you parked?"

"Two blocks over." Her voice caught in her throat. He was drawing slow concentric circles on her palm with his thumb. "W-we didn't want Ben and Abby to see our cars and spoil the surprise. It—it wasn't raining quite so hard then."

"Well, it's teeming now. I'll drive you to your car. No use getting soaked."

Before she could refuse—and she would have—he scooped her up and headed out the kitchen door. Hannah gave a squeal of shocked protest when she found herself lifted high in his arms, and then they were outside in the cool driving rain. A humid breeze whirled around them, splattering them with raindrops.

Just as suddenly they were out of the element, warm and dry, inside a big black van parked directly behind the boarding-house.

Hannah knelt on the bucket seat where she'd been deposited and looked around her. The van's interior had been custom-ized with a storage area behind the entire width of the front seat. Behind the storage area, the floor, walls and ceiling of the van had been covered with thick, dark carpeting. An air mat-tress, covered by a thick quilt and lots of pillows, filled most of the back.

Hannah gulped. "This isn't a van. It's a traveling lair."

"It suits my needs," Matthew drawled.

"I'll bet." Her eyes darted nervously around the interior. He could camp comfortably while casing his target site, then load up and leave the area before his prey ever realized they'd been relieved of their possessions!

"I think we'll both find it useful, since you live in a house-ful of chaperons and this boardinghouse seems to be over-flowing with Cloverites." His white grin seemed to glow in the darkness. "We'll have guaranteed privacy in here."

It took Hannah a moment to get his drift, and when she did, her cheeks flushed scarlet. "I have no use for a bedroom on wheels! Especially not one with *you* in it!"

Matthew merely laughed, a confident, arrogant laugh that enraged her. It was as if he knew that she was picturing herself lying on that air mattress with him beside her, the van parked in some secluded, woodsy spot! A piercing heat coiled ach-ingly inside her. She tried to ignore it, tried to push the pro-vocative images from her mind.

She flounced down in the seat and pulled the seat belt around her, snapping it with a vicious click. "Drive me to my car right now!" she commanded.

"Ah, the imperious Lady of the Manor emerges," Matthew taunted. "You keep that side of yourself well under wraps when you're playing your egalitarian role and socializing with the masses."

She lifted her chin higher. "I do not have to sit here and be insulted by you. If you say another word, I'll—I'll get out and walk to my car!"

"The lady certainly knows how to inflict punishment on those who dare to displease her! I don't know how I'd be able to live with myself, knowing that you'd walked two blocks in the pouring rain. Would you really deprive me of the honor of delivering you to your car door?'' Matthew pretended to look wounded but his derisive tone canceled out that pretense. "What a heartless woman you are, Hannah Kaye!"

Having made her threat—and listened to him gleefully ridicule it—Hannah knew she must fling open the door and stomp off to her car. The rain seemed to pound even more heavily against the van, making the prospect of that two-block walk an unappealing, drenching one.

But just as she reached for the door handle, Matthew started the van and steered it away from the curb into the street. "Direct me to your car, my lady," he said with an obsequiousness so phony that she was torn between laughing and grinding her teeth with vexation.

But she gave him the directions to her car, and moments later, he pulled the van alongside her sporty blue Cabriolet.

"Thank you for allowing me the privilege of chauffeuring you, princess. It's an honor I'll cherish for the rest of my humble life."

"I should have walked," Hannah muttered. "I don't know why I didn't. You're far more troublesome than getting soaked in the rain."

"Which is why you're still sitting in my car, egging me on. You're bored with all your would-be Clover swains toadying to you. You want someone to stand up to you." He reached over and captured her hand, lifting it to his mouth. "It excites you. *I* excite you."

Four

——

Matthew pressed her palm against his lips, then tugged on her wrist to draw her closer. "Come here." His smile was sexy and roguish, enticing and exciting.

Hannah closed her eyes and fought the melting warmth surging through her. Matthew was right. Being with him excited her. *He* excited her in a way no other man ever had. And he was all wrong for her. He was a transient with a gun and questionable motives for being in Clover. Hannah drew a sharp breath.

"Thank you for the ride," she said primly, yanking her hand from his grasp. "But I'm afraid you're harboring a delusion if you think that I ... if you think that you ... I think you're exciting—I—I mean, I don't! You are—"

"Delusion, huh? I don't think so, honey." Matthew chuckled. "You're so excited right now, you're stammering like a wide-eyed little schoolgirl with her first crush."

She was temporarily mesmerized by that smile of his, which tempted and challenged. Later, she would come up with scores of stinging retorts she ought to have hurled at him, but in the dark confines of his van she sat silent and still, her heart thumping, her gaze affixed to his face.

Suddenly, swiftly, Matthew moved closer to her, bracketing her face with his hands. His eyes, dark and glittering, searched her luminous gray eyes for a single moment, then he lowered his head to hers.

Hannah felt the firm touch of his lips pressing against hers, nudging them apart. She was determined to resist, and for nearly a second or two, she did manage to keep her lips locked tightly together. But his tongue was coaxing for admission, flicking lightly over her lips, tracing the shape of them, tantalizing her to allow him entry.

An insidious combination of pleasure and temptation undermined her resolve to push him away. She heard a small moan and realized that it had come from her. Hannah tried to remember why kissing him was such a bad idea, but the only thing she could summon to mind was the thrill of his kiss. Her senses recalled every single detail of his touch and his taste and were demanding to experience it all again.

Finally she gave in, her usual strong-willed stubbornness conceding to the urging of her body. Without any force from him, her lips relaxed and parted, and he thrust his tongue deeply inside her mouth.

Hannah's whole world careened into a timeless, sensual realm where nothing mattered except the heat and hunger and passion of their kiss. His hands still cupped her face, holding her mouth firmly under his as he slanted his lips over hers, first at one angle then another, drinking deeply from the moist warmth within. His tongue moved masterfully against hers in an erotic stimulation that she found exquisitely arousing.

She clutched his shirt with her hands, trying to pull his body closer, wanting—*needing* to feel his hard male frame against her. Heat spilled from her breasts to her belly and ribboned lower, surging into a hot river of desire. Hannah whimpered and swayed closer in sweet surrender.

Matthew abruptly raised his head. Placing his hands on her shoulders, he eased her back against her seat. She slitted open her eyes to see him reach across her and fling open the door on her side of the van. His body momentarily brushed hers but he slipped back into his own seat behind the wheel as she slumped bonelessly against the dark upholstery.

A gust of wind blew raindrops inside through the open door. Hannah felt the cool moisture against her skin and shivered. The blood was roaring in her ears and she was gulping for breath. She opened her eyes wider and turned her head to look questioningly at Matthew.

He was watching her. "Ever hear about being in the wrong place at the wrong time? Well, it applies here and now." He shrugged. "We were getting ahead of ourselves. If we'd followed through with what we both wanted to do, you would've missed your curfew, little girl."

His words punctured her sensual daze as effectively as a pin-prick to a helium balloon. Hannah bolted upright in her seat. "I don't have a curfew!" She hurled the words at him, suddenly as furious as a spitting cat. He'd kissed her senseless, ended it when she was quivering with urgency and now had the nerve to quote song lyrics and make jokes at her expense! "And the only thing I want to do is—is to get away from you!"

He laughed softly. "Now why am I having trouble believing that?"

"Well, believe it!" As an exit line, she conceded that it lacked flair and originality, but her mind was too muddled to come up with the devastating rejoinder that the situation required. Her emotions churning, Hannah climbed out of the van and rushed into the dry safety of her own car, pulling the door closed with a hard, satisfying slam.

Matthew idled the van alongside her car until she turned the key in the ignition and the engine roared to life. Then he drove away, retracing the route back to the boardinghouse. Hannah waited until her breathing and pulse rate had returned to normal before beginning her drive home.

It was a short, fast drive with the radio blaring in an attempt to displace the thoughts tumbling kaleidoscope fashion through her head. And though she arrived home in record time, Matthew Granger continued to dominate her thoughts, no matter how loud the music blasted over the airwaves.

Contrary to Matthew's taunt, she did not have a curfew and the house was dark and quiet when Hannah let herself in the front door. She was relieved that her parents had already retired to their suite for the night; she wasn't up for even a superficial conversation with them. Hannah removed her shoes, and for a moment, let her toes curl luxuriously into the thickness of the Oriental carpet in the hallway. She was halfway up the stairs when the soft hum of her grandmother's wheelchair caught her attention.

"Hannah? Hannah, is that you, dear?" her grandmother's voice called from downstairs. The noise of the motor grew louder, indicating that the wheelchair was drawing nearer.

Hannah stifled a sigh. Though she loved her grandmother dearly, she wasn't up to a chat with her just now. But she turned and padded back down the stairs, her shoes dangling by the straps from her fingers. "Hello, Grandmother."

She smiled as the older woman steered the motorized wheelchair into the vestibule. Her grandmother had selected the chair after her stroke, when it had become clear that walking was no longer an option for her. Now Lydia Farley was an accomplished driver, something of a speed demon, able to commandeer the chair to take her any and every place she wanted to go. She was also a night owl with a sweet tooth and held a plate of iced sugar cookies on her lap.

"I'd just come to the kitchen for a snack when I heard your car," Lydia explained, holding up the plate of cookies and offering them to Hannah. "Do join me, my dear. Come into the parlor."

Hannah followed her into the cozy sitting room down the hall from the large formal living room. She reached for a cookie and took a dainty bite. It was rich and buttery and melted in her mouth. She took another bite and sighed, feeling herself begin to unwind at last. "Thank you, Grandmother. I really needed this."

Her grandmother nodded approvingly. "Sometimes it's cognac or sherry and sometimes it's cookies or chocolate ice cream. One must be aware which panacea works best and when."

"In that case, after a night like tonight I probably should be downing a triple whiskey in one gulp," Hannah said wryly.

"My goodness, it sounds like you had quite an evening. Wasn't the surprise engagement party the success you had hoped for?"

Hannah devoured another cookie. "Oh, yes, I suppose it was. Abby and Ben were very happy and everybody seemed to have a good time. Yes, the, uh, the party was . . . very nice."

"Very nice," her grandmother repeated. "How very bland. I can't remember the last time you described anything as 'very nice,' Hannah Kaye. I've heard you use 'fabulous' and 'heinous' and all sorts of terms in between. But *nice*? The party must have been dull indeed."

"I wish it had been dull!" Hannah exclaimed fervently. "I would've gladly settled for dull. Dull would be preferable to the—the ... fiasco that—" She broke off, aware that she was blushing.

"Ah, a fiasco. That explains it." Her grandmother nodded. "You met a new man at the party. And from the looks of you, he has you in quite a tizzy."

"Grandmother, I am not in a tizzy!" Hannah paused to glance curiously at her grandmother, who was regarding her with amused gray eyes. "How do you know he's a new man?"

"Because you wouldn't have been kissing the ones you already know. And you were kissing this man, my dear. Don't bother to deny it. Your hair is tousled, your lipstick is all rubbed off and I haven't seen you blush in years. Now tell me, who is this mystery man? What is his name and when did he come to Clover?"

"He's a mystery, all right. And the biggest mystery is why I ever ... why I let him ... Ohhh, Grandmother." Hannah sank onto a silk upholstered walnut settee and clutched her head with both hands. "He's trouble. He's aggressive and moody, and— and he's way too macho and self-confident. He makes me shaky. He makes me furious. I should've slapped him down—"

"But you didn't," Lydia concluded. "You kissed him instead. And the evening was far from dull. I believe 'nice' is a bit out of context, too."

Her grandmother seemed pleased. Hannah frowned. "Grandmother, this is not a man you would ever want me to get involved with."

"That doesn't tell me much, Hannah. I practically begged you not to get engaged to that cold-fish Milquetoast, Carter Moore, but you went right ahead and did it anyway."

"Believe me, Grandmother, Matthew Granger is nothing like Carter Moore."

"That is definitely a point in his favor," Lydia said succinctly. "At least this new man, this Matthew Granger, sounds as if he has blood in his veins instead of liquid refrigerant like the glacial Mr. Moore."

"Carter was a human iceberg, wasn't he?" Hannah grimaced.

"And marriage to him would be like setting sail on the *Titanic*. I was positively thrilled when you broke your engagement to him, my dear."

"You were the only one who was, besides me, of course." Hannah heaved a sigh. "Mother and Daddy still lament the loss of Carter as their son-in-law."

Lydia dismissed the laments with a shrug and a wave of her hand. "I know they are your parents, I know your father is my son, but Baylor and Martha Lee are stuffy bores. You grandfather and I could never understand how our son grew up to be so stiff and humorless. He considered us too frivolous. We did not fit with his rigid notions of propriety and so he chose to marry your mother who, as we all know, is very, very proper indeed."

"And so are Sarah and Deborah and Bay." Hannah smiled. "How come I turned out to be the only capricious throwback to you and Granddaddy?"

"Perhaps because you are the result of the only moments of spontaneity that your parents ever experienced." Lydia grinned wickedly. "I've often speculated about it. That summer Baylor and Martha Lee vacationed in the south of France—their family quite complete—with absolutely no plans for any new little additions and then ... suddenly they are carried away by an inexplicable bout of passion that resulted in you, Hannah. You simply had to be different, and I am thankful every day that you are who you are."

"Careful, Grandmother, you're encouraging me again," Hannah teased. It was a long-standing joke between them. Baylor Carleton III and Martha Lee were forever admonishing Lydia for 'encouraging' Hannah in un-Farley-like behavior.

"And I shall continue to do so, my dear. Now, back to your new young man—"

"Grandmother, he is *not* my new anything. He can't be. He's—he's too unnerving."

"I think that the same characteristics that unnerve you attract you to him, too." Lydia took a contemplative bite of another cookie. "And it sounds to me as if it isn't his virility that frightens you as much as your own response to it."

"Grandmother!" Hannah admonished. "Did I mention a thing about virility?"

"You didn't have to, child. I'm not blind. I can see the effect this man has had on you. And I—"

She stopped in midsentence when they heard the front door open and then close. Hannah's brother, Baylor Carleton IV, strode down the hall, stepping into the parlor when he noticed the lights on.

"Grandmother, what are you doing up at this hour?" Bay frowned his disapproval. His eyes darted to his younger sister, took in her unabashedly sexy silver dress, and his countenance grew even more stern. "Hannah, please tell me you did not leave the house in that...that—"

"It's called a dress, Bay." Hannah arched her brows. "And I wore it to Ben and Abby's engagement party at the Clover Street Boardinghouse."

Bay's frown eased somewhat. He had no interest in Hannah's friends who were outside the Farley family social circle. "Well, as long as you weren't at the club or anywhere where you could be seen by anyone that matters... But as far as dresses go, yours is a bit extreme, Hannah, even for that particular...group of yours."

Hannah and her grandmother exchanged glances.

"Would you care for a cookie, Baylor?" Grandmother offered her grandson the plate.

Baylor shuddered. "At this hour? No, thank you. And you shouldn't be eating them at any hour, Grandmother. Consider the ingredients—sugar, butter, eggs. All are bad for you. If you must snack, carrot sticks or celery or perhaps even a rice cake would be far more suitable."

"My dear boy, when you've passed your eightieth birthday as I have, one can have a cookie whenever one pleases." Grandmother split the last cookie in two, handing one half to Hannah and nibbling on the other herself.

"Where were you tonight, Bay?" Hannah asked, glancing at her brother's custom-tailored tuxedo. Someplace insufferably stuffy and dull, she was sure of that. Though it was late, he looked immaculate, every hair in place, not even a single wrinkle in his clothing or a smudge on his polished shoes. She compared his impeccable appearance with her own and felt a tingle of pink stain her cheeks. Unlike herself, it was plain to see that brother Bay had not been necking with an impossibly inappropriate individual.

Bay actually smiled. "I was invited to dinner at the Wyndham estate," he said proudly. He sat down on the matching settee opposite Hannah's.

Grandmother looked bored. "I'm surprised that they didn't demand you appear in white tie and tails. Dining at the Wyndhams is more formal than a White House state dinner."

Hannah sat up straight, her every nerve on alert. It seemed queerly coincidental that her brother had spent the evening at the very place she'd seen marked in target red on Matthew Granger's map. Was it some kind of weirdly prophetic clue? At a moment like this in an occult-suspense movie, there would be a dramatic crescendo of blood-chilling music as a tip-off. But sitting here in the quiet Farley parlor, there were no such telltale sound effects.

"I was invited to be Justine's escort," Bay continued proudly.

"Now which one is that?" his grandmother asked.

"She is Alex's daughter, Justine Wyndham Marshall."

"Ah, yes." Grandmother nodded her recognition. "Alexandra is divorced from Justine's wretched father, Justin Marshall."

"*Alex?*" Hannah raised her brows. "You're certainly getting chummy with her, aren't you, Bay?"

Baylor glowered at his sister. "*Alexandra* would like nothing better than to see Justine and I make a match of it. Needless to say, so would I. It's almost unimaginable, but in all these years a Farley has never married a Wyndham. I would like to be the first to unite the two families. It will be nothing less than a historic joining!"

"But Justine just turned twenty—she's still in college," Hannah noted. "And anytime I've seen her, she's been quiet and anxious, not your type at all, Bay."

"An eight-year difference hardly matters later on, but the difference between twenty and twenty-eight is crucial," their grandmother interjected. "And I firmly believe that a twenty-year-old is too young to marry anybody. Why, imagine if Hannah had wed at that age!"

"Grandmother, there is absolutely no comparison between Hannah and Justine, and for that I am immensely grateful. A girl like Hannah would drive me mad in less than a week, but Justine is very quiet—irritatingly so—but she is also quite pliable. I can mold her into the type of wife who will suit me. And Alexandra agrees. She wants Justine to have a husband who is a stabilizing influence."

Hannah was appalled. "What a disgustingly retro viewpoint! What about what Justine wants? And what about love?"

"Hannah, you are so naive." Bay rose to his feet and glared disparagingly at his sister. "Romantic love is nothing but a childish delusion, fostered by the media and the advertising-industrial complex. It is definitely an impractical and unrealistic basis for marriage. I want to marry a Wyndham to enhance my personal wealth and my social standing. Alexandra wants me to marry Justine to keep her from falling for some totally unsuitable idiot who will not match the standards of the Wyndham family. Justine is a biddable girl who will do as she's told."

"And Baylor Carleton Farley IV more than meets the high standards of the illustrious Wyndhams, I suppose," Hannah said caustically. She was incensed. Alexandra Wyndham was a snob and worse if she were willing to push her daughter into a loveless marriage with the blatantly social-climbing Bay! Maybe she deserved to have Matthew Granger pay a midnight visit to her jewelry box after all!

Bay either missed or ignored the caustic note in his sister's voice. "One could argue that I exceed the Wyndham's requirements," he replied smugly. "I am a successful stockbroker, an excellent golfer and a lively conversationalist. I am the ideal candidate for Justine's hand, and I intend to be engaged to her by the end of the summer." He bent down and dutifully kissed his grandmother's cheek. "Good night, Grandmother. Please go to bed soon. You need your rest. Don't let *her* keep you up too late." He shot another disapproving glance at Hannah.

Bay marched grandly from the room. Hannah and her grandmother sat quietly until they heard him mount the stairs.

"You go first, Grandmother," Hannah offered eagerly.

"My dear, I cede the floor to you. I can see you're absolutely bursting with the need to comment on your brother's cold-blooded, coldhearted, self-serving plan."

"I wanted to shove a flashlight down Bay's throat!" Hannah exclaimed. "Have you ever heard such an ego?"

"I'm sorry to say that young Baylor heads his own admiration society," Lydia said, sighing.

"He's the only member in it."

Lydia's gray eyes, so like Hannah's gleamed with mischief. "I'm unfamiliar with his success in the stock market or on the golf course, but I have *never* thought of young Baylor as a lively conversationalist."

"Poor Justine! I wish we could rescue her." Hannah looked troubled. "I don't know her very well—I don't think anybody does—but from what I do know of her, she is shy and seems to be totally dominated by her mother."

"Sad." Lydia tsked with sympathy. "A pity."

"Why would Alexandra Wyndham want to marry off her only child to Baylor, Grandmother? He'd cold and pompous and he doesn't even make a pretense of loving Justine. He doesn't love anything except himself—and money and social status, of course."

"Heaven only knows." Lydia shook her head. "But I certainly don't think that Alexandra is qualified to pick a husband for anyone. She did such a poor job of selecting one for herself. Justin Marshall was simply vile, a country-club Casanova with a drinking and gambling problem. Why she ever married him in the first place is beyond me, but I do recall hearing certain rumors about her when she was just a girl."

"Rumors about Alexandra Wyndham?" Hannah laughed at the very idea. "Did she do something socially scandalous, like wear white shoes after Labor Day? Frankly, I can't imagine a Wyndham doing anything improper."

Lydia leaned forward in her chair and lowered her voice, though there was nobody else around but the two of them to hear. "There were rumors that she had a wild streak and caused her parents much pain. And now, perhaps she fears her daughter might make a similar mistake."

"Alexandra Wyndham with a wild streak?" Hannah grinned. "You must've heard wrong, Grandmother. The wildest that woman gets is wearing a hot-pink golf skirt on the links. Oh, and I heard she ventured into Clarke's Steak House once and actually ordered chocolate cheesecake for dessert. Shocking!"

"You forget that Alexandra was once as young as you are, my dear. She wasn't always an uptight, middle-aged paragon of etiquette."

Hannah's eyes danced. "Next you'll be telling me that Mother was wild until Daddy's stabilizing influence molded her into a proper wife!"

Lydia sighed. "I would love to tell such a story but it would be a blatant untruth. Your mother has been correct and proper since emerging from the womb." She glanced at her watch. "Gracious, it is getting late. As much as I hate to take Baylor's advice, we really ought to get ourselves to bed, child."

"I guess so." Hannah stood up and walked to the window. It was still raining, and the sight and sound of the storm reminded her of Matthew. His fury when the roof over his room was leaking. The way he'd picked her up and carried her out to his van while the rain swirled around them. His mouth on hers.

Hannah gulped as tempestuous memories of those hot kisses on the dance floor and in his van assailed her. She felt restless, her body throbbing. She knew she wasn't going to sleep very well tonight. When she turned, she found her grandmother watching her.

"Will you see him tomorrow, Hannah?"

Hannah didn't bother to feign ignorance. "I don't know. I hope not," she added fiercely.

"'The lady doth protest too much, methinks,'" Lydia quoted cheerfully.

"That's what *he* said!" Hannah scowled.

"He quotes Shakespeare?" Her grandmother was delighted. "Now I am definitely intrigued. You will bring him by to visit, won't you, dear?"

And give him an opportunity to case the place? Hannah shook her head vigorously. "I intend to stay far away from Matthew Granger, Grandmother. And with any luck, he'll quickly grow bored here in Clover and go prowl somewhere else."

The sky was gray and overcast the next morning when Hannah drove into town after spending the restless night she'd anticipated, tossing and turning, too wired to sleep until nearly dawn. It was raining again, a steady drizzle without the sound-and-light show provided by yesterday night's thunderstorm. According to virtually every forecast, the rainy weather was socked in, with showers predicted not to end until evening. That meant those vacationers who's hoped to spend their time on the beach and/or swimming in the Atlantic would be forced to find other things to do instead. One of those things would be shopping. It promised to be a banner day for Clover merchants.

As Hannah let herself into her shop, Yesterdays, she noticed that most of the other shops along Clover Street were opening a bit earlier than usual this morning, too. Yawning, she turned on the inside lights.

A soft glow lit the long narrow room crammed with pieces of antique furniture and bric-a-brac. An adjoining room held more, including a charming assortment of antique dolls arranged in wicker doll carriages and small carved chairs. Vintage tin toys and painted-metal toy soldiers were strategically placed for browsing, and the male customers who came into the shop were inevitably drawn to them.

The collectibles, which she had carried on a trial basis and recently expanded to greater numbers when they'd proved immensely popular, were farther in the back. The collectibles did not qualify as bona fide antiques because of their age. She had some baseball memorabilia, jelly-jar glasses with cartoon and TV characters from the fifties and a whimsical collection of ceramic cookie jars, among other things she'd found while canvassing flea markets and yard sales.

Hannah checked her inventory, made sure the items were dust free and invitingly positioned, then returned to the counter. She was about to start up the computerized cash register when her stomach growled, protesting its emptiness. She'd skipped breakfast at home—she couldn't bear to listen to Bay boasting of his Wyndham coup yet again—but she needed sustenance now. Not to mention a bolstering jolt of caffeine to counteract this sluggish, groggy feeling enveloping her.

She thought longingly of Peg's Diner. The coffee there was the best—dark, rich and strong—and the homemade muffins, baked daily, were indescribably scrumptious.

Yesterdays wasn't open for business yet, Hannah decided. There were no potential customers in immediate sight anyway. The lure of the coffee and muffins at the diner drew her like a siren's song. Grabbing her still-damp umbrella, she hurried down Clover Street to Peg's Diner.

The place was filled to capacity with locals and tourists crowded into booths and onto the round stools that lined the long counter. Waitresses, balancing plates halfway up their arms and proffering pots of hot coffee for cups that required constant refilling, bustled back and forth between their customers and the kitchen.

Hannah decided that a take-out order would be faster and more convenient than waiting around for a place to sit down. A hand-lettered sign beside the cash register served as the take-out checkpoint. Peg Jones, Katie's aunt, a matronly, handsome woman with short blond curly hair and pale blue eyes commanded both stations.

"Good morning, Hannah," Peg greeted her. "Don't you look pretty today! Violet is definitely your color."

Hannah smoothed the flared skirt of her violet sundress with its shirred bodice and spaghetti straps. The dress was simple and cool, though her sisters and brother had disapproved of the short length. There were very few items in her wardrobe that met with full Farley approval, a fact which troubled Hannah not at all.

She thanked Peg for the compliment.

"You just missed Katie," Peg continued chattily. "She was here to help with the first breakfast shift, but she had to go back to the boardinghouse to meet with a roofer for an estimate. She told me about the party last night. Even though Abby and Ben weren't surprised, it sounds like it was a wonderful success." Peg beamed. She adored her niece and enjoyed talking about anything involving her.

"Oh, yes, it was, Peg. Katie is a natural hostess and the boardinghouse has such a marvelously homey atmosphere. It's just the right place for a special party," Hannah affirmed, her social smile and manner gracious and warm and firmly in place. "Everybody had a lovely time."

"I didn't."

Hannah froze. She didn't have to turn around to know who'd uttered that cryptic remark. She'd heard that voice—*his voice*—echoing in her ears during most of last night as she had thrashed around in bed and tried desperately not to think of Matthew Granger.

She kept her eyes straight ahead, fixed to the rainbow-lettered take-out sign, even as she felt him come to stand behind her. Very closely behind her. She could feel his breath against her hair, and though he was not touching her, his body heat seemed to burn her.

Hannah steeled herself against him. "Just ignore him Peg," she said trenchantly. "He's a chronic complainer. He doesn't like water. He doesn't like music. He claims that he prefers the company of insects to people, so his opinion of the party hardly counts."

But Peg was smiling fondly at Matthew. "I heard all about poor Matthew's evening at the boardinghouse from Katie, and

I think he's been wonderfully good-natured about everything."

"Poor Matthew?" Hannah echoed incredulously. Peg felt sorry for him?

Hannah whirled around and saw Matthew grinning at her, his dark eyes agleam. He was dressed in well-worn jeans and a charcoal gray polo shirt, faded from many washings, and he looked as rugged and virile as he had last night—in person and in her restless dreams. Her stomach took a dive as if she'd just plunged down a seventy-five-foot drop on a roller coaster. She quickly dragged her gaze away from him.

"Katie and I both feel terrible at the inconvenience Matthew had to suffer. Imagine being rained on in your own room!" Peg was clearly appalled by the episode. "As Katie told you, breakfast this morning is on the house, Matthew. I do hope you enjoyed your blueberry pancakes?"

"They were fantastic," Matthew said sincerely. "And I'm not exaggerating when I tell you that your coffee is the best I've ever tasted. I could write accolades about it."

"I thought you wrote exclusively about bugs," Hannah muttered. "Wouldn't an accolade for cockroaches be more your style?"

"Irritable this morning, aren't you, princess?" taunted Matthew. "Did you get up on the wrong side of the bed? Or maybe you're all black-and-blue from that pea under your stack of mattresses. You blue-blooded aristocrats are extremely sensitive, so I've been told."

Hannah decided to ignore him. She lifted her chin and focused her attention on Peg. "I'd like to order a large black coffee and a muffin to go, please."

Peg chuckled softly. Katie had told her everything about the party last night, including Hannah Farley's and Matthew Granger's instant, volatile fascination with each other. But she merely said benignly, "We have blueberry or banana nut muffins today, honey. Which would you prefer?"

"Give her one of each," Matthew spoke up, handing Peg a twenty-dollar bill at the same time. "It's on me, and keep the change."

Peg thanked him effusively and gave Hannah's order to the counter waitress. A customer approached the register with his check and money in hand, and Hannah and Matthew automatically stepped aside while Peg busied herself with the transaction.

"There's no need for you to buy me breakfast," Hannah told Matthew. She was completely floored by the gesture. Unlike his gibes or his anger, his rather renegade gallant streak—driving her to her car last night in the rain, buying her breakfast this morning—threw her off-balance.

"I wanted to." Matthew shrugged. "And it gives me a credible way to pay for my own breakfast. Both Peg and Katie insisted it was on the house but I don't feel comfortable with all this free stuff."

"So you're sort of like Robin Hood," Hannah blurted out. "You don't like to take from the poor but you—" Just in time, she caught herself before she'd finished her thought and uttered the incriminating phrase "rob the rich." "Not that Katie and Peg are poor," she amended hastily. Her face felt hot; she was sure she was as red as the strawberries featured at the annual festival. Why couldn't she keep control of her tongue around this man?

"No, not poor, but hardworking," Matthew agreed. "The opposite of the Polks, who are both poor and lazy, among other things, according to the good citizens of Clover."

There was something in his tone that drew her attention immediately. Hannah stared at him. His expression was bland and blank, totally unreadable. And though she'd known him a very short while, one absolute she'd discerned about him was that there was nothing bland or blank about Matthew Granger. His current expression was as much a mask as anything worn at Halloween.

"Last night at the party, people were talking abut the Polks," she said carefully, wondering why on earth she was discussing the Polks with Matthew Granger. But he'd introduced the subject, not her.

Matthew nodded. "There was another lively discussion about them last night after the party at Fitzgerald's Bar and Grill." He grimaced wryly. "Everyone had a Polk-related tale to tell. Maureen had dozens."

"You went to Fitzgerald's after the party?" Hannah was pleased to have injected just the right note of insouciance into her voice. She sounded cool and indifferent to the news of the impromptu party-after-the-party.

But indifferent she was not. She visualized pretty red-haired Maureen Fitzgerald chatting cozily with Matthew at the bar into the wee hours of the morning. Maureen, who'd been so smiley and friendly to Matthew yesterday at the party, even though he'd almost decked her cousin Sean! Hannah felt a sickening surge of jealousy and was horrified by it.

"A group of us went. Blaine and Judy, Emma and Ken, and Susan and Sean and Maureen and I," Matthew said. "Don't ask me last names. I didn't get any of them."

Hannah felt acutely left out, and she hated the feeling. Even worse was this irrational streak of possessiveness she seemed to have developed concerning Matthew. She found herself mentally reviewing the women in the group who'd gone to Fitzgerald's last night. Judy was dating Blaine, and Emma was dating Ken; they would have little interest pursuing a fling with a newcomer in town. But Susan, an attractive brown-eyed blonde who'd recently been divorced, was very available, and Maureen was single and fun and had never lacked for admirers.

Hannah pictured Susan and Maureen vying for Matthew's attention, trying to win his favor in a feminine charm-off. And all the while, he was probably smiling that too-confident, all-knowing smile of his, accepting the competition for him as his due.

Hannah was outraged. Well, she refused to participate in such demeaning games! Let the others pander to the man. She was not going to chase after a disreputable cat burglar—or worse!

"The waitress just handed Peg my order," Hannah told him with icy dismissal. "I insist on reimbursing you. I'll send the money to you today via Katie." She flounced off, without a backward glance at him.

Moments later, huddling under the small overhang in front of the diner to keep out of the rain, Hannah clutched the paper bag containing her breakfast with one hand and tried to push open her stubborn umbrella with the other.

"Does it ever stop raining here?" Matthew said wryly as he took the umbrella from her and opened it easily. "I'm starting to wonder if an ark would be more useful than my van in this town." Hooking one hand firmly around her waist, while holding the umbrella above their heads with the other, he walked her out into the rain. "Which way, right or left?"

"I'm going left to my shop. I don't know where you're going," Hannah said coolly. She reached for the handle of her umbrella, but Matthew didn't cede it. Instead, he placed his hand firmly on top of hers, covering it.

"I'm going wherever you are, honey. I feel like doing some shopping in your store this morning."

"You don't even know what kind of store I have."

"Yes, I do. Antiques. And some collectible stuff."

She shot him a wary glance. "How do you know that?"

"I asked Katie," he admitted. He wrapped his arm more firmly around her waist, bringing her back against his chest. The closeness of their bodies made the umbrella's protection quite effective. "Now neither of us will get rained on," he added huskily.

He had asked Katie about her. While Hannah was pondering that, she felt a warm flush suffuse her body. The back of her head was touching the hollow of his shoulder and her bottom nestled against the powerful strength of his thighs. His arm lay like an iron band across her waist, radiating heat to her belly and lower limbs. Hannah restrained the urge to lean back into him, to turn her head and lift her lips to his....

"I—I feel dizzy," she said breathlessly. "It must be low blood sugar. I haven't had anything to eat today."

"Do you want me to carry you? I don't mind, short stuff. You're not any heavier than a kid."

It was hardly a romantic offer. The heroes in the historical romances she enjoyed did not make reference to the heroine's height or weight.

"Short stuff?" Hannah was truly galled. And no longer dizzied by sensuality. "If you only knew how sick I am of being accused of being short! Forced to stand in the front row of every single class or group picture by insensitive photographers who discriminate by arranging people according to height and—"

"Whew, I guess I really hit a nerve!" Matthew laughed. "But you have to admit, you're a lot shorter today than you were yesterday. By about four or five inches?"

Hannah decided never to wear flat-heeled shoes again. Her head held high, she started walking along the sidewalk toward her store.

Matthew, still holding her and the umbrella, allowed her to set the pace. "I take it you don't want me to carry you, then?" he drawled.

"What I want is for you to leave me alone!"

"I would, if I thought you really meant it, little girl."

"I do!" she snapped. "What else do I have to say to convince you?"

"It's not what you say, it's what you do. Actions speak louder than words, remember? And you act as if you want me around."

"I do not!"

"I saw the way your eyes lit up when you first saw me in the diner this morning. I also watched you practically turn green with jealousy when I mentioned I'd gone out after the party. And last but not least, you've been snuggling back against me the whole time we've been walking. Oh, you want me around, honey. I don't have a single doubt about that."

Hannah was speechless. He read her so clearly! That was a first for her. She'd always been the perceptive one, skillfully assessing and interpreting the signs and signals of the opposite sex while carefully concealing her own. But she was like an open book to Matthew. He looked at her and seemed to divine all her secrets, her thoughts and her desires. It was unnerving; it was infuriating!

She was too shaken to look where she was going, and she stumbled a little over a tree root growing up through a crack in the sidewalk. Matthew tightened his grip on her, steadying her, then drew her under the ornate portico of the Clover Street Hotel. He set the umbrella on the ground. The usual busy entrance to the hotel was deserted. Obviously the hotel guests were not eager to venture out early on this gray, rainy morning. Hannah and Matthew stood face-to-face, toe-to-toe, their eyes locked.

"Well?" Matthew's smile was challenging, inviting, daring her to disagree with his analysis.

Naturally, she did. "You're delusional!"

"You like to fling that charge around." He placed both his hands on her waist and held her lightly. "Well, I disproved it last night and I can do it again right now."

She could have moved away from him without exerting any force and with hardly a shred of effort. But she stayed right where she was. "I won't let you kiss me again!"

He grinned wolfishly. "Now that's an invitation if I ever heard one."

"No, it isn't. But you're certainly vain enough to think so!"

"You're flattering me again." He lowered his head and kissed the soft lobe of her right ear, then the sensitive skin behind it.

"And you're...you're demented!" He brushed her lips with his, briefly, almost experimentally. "The compliments just keep on coming. I've always heard about the fabled charm of Southern women and now I know it's not a myth. You steel magnolias really do know how to make a man feel like he's a king."

"Stop making fun of me," she ordered breathlessly. "You'll notice I'm not laughing."

"Believe me, baby, I'm not laughing, either. In fact, I've never felt less like laughing in my life." His voice held a desperate ring. He scooped up a fistful of her long, dark hair, baring her neck. "Too bad, because I think the joke is on me."

His tongue touched the white softness of her neck. He stifled a groan of pleasure at the feel and taste of her skin.

Hannah closed her eyes. His lips were warm and soft, and she ached, remembering the sensual pressure of them against hers. She wanted it again; she wanted his mouth open and hot and covering hers. She wanted his tongue deep inside her mouth, rubbing hers, making her squirm with liquid desire. Yearning swelled inside her, so strong and heavy she could scarcely breathe.

Matthew pulled her deeply into his embrace. She went willingly, raising her mouth to his as he lowered his to hers.

Five

Their lips came together lightly, fleetingly, rubbing and lifting, before touching again. They savored the contact, repeating the seductive sequence again and again. Hannah trembled with anticipation, waiting for his mouth to take hers in a deep, hard and intimate kiss, the kind they'd shared while dancing, while sitting in the van with the rain pounding around them.

But the hungrily awaited kiss never happened. Out of nowhere came three young boys about eleven or twelve years old, roaring down the sidewalk on their bikes. They were laughing and cussing and one of them careered into Matthew and Hannah, knocking them into the wall of the hotel. Matthew took the brunt of the hit but maintained his balance, his body sheltering Hannah, protecting her from the full impact of the bike and the wall. She clung to him gasping, knowing that if he hadn't been holding her, she would've been knocked to the ground.

At the same time, another young biker swooped down and snatched Hannah's umbrella, which Matthew had set on the ground nearby. Whooping with triumph, he rode off with it. Moments later, a gust of wind caught the open umbrella like a sail, and the velocity nearly unseated the young rider. The boy let the umbrella go and it flew into the street, where an oncoming car promptly ran over it, smashing it to smithereens.

"You little hoodlums!" Matthew shouted. His body was taut with fury, his black eyes flashing with rage as he started down the sidewalk after them. "You'd better pray I don't catch you because if I do—"

"Matthew, don't." Hannah hung onto him, holding him back. "Let them go. They're just kids."

The boys laughed, called a few taunts over their shoulders and then sped off, causing a party of senior citizens to scatter. The seniors turned to glare at the boys, who had already vanished around the corner.

"They're juvenile sociopaths!" Matthew grated.

Another car drove over the remains of Hannah's umbrella.

Hannah heaved a sigh. "Well, you just had your first run-in with some of the Polks. Literally. Now you have a story to contribute next time everybody's hanging out at Fitzgerald's Bar and Grill, trashing the Polks."

"Polk?" Matthew croaked. His face was suddenly, oddly ashen. "Those little thugs? Are you sure?"

Hannah nodded. "Absolutely sure. All the Polks have that dark hair and dark eyes and swarthy complexion. And of course, their behavior was a dead giveaway."

"No other kids in town knock over pedestrians, grab things and then toss them in front of cars?" Matthew questioned grimly.

Chances were likely that those maddening little monsters who'd all but knocked him and Hannah down, who'd stolen her umbrella only to see it carelessly destroyed, were related to him. How closely? he wondered bleakly. Cousins, preferably distant? What if he had sisters and brothers who had kids, and those bicycle-riding young terrorists were his nephews? Suppose Jesse Polk, the man who'd fathered him at eighteen, was still reproducing at the ripe old age of fifty, and those brats were his kid brothers?

All of the prospects depressed him. He began to more fully understand the stigma of being a Polk in Clover. It was not a name and heritage to be proud of.

He gazed down at Hannah, who was staring at him, her wide gray eyes curious. "Are you all right?" he murmured huskily. She nodded her head. "I'm sorry," he added, apologizing for his kinfolk and their atrocious behavior. He felt as if he owed the entire town an apology!

Hannah was perplexed. She couldn't detect whether he was angry or sad. Or both. And his apology made no sense, unless he felt responsible for the loss of her umbrella. Perhaps he blamed himself because he'd been the one to put it on the ground for the young Polks to grab.

"It doesn't matter," she assured him. "The umbrella was cheap, only a few dollars. It's certainly no great loss. I bought it at the five-and-ten because I'm always losing umbrellas. I'd never invest in an expensive one."

The way he was staring at her made her nervous. The umbrella incident had clearly rattled something within him. Certainly *he* minded the young Polks' transgressions far more than she did. She realized once again how very little she knew about him. Far too little to be allowing him the intimacies she was freely granting! A chill of danger tingled along her spine, and this time it alarmed her instead of exciting her.

"I—I'd better get to my shop right away," she said uneasily. "The rain is starting to come down harder." She scurried off, leaving the shelter of the hotel portico, feeling the need to put distance between them.

But Matthew followed her down the block to Yesterdays. Though not soaked, they were both wet, before they ducked under the striped awning protecting the entrance to the shop. She unlocked the door and went inside, Matthew right behind her. He trailed her to the counter, where she removed her cup of coffee from the bag and took several bracing gulps of the hot brew.

"So this is your shop." Matthew glanced around him, his eyes resting on the tall, narrow nineteenth-century dresser decorated with delicately detailed hand-painted flowers, then moving to the petite eighteenth-century rosewood reception desk.

Both were rare and among the most valuable pieces in the shop.

Hannah watched him nervously. Was he taking inventory of her inventory?

"Nice-looking stuff," Matthew remarked. "I've seen a lot of beat-up junk labeled antiques. The word bestows a certain cachet and an excuse to charge exorbitant prices. But you aren't running that scam here."

"I've never run a scam anywhere!" Hannah said fervently. If he were entertaining thoughts of recruiting her as a fence for his purloined booty, she wanted to quash the notion immediately.

Matthew wandered into the other room, and Hannah shifted position behind the register so she could watch him. He studied the toy soldiers, lifting each tiny figure to admire the rightly colored uniforms and old-style weapons more closely. Then he noticed the dolls. He picked one up and stared at it.

Hannah fairly flew into the other room. He'd unerringly chosen the most valuable doll in her shop, a Bye-Lo Baby, circa 1922, with a porcelain head and muslin cloth body, its blue-green glass eyes and dainty painted features in mint condition.

"My mother had a doll exactly like this," he told her. "It was dressed in a christening gown and she kept it in a carved wooden doll cradle. It was one of the few things she owned that was off-limits to me as a kid. Not that I had any interest in dolls whatsoever. I was strictly a toy-car-and-truck kind of guy."

He laid the baby doll in Hannah's arms. She relaxed and smiled up at him. "It's a wonderful doll." She was always ready to discuss one of her major interests. "The Bye-Lo Babies were extremely popular in the twenties. The first Christmas they were released, people lined up for them, and the doll became known as the Million Dollar Baby."

"Sort of a forerunner to our toy fads today, huh? Who would think that people would be chasing after dolls back then?"

Hannah set the doll back in its wicker carriage. "One thing I've learned from talking to my grandmother and from the antiques business in general is that people aren't all that different, regardless of the age they lived in."

"Maybe not. But the ages sure are different. Imagine someone from seventeenth-century Clover being set down here in the town today. Or vice-versa." Matthew grinned. "Imagine if you and I were transported back in time to the Clover of 1795?"

"The Farleys would be there. And they'd probably accuse me of not behaving with the proper decorum befitting the family's position in the town," Hannah added wryly.

"I wonder if the Polks would be around." Matthew mused.

"Probably. One legend has it they're descended from pirates who sneaked into the country while the king of England still ruled the Carolinas. Another has them as escaped convicts who stowed away and then arrived in Clover to carry on as usual."

"How would the young Polks terrorize the town back in those days?" Matthew mused. "By placing burrs under the saddles of the horses?"

"How about untethering the horses' bridles and stampeding them through the center of town?" suggested Hannah.

They both laughed.

"Of course, the Wyndhams would still be the wealthy patricians, ensconced in their mansion," Matthew continued. "Probably the same stuff that was there then is still there now, except today it's priceless. Wouldn't you like to get your hands on some of *those* things for your shop?"

"No!" Hannah cried. "I—I mean, they'd never sell it." She ran her hand nervously through her thick dark hair. "And I would never, ever deal in stolen goods," she added with righteous fervor.

"Very commendable of you," Matthew said dryly.

He walked back into the main room and she followed him. Was it her imagination or was he eyeing her new cash register, a computerized high-tech wonder, with uncommon interest?

"I, uh, I don't keep much money in the cash register overnight," Hannah felt compelled to inform him. "Some change, a few bills. I don't like keeping a lot of cash around in case of—of robbery."

"You make a bank deposit every day?"

"If I've made enough sales." Hannah's hands were shaking as she tore off a piece of banana nut muffin. "I don't have any set routine. I vary the time I go to the bank every day, if I go at all. Sometimes I hardly sell anything and the day's receipts don't warrant a deposit."

Matthew glanced at her sharply. "You're awfully jumpy. What's the matter?"

"Maybe I don't like being grilled on my banking habits!" Hannah snapped. She stuffed half the muffin in her mouth to prevent further indiscretion.

Matthew studied her. "I've been thinking about something you said earlier."

"What did I say?" she demanded warily.

"You mentioned that everybody last night was trashing the Polks. And you were right, they were trashing them, each person trying to top the other's tale about how low-down and reprehensible that family is." His dark eyes were intense and piercing and never left her face. "Everybody had something bad to say—that is, everybody but you. You didn't say a word against the Polks last night at the party or today, not even when those kids swiped your umbrella and practically knocked you over. Why not?"

Hannah swallowed convulsively. The muffin hit her stomach like a ball of lead. She was utterly confused. "They're just kids," she reminded him again. "What they did was hardly the crime of the century."

In truth, she was grateful the kids had come along when they did. In broad daylight, she had been kissing Matthew—and wanting to do much more—right in front of the Clover Street Hotel in the middle of downtown Clover's busiest street. A most shocking breach of good judgment and common sense!

She'd been lucky it was the Polk children who had interrupted them and not the Reverend Mr. Smith or Father Peterson or, worst of all, Jeannie Potts, who would've promptly reported what she'd seen to everyone who set foot in the Beauty Boutique.

"Do you know any of the Polks?" Matthew persisted.

He couldn't stop himself from seeking information from the only person he'd met in town who seemed to hold a nonjudgmental attitude toward his birth father's family. Or perhaps she was merely indifferent? Perhaps a highborn Farley did not bother to have an opinion about the downtrodden Polks. Matthew didn't mind. Indifference was preferable to the scathing indictments served up by everybody else.

"I know some by sight," Hannah replied, puzzled by his interest. Where was this conversation leading? She couldn't begin to guess. "I went to school with some, although by high school we were on different academic tracks."

"You were headed toward college. They were headed toward prison," he said flatly.

"Something like that. The Polk girls tended to get pregnant and drop out. The Polk boys tended to drop out and get in trouble with the law."

"What about the adults? Surely not everybody in that family is stupid or lazy or amoral. Don't some of them work for an honest living?"

"I don't know," she replied uncertainly.

"Of course you don't. Nice girls from good families are taught to assiduously avoid the town pariahs."

"You sound bitter. Did you—" Hannah took a deep breath. She simply had to ask him. "Did you grow up in a family like the Polks, Matthew? Is that how...is that why you ended up—" She paused, her gaze meeting and holding his. "Is that why you do what you do?"

He made no reply but she watched his expression turn guarded and tense.

She was anxious, but there could be no turning back now. Confirming the information she'd gathered about him, no matter how painful, was preferable to this pretense they were maintaining between them. "Matthew, it's time to drop the subterfuge, to stop dancing around the truth. I know what you are and what you do. On some level, you probably already know that I know."

She was so very serious, so earnest. Her lips were slightly parted, her gray eyes shining with concern. Matthew gazed at her. She almost took his breath away.

"You know who I am and what I do?" he rasped.

"Yes. No more games, Matthew. I know. I—I looked in your bag yesterday."

His face hardened. "What did you see?" He stepped behind the counter and caught her shoulders with his hands. "Tell me."

Hannah refused to cower. She would not be bullied by anyone. "I saw the book about the first families of South Carolina. And I saw the map marking the Wyndham chapters, where you circled the location of their estate with red ink." She squared her shoulders, no easy task under his heavy hands. "I know you're either a jewel thief or a cat burglar, Matthew. I know you're in town to hit the Wyndham estate and pull a—a heist."

She flinched, dreading his reaction. What if he turned violent? Fear gripped her.

"A heist?" Matthew echoed. "A cat burglar?"

The one thing she did not expect him to do was burst into laughter.

But he did. He dropped his hands from her shoulders and leaned against the counter, laughing long and loud. He laughed so hard that tears filled his eyes and he had to clutch his aching middle because the force of his laughter had strained his stomach muscles. Hannah watched, her face flushing, her expression growing more mutinous the longer and harder she laughed. She didn't need him to tell her with words that she had spectacularly misinterpreted the evidence in his bag; his unrestrained peals of laughter said it all. Even more embarrassing, as she thought back to the evidence on which she'd based her theory—the books, the map, the Wyndham clues—was how ridiculously flimsy it all actually was. She was silently grateful that she hadn't gone running to Sheriff Maguire with her suspicions. He would've never let her forget it!

Finally, Matthew calmed down, his laughter subsiding, though he grinned widely every time he looked at her. "I guess I should be flattered." His dark eyes still gleamed with mirth. "In movies and on TV, jewel thieves and cat burglars are usually romantic figures, the suave, sophisticated Cary Grant or Robert Wagner types. Basically good guys with a charming flaw or two. I'm glad you didn't cast me as a serial killer since I had books on—"

"I know," Hannah muttered. "I saw them."

"Did you share your suspicions with anybody else or did you plan to stop my . . . heist all by yourself?"

"I didn't tell anybody or make any plans." She folded her arms across her chest and glared at him. "I was mulling things over. And I still have a few unanswered questions about—"

"By all means ask. I can't wait to hear them." He looked ready to succumb to another fit of laughter.

Hannah fumed. "Why did you mark the Wyndham estate on that map? Why did you write Alexandra Wyndham's name at the bottom of the page in the book? And what are you doing with a gun? I saw it when I got your shirts from the closet."

A dull flush stained Matthew's neck. "My, you are an inquisitive little girl, aren't you? A busy one, too. Not to mention imaginative."

Hannah refused to be diverted. "It seems to me that you're being awfully evasive for somebody who has nothing to hide."

"You didn't look in my files?"

"I didn't have time," Hannah said defiantly. "You and Katie came back into the room before I had a chance."

Matthew felt inordinately relieved. He was not ready to share the truth about his parentage with anyone, not even Hannah. *Especially* not Hannah!

"Is the real reason why you came to Clover in your files?" Hannah demanded. "And don't even try to use that lame story about researching insects for a book!"

"You're right. That story was lame. But I really am a writer." *When being evasive or lying, always stick as closely to the truth as possible.* Matthew followed the course taken by his protagonists in his books. Reveal as much as necessary and as little as possible.

Hannah was regarding him with frank disbelief.

"It's true," he insisted. "Among those paperbacks in the bag, didn't you see three by Galen Eden?"

"I don't remember. Maybe. I don't know who that is."

"You don't know who Galen Eden is and you haven't read anything he's written?" Matthew arched his brows and his mouth quirked into a wry smile. "My overinflated ego is quickly deflating. A few more minutes talking books with you and it'll be flatter than a burst balloon."

"Are you trying to say—"

"And doing it poorly, it seems," Matthew interjected dryly. "My pen name is Galen Eden, after the first names of my father and mother. I've written three books, suspense thrillers, which have sold very well, and I'm here in Clover to—" He cleared his throat. It was always tricky when it came time to alter the truth. Or to veer away from it altogether. "To do some research for my next book."

"And there's going to be a serial killer in it!" guessed Hannah. Why, it all fitted now, like pieces in a well-cut puzzle. "That's why you have those non-fiction books—to study psychopathic personalities. And the book about the first families of South Carolina?" She frowned. No, the puzzle wasn't in place yet after all. "Why are you interested in the Wyndhams?"

"What if my serial killer was from a well-respected, wealthy family with connections and influence everywhere in the state?" improvised Matthew. She'd accurately guessed that he'd planned to write a mystery about a serial murderer, though thus far he'd been unable to develop a plot. His impromptu synopsis was merely an on-the-spot device to divert her, but he was beginning to warm to it. Maybe he had the germ of an idea for a new book! He felt excitement kindling within him. He hadn't felt a creative spark in months, and now, finally, he felt his imagination lumbering slowly back to life.

"You're going to model that family after the Wyndhams?"
Hannah exclaimed.

"Suppose my fictional family has no idea that their seemingly charming son has a dark, treacherous side? Or maybe they
do and are trapped in a conspiracy to cover up for him."

"Is he threatening them? Has he hurt anyone in their exalted circle?" Hannah speculated eagerly.

"This is turning into a regular brainstorming session." Matthew smiled at her enthusiasm.

"A Wyndham who is secretly a vicious criminal. Wow!"
Hannah grinned mischievously. "Dr. Wyndham and Mr. Hyde.
They'll hate that."

"The family will be entirely fictitious. The Wyndhams will
never know they were my, er, inspiration."

"But you wanted to see the Wyndham estate to get an idea
of where and how such a family might live," guessed Hannah.

Matthew built on her supposition. "I'm not a very good de-
scriptive writer. I can plot and envision action, but I have
trouble picturing places in my mind. It helps if I can see what
I'm trying to describe."

"What will you tell Alexandra Wyndham when you call and
ask permission to visit?" Hannah asked. Without asking, she
had figured out why he'd written the woman's name in the
book. Alexandra handled the Wyndham family matters, unre-
lated to business. Anybody would've been told so when making inquiries about the family.

"I haven't come up with what to say to Alexandra." Matthew shrugged. Truer words have never been spoken. He had
no idea what to say to the woman who had given birth to him
if and when he actually did call on her. "Any advice? Any
ideas?"

Hannah tilted her head and frowned thoughtfully. "Don't
tell her you're writing a book about crime. Especially not a
potential bestselling thriller."

"Too sensational and sleazy for their refined tastes?"

"Exactly. You can say you're a writer but don't mention
what kind of books you write. It's best to stick close to the truth
when you're telling a fib and—"

"Useful advice," Matthew interrupted drolly. "I'll have to
remember that."

"Not that I'm a liar or anything," Hannah defended herself. "But there are times when something a little less than the truth is required."

"I couldn't have put it better myself."

"I've got it! You can pretend to be doing research for a serious historical novel."

"A hagiography about a glorious and beloved old Carolina family?" Matthew suggested dryly.

"The Wyndhams are active members in several historical societies. They'll probably even like the idea that you're a writer if history is involved." Hannah suddenly clapped her hands. "I have an idea! I'll introduce you to my grandmother—she'll be delighted to meet a writer—and then I'll ask Grandmother to ask Alexandra to allow you to visit the Wyndham mansion."

"And will . . . Alexandra do as your grandmother asks?"

Hannah nodded confidently. "If Grandmother asks a favor of her, especially such a minor one, Alexandra has no choice but to say yes. You see, Grandmother was a lifelong friend of Alexandra's parents, and the Wyndhams honor such ties."

"So she's well and truly stuck. Good plan!" Matthew took both Hannah's hands in his. "I appreciate your help, Hannah. I mean it."

The warmth of his smile and the strength of his hands clasping hers went through her like a heady gulp of potent wine. Within seconds, Hannah felt half drugged with a delicious lassitude. It would be so easy, so natural, to take the few steps necessary to close the gap between them. Then she would be back in his arms, where she'd been before the Polks' untimely intrusion.

The Polks . . . The thought of them proved to be as intrusive as their actual presence. And once again, Hannah was grateful for the diversion. All Matthew Granger had to do was look at her or touch her, and her mind seemed to short-circuit, leaving her body in charge.

It was exciting, yet it was unnerving. Every time they were together, things got too hot too fast. And though Hannah walked the walk and talked the talk quite convincingly, she had never been governed by her sexual impulses. Flirting was as far as she went, and it was a game she controlled with ease.

But not with Matthew. With him she was out of control, and while the adventurous rebel within her reveled in the danger, her strong self-protective instincts failed to restrain her. She pulled her hands away and reached for her coffee, clutching the cup as if it were a shield protecting her from the devastating effects of his touch.

"What's the matter?" Matthew asked huskily. Her abrupt withdrawal rankled. He'd been about to take her into his arms, and he knew damn well she'd wanted him to. Already his body was flooded with heat from simply holding her hands. That brief, innocent contact had fueled the fires that he'd managed to bank after their last physical encounter under the hotel portico. He didn't know if he had the willpower to bank them again.

"There are still too many things I don't know about you," Hannah murmured, keeping her eyes averted from him. It was easier to keep her wits when she wasn't drowning in his deep dark eyes.

"Such as the inevitable query—am I married?" Matthew drawled. "The answer is no, I am not now nor have ever been married."

Hannah blushed. "Your marital status doesn't interest me in the least," she said coolly.

"Not much," muttered Matthew. "You're not the type to have a fling with a married man."

"Let's add that I'm not the type to have a fling with you, either." She lifted her chin haughtily. "In fact, I'm not the type for flings."

"That's true. You don't have flings. You have engagements. Three at last count, I believe."

Hannah was completely taken aback. "Who told you?"

"Your good friend, Sean, last night at Fitzgerald's Bar and Grill over pitchers of beer and plates of nachos. I detected a certain sour-grapes attitude in him. Perhaps because he's never advanced to the coveted position of fiancé?"

"So during a lull in the Polk-bashing, they bashed me!" Hannah was hurt. "I thought they were my friends."

"They are." Matthew moved closer. His hands actually ached from wanting to touch her. "But I think they're a little in awe of you. My new best friend, Blaine, said you were the most beautiful girl in Clover and then went on to rhapsodize about your perfect teeth. He's proud to be your dentist."

Hannah laughed in spite of herself.

"So what about all those engagements, Hannah?"

She shrugged. "I got engaged three different times to three different Mr. Wrongs. I wasn't their idea of Miss Right, either. I guess that about sums it up."

"No melodramatic tales of broken hearts and love gone wrong?"

"Is that the past you've invented for me? Sorry to disappoint you, but I'm not a heartbreaker who casts off fiancés the way a dog shakes off fleas."

"Just as I'm not a cat burglar in town for a, uh, a caper."

"What about the gun?" Hannah asked. Her hand trembled. "You haven't explained that away yet."

"I wish I could come up with a story as inventive as yours, honey. The gun isn't a Saturday night special. It's a World War I vintage German Luger that belonged to my father. He and I used to go target shooting together, and when I heard there's a shooting range a half-hour drive from Clover, I decided to bring the Luger along and get in some practice. I almost forgot it and stuck it into the pocket of my suit jacket at the last minute."

"I don't like guns," Hannah said tightly.

"Duly noted." He reached out to stroke her cheek with gentle fingers. "I won't take you target shooting with me."

They stared at each other for a long moment. "Why all the secrecy about your writing?" she asked quietly.

"I didn't feel like dealing with the questions and comments people sometimes make when they find out what I do. Offering plot lines, asking me to read their own or a relative's manuscripts. All that gets distracting. I want to concentrate my time and energy on what I came here to do." His fingers curved around her jaw. "Are you going to blow my cover, angel face?"

"Not if you don't want me to." Hannah covered his hand with her own. She liked the idea of sharing his secret. It created an intimacy between them, a sense of exclusivity, and she wanted that, she acknowledged achingly.

"Thank you." He leaned forward, his dark eyes flaring with a passion that made her shiver with anticipation.

Hannah stared at the fine sensual lines of his mouth and felt a syrupy warmth flow through her. He was not a criminal and he was going to kiss her. At that moment, nothing else mattered.

Matthew drew her to him, his gaze tracking downward from her luscious mouth to her breasts straining against the bodice of her sundress. They were full and round, the nipples already peaked and prominent beneath the soft violet cotton. He couldn't stop himself from running his thumb over the outline of the rigid crest.

His touch electrified Hannah. She whimpered softly and breathed his name. It was an intensely private time, one that might have led anywhere.

Except that the door to the shop opened, and two sportily dressed couples in their thirties hurried inside. Hannah and Matthew sprang apart.

"It's really starting to pour!" one of the women announced. "Are we ever glad we made it in here before we got completely soaked!"

Matthew wasn't. He wished they would've taken refuge somewhere, *anywhere* else. Those explosive, seductive moments with Hannah left his body rigid and aching for sex—and something more. For the first time in months, he'd felt a connection with another person, one so strong it was primal in intensity.

He experienced a sense of loss as he watched Hannah move away from him to welcome the prospective customers. Who probably wouldn't even buy a thing, he thought disgustedly. They would hang around until the rain lessened and then leave empty-handed, wasting time he and Hannah could've spent alone together.

He watched Hannah engage the couple in conversation, probing their tastes, offering information on the items that attracted their attention. She concentrated on the women, sharing likes and dislikes, listening attentively to their replies. The men, Matthew noted, trailed dutifully after their wives, while casting covert admiring glances at Hannah. She occasionally smiled at them or directed a comment their way.

Matthew remembered Blaine Spencer's observation. "Every guy in town has been slavering over Hannah Farley for years." Apparently, vacationing husbands weren't immune to her beauty, either. Matthew knew he wasn't. He was falling hard and fast for her, and it worried him.

He hadn't been himself since arriving in Clover. The deception, the false pretenses under which he was here—it was all so unlike him. And so was chasing after a young woman who, until a short while ago, had believed him to be a criminal! Had it been the risky thrill of potential danger that attracted her to him?

The thought troubled him. He knew that Hannah Kaye Farley was accustomed to men throwing themselves at her. Any woman who was beautiful, sexy and rich was able to pick and choose among many suitors. But unlike quite a few of the beautiful, sexy and rich women he'd met, Hannah actually had a personality. She was charming and feisty, which only increased her allure.

But she wanted him. At least she had until now. Would she lose interest in him now that she knew he was a solid citizen rather than a glamorous rogue? She was not at all impressed by his success as a writer; she'd never even heard of his books till he had told her about them, and even then she hadn't expressed a desire to read one.

And didn't her three broken engagements seem to indicate a rather short attention span when it came to men? Sort of a Relationship Deficit Disorder. RDD? If such a term didn't exist, it probably soon would, with reams of talk-show guests and self-proclaimed therapists discussing the symptoms.

Matthew scowled, annoyed at his own ruminations. Was this really him, Matthew Granger, moping around an antique shop, wondering and worrying if Hannah Farley liked him? How humiliating! How ridiculous! He was a thirty-two-year-old experienced man of the world, not an infatuated fourteen-year-old!

He was feeling belligerent and ill-used when Hannah returned to the cash register with the two couples, who each carried several items. They couldn't seem to stop exclaiming over their lucky finds. When Hannah rang up the totals, Matthew was astonished at the sum.

"They had no intention of buying anything when they walked through that door," he murmured as the couples left, their purchases wrapped well to protect them from the rain. He stared at Hannah, awed. "You can really sell!"

She smiled, pleased with the sale and with Matthew's astonished acknowledgement of her prowess. "I enjoy it. It's a challenge. Some shop owners sit back and don't even glance at their customers. They let them wander around the shop and walk out without even trying to make a sale. I don't understand that. I like to talk to people, figure out what they like and what I have that would appeal to them. To make a match." Her gray eyes sparkled. "It's like a game. And when I find things to sell to people who didn't even know they wanted them, well, I win."

"And you enjoy winning." He felt a tidal wave of sensual hunger rise up in him and fought the urge to pull her into his arms and kiss her until she was weak and soft and clinging to him. The way she'd been each time he'd kissed her before.

"Of course." She arched her dark brows, her smile one of sultry challenge. "Who doesn't?"

Matthew's mouth was dry. He knew he had it bad when simply one of her smiles had a throbbing, visceral effect on him. "You're a dangerous woman, Hannah Farley."

And he would do well to remember that. Especially at this particular time in his life when the uncertainties of his newly discovered past were wreaking havoc on his equilibrium. He had to make a conscious effort to tame the lust that intensified every time he looked at her; he had to prove to himself that he wasn't so captivated by her that he couldn't master his desire.

He quickly calculated a plan, one that kept him firmly in control. He would make use of Hannah Farley socially—her acquaintance with his birth mother was an invaluable aid to his quest—and sexually, if she let him. And oh, how he hoped she would let him! But he would *not* become emotionally entrapped by her. He intended to leave Clover as romantically unencumbered as when he'd arrived.

Hannah was watching him. She saw the range of emotions play across his face. His intensity excited her. And though they were in the shop with the possibility of more customers entering at any time, she had to be closer to him. She wanted him to kiss her, right here, right now.

She sauntered over and stopped in front of him, so close that their bodies were almost touching. Tilting her head, she gazed up at him through her thick dark lashes. "Matthew?"

She was flirting with him, teasing him. Challenging him to make his move. She *expected* him to grab her. Matthew clenched his jaw so tightly his teeth were grinding together, but he didn't lay a hand on her. He would prove that he was strong enough to resist little Miss Irresistible.

"Now that I know you're a writer, I would really like to read your books." Hannah laid one slim-fingered hand on his chest. Her crimson nails provided a sensuous contrast against the backdrop of his charcoal gray shirt. "There's a bookstore on

Clover Street run by my friend, Emma Wynn. You met her last night at Fitzgerald's with her friend, Kenneth Drake." One well-shaped nail traced the small signature emblem on his shirt. "Do you think your books will be in stock at her store? Or can I order them?"

Why isn't he touching me? Hannah thought. *A short while ago, he couldn't resist me. Did he decide to be offended because I thought he was a thief? Was his ego bruised because I didn't know a thing about his books or his success as a writer?*

Determinedly she moved closer. The peaks of her breasts touched the muscular wall of his chest; her thighs skimmed his.

Matthew felt as if a lightning bolt had zapped him. His body was so hot and wired, he could probably serve as an electrical conductor. "I brought some copies of my books with me." His voice sounded strained and unnatural. *If you touch her, she wins,* he reminded himself. "You saw them in my bag. I'll give them to you."

"Thank you, Matthew." Hannah was in despair. *Doesn't he want me anymore? How could he change his mind so fast?* And then he involuntarily shifted his body, and she felt the hard rigid length of his erection against her.

Oh, he still wanted her! There was absolutely no mistake about that! But for some stupid reason, he'd decided to restrain himself from making the first move. Hannah was perplexed. What should she do now? She wasn't used to initiating physical advances; she was usually busy fending them off. But if she didn't feel his mouth on hers soon, she would die!

Matthew studied her face, thoroughly enjoying her dilemma. She wanted him as much as he wanted her. The realization thrilled him far more than it should have, but he didn't care. He waited for her to make her move, for he was certain that she would. He was going to win this round!

But victory eluded him as the door to the shop opened, and a tall, dark-haired young man strode inside as if he owned the place. Matthew felt frustration roiling through him. It took considerable control to keep from uttering the curses that were running through his head. He waited for Hannah to scurry away from him, to run off to charm her latest customer into buying something he didn't know he wanted.

But Hannah stayed where she was. Groaning softly, she turned toward the man, but stayed close enough to Matthew so that her hip and arm were touching him. "It's my brother." She did not sound pleased. "What do you want, Bay?"

Bay Farley headed toward them, glanced briefly at Matthew and dismissed him as not worth acknowledging. "I want a special gift for Justine," Bay announced importantly. "Can you tear yourself away from your latest boyfriend to pick something out for her?"

Six

___

Her brother's words hit Matthew like a bucket of cold water and strengthened his resolve. *Her latest boyfriend?* Oh, no, not him! He was not going to allow himself to join the hapless club of Hannah Farley's castoffs.

Matthew laid his hand on the small of Hannah's back and leaned down to murmur in her ear, "This time it's a draw, you little tease." His fingers kneaded the sensuous hollow at the base of her spine, and shivers of pleasure tingled through every nerve ending. His thumb traced the outline of the hip-hugging lacy band of her panties through the material of her sundress. "But keep in mind that until Big Brother showed up, *I* was winning."

She whirled her head around so fast that her long dark tresses flew out and whipped his face. "I didn't realize there was a competition going on," she said tersely. "If I had, you can believe that—"

She didn't get to finish her threat. Bay was upon them, his expression petulant. "Mother says I ought to bring Justine a special little gift when I go over there tonight. She said you'd be able to suggest something, Hannah. I certainly have no idea what to give the girl."

"Me?" Hannah moved away from Matthew, as annoyed with him as she was with her brother. "If you're almost engaged to her, you have to know Justine a lot better than I do, Bay. What do you want to give her? What sort of things does she like? What are her interests?"

"How am I supposed to know?" snapped Bay. "She's practically mute when she's around me. Alexandra and I carry on splendid conversations while Justine hovers in the background like a wraith. For a Wyndham, she is certainly socially inept! I shall expect her personality to improve drastically when she is Mrs. Baylor Farley."

"Well, if Justine's personality doesn't suit you, and you and Alexandra get along so well, why don't you marry *Alex*, Bay?" Hannah asked snidely. "She's divorced and available. So what if she's twenty years older than you? Older-woman-younger-man relationships are quite trendy these days. Then you would be Justine's wicked stepfather, just like in the fairy tales except for the gender change. I think it's a role you were born to play."

"Alexandra Wyndham?" Matthew didn't realize that he'd spoken aloud until he heard his own voice.

"This doesn't concern you." Bay glanced impatiently at Matthew, not bothering to conceal his disdain for someone he considered a lesser being. It was the way he treated all Hannah's friends unless they possessed the requisite social pedigrees.

And though Matthew's flippant sexual arrogance had her seething only moments before, Bay's attack on him triggered Hannah's rebellious streak—and a sudden inexplicable loyalty to Matthew that she hadn't been aware of until right now.

She gave him her warmest smile to make up for Bay's snub. "We're talking about Alexandra Wyndham and her daughter, Justine, who just turned twenty. The poor kid is being railroaded into marrying my viperous brother here." Hannah faced her brother, a steely glint in her gray eyes. "And Bay, this *does* concern Matthew because he's been asked by a very prestigious historical society to write a book about the Wyndham's role in South Carolina history. He has a meeting scheduled with Alexandra, and Grandmother is going with him to make the introductions. Didn't I mention Matthew's grandparents were great friends of Grandmother and Granddaddy? They're the Grangers of—"

NO RISK, NO OBLIGATION TO BUY… NOW OR EVER!

PLAY

"ROLL A DOUBLE"

AND GET UP TO

FIVE FREE GIFTS!

HERE'S HOW TO PLAY:

1. Peel off the label from the front cover. Place it in the space provided in the coupon to the right. With a coin, carefully scratch off the silver dice. Then check the claim chart to see what we have for you – up to four books and a gift – ALL YOURS! ALL FREE!

2. Send back this card and you'll receive specially selected Silhouette® novels from the Desire™ series. These books are yours to keep absolutely FREE.

3. There's no catch. You're under no obligation to buy anything. We charge you nothing for your first shipment. And you don't have to make a minimum number of purchases – not even one!

4. The fact is, thousands of readers enjoy receiving their books by mail from the Reader Service™. They like the convenience of home delivery and they like getting the best new romance novels at least a month before they are available in the shops. And, of course, postage and packing is completely FREE!

5. We hope that after receiving your free books you'll want to remain a subscriber. But the choice is yours – to continue or cancel, any time at all! So why not accept our no-risk invitation. You'll be glad you did!

You'll look a million dollars when you wear this lovely necklace! Its cobra-link chain is a generous 18" long, and the lustrous simulated pearl completes this attractive gift.

ENLARGED TO
SHOW DETAIL

"ROLL A DOUBLE!"

PLACE LABEL HERE

SCRATCH HERE

SEE CLAIM CHART BELOW

YES! I have placed my label from the front cover into the space provided above and scratched off the silver dice. Please rush me the free books and gift for which I qualify, as shown on the claim chart below. I understand that I am under no obligation to purchase any books, as explained on the back and on the opposite page. I am over 18 years of age.

D8EI

MS/MRS/MISS/MR _____ INITIALS _____

BLOCK CAPITALS PLEASE

SURNAME _____

ADDRESS _____

_____

POSTCODE _____

C L A I M   C H A R T

⚅ ⚅	**4 FREE BOOKS** PLUS FREE PEARL DROP NECKLACE	
⚅ ⚃	**3 FREE BOOKS**	
⚅ ⚀	**2 FREE BOOKS**	

CLAIM NO. 37-829

THE READER SERVICE : HERE'S HOW IT WORKS

Accepting the free books and gift places you under no obligation to buy anything. You may keep the books and gift and return the despatch note marked "cancel". If we don't hear from you, about a month later we will send you 6 brand new books and invoice you just £2.50* each. That's the complete price - there is no extra charge for postage and packing. You may cancel at any time, otherwise every month we'll send you 6 more books, which you may either purchase or return - the choice is yours.

*Prices subject to change without notice.

THE READER SERVICE™
FREEPOST SEA3794
CROYDON
Surrey
CR9 3AQ

▼ DETACH AND RETURN THIS CARD TODAY. NO STAMP NEEDED! ▼

"Florida," Matthew supplied promptly. He accorded her imaginative powers and the speed with which she exercised them his greatest respect. On the spur of the moment, she'd conjured up a far more clever and legitimate reason for his presence in Clover than his insipid insect tale.

"Florida," Hannah repeated. She saw the look of chagrin on Bay's face and exulted. "Oh, Baylor, just wait till I tell Grandmother and Alexandra how rude you were to Matthew Granger!" she exclaimed gleefully. "They'll be appalled!"

Bay shot her his I-don't-know-why-Mother-and-Daddy-ever-had-you look, the one he'd been giving her ever since she'd been placed in her bassinet upon her arrival in the Farley home. Then he turned to Matthew with a forced, sickly grin and held out his hand. "I truly apologize, Granger. I had no idea who you were. Hannah should have introduced us immediately, but of course she's too perverse for conventional etiquette. I would like to extend to you my warmest welcome to Clover, and I do hope you'll see fit to forgive my, uh, unfortunate lapse. I'm on the verge of getting engaged, you see, and I'm afraid my bachelor nerves are a tad strained."

Hannah watched Matthew shake her brother's hand and accept his apology with a cool smile. At least she assumed it was a smile. There was definitely a flash of straight white teeth but the effect was more carnivorous than congenial.

Matthew resisted the urge to crunch the bones in Bay Farley's hand during their obligatory handshake. Perhaps he would have if he hadn't still been reeling from the stunning news. *He had a little sister!* Justine, age twenty, who, according to Hannah, was being pushed into marrying this insufferable snob.

His eyes narrowed as he studied Bay Farley's fine aristocratic features, and he made a promise to himself and to the sister he had yet to meet. From this moment on, no one could malign his little sister the way Farley had disparaged Justine and get away with it. Matthew burned with newfound sibling fervor. Baylor Farley's prospective engagement to Justine was never going to happen. Her big brother would see to that!

"Bay, I think I know what you can give Justine," Hannah said sweetly.

Matthew was immediately suspicious of that saccharine tone of hers. One glance at her slitted gray eyes and arched brows confirmed his hunch. She was definitely plotting something treacherous. But her self-absorbed brother did not pick up on it, assuming that she was finally, inevitably, willing to oblige him.

Shortly thereafter, Bay left the shop several hundred dollars poorer, carrying the wrapped gift for his young bride-to-be.

"A mourning picture?" Matthew murmured as Bay strode grandly out the door. "I've never heard of such a thing. It's downright creepy."

He grimaced, thinking of the small original watercolor dated 1840, which commemorated a young boy who had died that year at the age of five. The picture showed two somber adults, presumably the parents, flanking the tombstone lettered with the child's name and dates of birth and death. A small portrait of a child's profile was sketched in the right-hand corner. There was a distinct melancholy feel to the sad little painting.

"Mourning pictures were common before photography was available to families, especially as a memento of a dead child," Hannah said. "I think the watercolor is touching, but it isn't an appropriately romantic gift from a would-be fiancé. I'm hoping Justine will take one look at it and another look at Bay and run for her life!"

"You think they're that ill-matched?" Matthew watched her intently.

"It's not a match. It's a train wreck! And I feel like I'm being made to stand and watch and do nothing to stop it."

"But you are doing something," Matthew reminded her. Her distress was real. Just as she hadn't maligned his paternal relatives, the Polks, she wanted to help his young Wyndham half sister. The surge of warmth that he felt for her as he gazed at her beautiful face was far more compelling than sexual urgency. "I think we could describe your intervention as sabotage by antique artistry."

"I hope the Wyndhams will think Bay is morbid and insensitive and not the suitable choice they've imagined him to be." Hannah crossed her fingers on both hands. "And I really hope Justine will tell her mother that she'd rather be featured in her own mourning picture than marry Bay Farley."

"Marriage to your brother strikes you as a fate worse than death?" Matthew asked wryly.

"Maybe not for some social-climbing narcissist just like him, but for Justine it would be sheer hell. I feel so sorry for her. It must be awful to be a shy Wyndham. I can really identify with someone whose nature doesn't fit the family mold and expectations. But I'm luckier than Justine. I've always had my grandmother firmly on my side. From what I can tell, there is no one in the Wyndham family to champion Justine. She's quiet and insecure. Her father is a womanizing drunk who rarely sees her, and her mother is domineering in that terrifyingly self-confident Wyndham way. Marrying poor little Justine off to Bay, who doesn't have a sensitive cell in his body, strikes me as cruel and unusual punishment!"

"Cruel and unusual punishment is unconstitutional," Matthew remarked, striving to remain calm. "So we can't let that happen, can we? Did I tell you that I'm also a lawyer? I gave up practicing law to write full-time."

"A lawyer? And here I'd pegged you on the wrong side of the law." Hannah stared at him, her gray eyes alert and curious. "Any more secrets, Mr. Granger?"

"You would be amazed, my sweet."

She was about to ask him what a lawyer could do to save Justine from a loveless marriage to Bay when the door to the shop opened again, and a group of middle-aged women entered the shop, talking and laughing among themselves.

"Now there's a challenge," Matthew murmured. "Seven women at once. Won't the intensity of your charming sales pitch be drastically diluted?"

Hannah responded instantly to the challenge. "I can sell something to every one of them. It might be just a little thing, but I bet I make seven sales."

"You're on, baby. I say you won't. The loser—"

"Pays for dinner at Clarke's Steak House tonight," Hannah said quickly.

"A steak house in a coastal town with fishermen supplying fresh fish daily? What a waste!"

"Clarke's is great!" Hannah said loyally. "*And* it features the catch of the day along with the best steaks in South Carolina."

"Good. I'll sit back and dream about dinner while you strike out with the ladies. I like to win, too, princess," he added imperturbably.

She left him sitting behind the counter and went over to join the women, smiling at them as if their presence in her shop was the most wonderful thing that had ever happened to her.

Forty-five minutes later, all seven ladies left, each one having found and purchased their own particular treasure.

Hannah and Matthew dined together later that evening at Clarke's Steak House on Clover Street, feasting on bowls of she-crab soup and steaks. Matthew had decided to forgo the catch of the day after all.

"I don't trust anything that is labeled as zesty," he muttered, upon hearing the seafood special was "Zesty Fillet of Sole." "I'm sticking with just plain steak."

"Sounds good to me. And since you're buying and everything on the menu is à la carte, I think I'll also have a salad and vegetables, and dessert, of course," Hannah announced mischievously.

"Going to soak me, huh?" Matthew took his loss good-naturedly. "I guess I deserve it. You could sell hamburgers to vegetarians. When it comes to the art of the sale, I'll never bet against you again." Having spent most of the day with her at Yesterdays, he'd seen firsthand that her success in selling was no fluke.

Tommy Clarke, one of several Clarkes who worked at the family restaurant, stopped by their table frequently to ask if everything was to their satisfaction.

"Maybe we should pull up a chair and invite him to join us," Matthew grumbled after Tommy's fourth foray to their table. "I feel as if we're being chaperoned."

"Life in Clover is something of a goldfish bowl," Hannah conceded. "And you're something of a curiosity, Matthew. You haven't moved here, but you don't fit into the tourist category, either. You were at Abby and Ben's engagement party, then you turned up at Fitzgerald's with a gang of Clover residents. And—"

"Let's not forget that I was seen making out with the town beauty while slow dancing with her," Matthew interjected glibly.

Hannah drew a shuddery breath. His mention of that wild hot kiss evoked a sweet surge of sensation within her. As if it were happening all over again, she could feel his mouth on hers, his body hard and hot against her. She touched her fingers to her lips.

Matthew gazed into her eyes, the candle flame flickering shadows over his face, his expression almost primitive. He slid his long muscular legs alongside hers and rested them there, letting her feel the sensual weight and strength of his limbs.

Hannah's heartbeat accelerated as she felt the firm warmth of his thighs, of his calves heating her legs, sending flames of sensation deep into the most secret, intimate part of her. The instant physical attraction she'd felt for him was rapidly intensifying, and the time they'd spent together today, the things she'd learned about him, heightened this natural affinity they seemed to share.

There was a sensual determination in his gaze that simultaneously thrilled her and kept her on edge. *"This time it's a draw, you little tease,"* he'd said in the shop when Bay had made his unwelcome appearance.

Was he playing games with her? Hannah tried to stem the vague hurt welling inside her. She'd never had trouble reading men before, normally she could trust her instincts. But Matthew's allure had all but obliterated them. For the first time in her life, she felt totally uncertain of herself. It was far worse than last night when she'd thought he was a thief. At least that theory had served as something of a restraint. Now she couldn't summon up any reason whatsoever to keep him at bay.

Except that he might be using her. Playing games to amuse himself while she fell deeper and harder for him. Caution warred with desire and won. She inched her chair farther down the table, drew her legs under the rungs of the chair and sat up very straight. If it was a game he wanted, she was a player.

"I'm glad the rain has finally stopped," she said in the bright, friendly tones he'd heard her use with her customers all day in the shop. "I know this is thunderstorm season, but enough is enough."

Matthew was frustrated because she had reverted to her social smile and social chatter, and he wanted her private self, the one she'd already shared with him. "Have I ever mentioned how much I hate to talk about the weather?" he growled.

"What do you like to talk about, Matthew?" She was flirting with him, harmlessly and impersonally, the way she might flirt with any other man.

He didn't want to be relegated to every-other-man status; he wanted to see passion and need flare in her eyes when she looked at him, the way she had a few minutes ago. Yet now she seemed bent on proceeding as if she were on a routine dinner date with any one of her Clover pals.

Matthew frowned. He was used to setting the pace and determining the course of events. Suddenly he was supposed to accommodate someone else's agenda, intentions and limitations?

"Are you really from Florida?" Hannah continued, determined to break the silence and draw him out.

Matthew knew what she was doing; he'd been watching her operate all day. If they'd been in Yesterdays, she would be trying to match him up with a set of Howdy Doody jelly glasses to take home.

"If you aren't from Florida, have you ever been there?" persisted Hannah.

Matthew heaved a resigned sigh. She wasn't going to give up. He might as well carry on the dull, getting-to-know-you conversation she was attempting to conduct.

"I have a condo in Pensacola, Florida," he admitted. "I wasn't raised there, though. My dad was a navy captain and I grew up on naval bases all over the world. My folks retired to Pensacola and I bought a place there, too, to be near them."

He felt the familiar pain of their loss welling within him. He knew he wouldn't continue living there now they were gone. He hated thinking about it, talking about it. Matthew frowned again. "So that's a summary of my geographic history. Okay?"

"Okay." Hannah smiled. "And I promise not to ask you a single thing about the weather there."

The dinner went surprisingly well from then on. They found a lot to talk about and it wasn't dull at all. Both had traveled extensively and been to many of the same places. They exchanged observations and opinions on cities and states and countries, sharing some, disagreeing on others. They talked music and movies, swapped political and celebrity gossip.

The conversation never flagged. They were still conversing animatedly as they left the restaurant and walked along Clover Street hand in hand. They paused frequently to gaze in the windows of the shops they passed. One was the Clover Street Drugstore.

"Do you mind if we go in for a minute?" Hannah asked. "I have to buy a couple of things."

"Not at all. I might need something, too."

They temporarily split up inside. Hannah bought a box of tissues to replace the nearly empty one at her shop, a roll of film and a box of coffee-flavored candies that her grandmother enjoyed. Matthew joined her at the cash register, carrying a small paper bag containing a purchase of his own.

"Candy?" Matthew was amused. "If you wanted more dessert, you should have told me. I'd've sprung for another piece of strawberry cheesecake."

"These are for my grandmother. She's the one with the colossal sweet tooth. She goes through a box of these every other day."

Hannah paid for the items and they strolled outside into the warm June night. There was a pleasant, offshore breeze and the humidity was comfortably low after the days of rain.

"I'm looking forward to meeting your grandmother," Matthew said. "I still can't believe she agreed to arrange a meeting with Alexandra Wyndham for me and to pretend to Bay that she knows me and my grandparents. I never even knew my grandparents."

"Grandmother is so cool," Hannah said proudly. "Don't worry. She'll invent a credible set of grandparents for you. She's always ready for adventure or intrigue."

"Or trouble. Which I imagine her granddaughter supplies in spades." Matthew rolled his eyes heavenward. "What a pair! All you had to do was ask her to be your accomplice over the phone this afternoon and she immediately agreed. She liked the idea of a mystery writer pretending to be writing a history book in order to dupe the Wyndhams. She was delighted to go along with your harebrained scheme."

"*Our* harebrained scheme," Hannah corrected him. "You're the one who wants to see the Wyndham estate, remember? I just dreamed up your historical-society cover."

"For which I owe you a great debt of gratitude. How shall I repay you?" They stopped near the steps of the picturesque Clover Town Hall. Matthew lifted her hand to his mouth, lightly kissing each fingertip.

Hannah's nerves tingled excitingly but she tried to play it cool. "Well, when you write your book about the nasty society-boy-turned-serial-killer, don't name one of his victims Hannah."

"Done," he agreed, then added, "I remember promising to give you copies of my books. Would you like them now?"

While she was nodding her head, he tucked her hand in his and started toward the boardinghouse. Tonight there would not be a spirited crowd of party guests to act as chaperones.... Her heart somersaulted wildly in her chest. She and Matthew talked as they went along, but she couldn't remember a thing they'd said, not even moments after saying it.

The place was quiet when they entered, although the hallway and the big living room were well lit. Hannah cast a quick glance into the room. It had been returned to its normal postparty state. The knickknacks were back on the tables, the furniture, which had been pushed aside to create the dance floor, was back in position. The long aluminum tables set up to hold refreshments had been folded up and put away.

Hannah waved to Katie, who was sitting on the sofa and talking to two silver-haired women occupying the chintz-covered wing chairs by the fireplace.

Matthew nodded and smiled at Katie and the two elderly women. "The Porter sisters, Dotty and Ella," He murmured to Hannah. "I met them this morning when they arrived for their annual six-week stay in Clover."

"Good evening, Matthew," one of the Porters called to him. "We were about to turn on the television and watch the ball game. You and your lovely young friend are welcome to join us."

"That's very kind of you, Dotty, but I'm taking her upstairs to see my etchings." Matthew flashed a lascivious grin.

"Matthew!" Hannah admonished, blushing.

The Porter sisters laughed heartily. One of them gave Matthew a thumbs-up.

"I have to talk to Katie," Hannah said desperately. Panicky qualms assailed her.

Matthew trapped her between the wall and his body. "What about?"

"I—I want to tell her that I was mistaken about your—identity. When I thought you were a cat burglar, I told her not to say anything about the Wyndhams to you. But since you're not a common criminal after all, I wanted to let her know that she can answer your questions about them."

"How much does Katie know about the Wyndhams?" Matthew was genuinely curious.

Hannah's blush grew hotter. "Well, nothing really. But I think she—"

"Are you afraid to be alone with me?" His dark eyes laughed at her. He seemed to find her rapidly crumbling composure immensely entertaining. "Is that what this sudden fit of nerves is all about?"

"No!" Hannah was aghast. It was horrifying, the way he seemed to see right through her. And for him to know that she'd been reduced to a state of adolescent jitters was a most embarrassing plight. She cringed. "I—I just wasn't expect- ing—" Half laughing, half scowling, she curled her fingers into a fist and aimed for him. "Your *etchings?*"

Matthew captured her fist easily, fitting his big hand around it. "Well, I couldn't say my *books,* could I? We're keeping my writing career a secret—at least with this crowd. We've in- vented a phony historical-writing career for the Wyndhams." He shook his head ruefully. "This is starting to get confusing. We have too many stories to keep straight."

"How does that old saying go?" mused Hannah. " 'What a tangled web we weave, when first we practice to deceive.' Or something along those lines."

Indeed, Matthew silently agreed. And she didn't even know there was yet another tangle in the deceptive web—his true reason for being here. To investigate his seemingly incompre- hensible Wyndham-Polk parentage. Matthew felt a flash of guilt for keeping that crucial secret from her. She'd proven herself to be trustworthy and a valuable ally. She deserved to know.

But he knew he wasn't ready to tell her. He didn't know if he would ever be ready to tell anyone.

"Come on, let's go up." He kept hold of her hand, leading her up the staircase. "I promise not to make a heavy pass at you, not unless you beg me to."

"A snowstorm at the Strawberry Festival is more likely. You can give me the books and be back down to join the Porter sis- ters for the game before 'The Star-Spangled Banner' is fin- ished being sung."

She followed him into his room, his hand still gloving hers. She would get the books and leave, Hannah promised herself. She stood in the middle of the room as Matthew switched on the bedside lamp, then walked calmly to the door and closed it.

"Do you want me to lock it?" His dark eyes gleamed with challenge.

Hannah fumed. He was testing her, baiting her. Trying to make her lose her cool all over again. Matthew Granger might not be a cat burglar but he was an incorrigible tease. A flirt. She gulped. He was a lot like her.

The sudden insight amused her. Now she knew exactly how to play this scene. "I don't care." She shrugged nonchalantly. "Do whatever you want."

"The perfect opening." Matthew grinned. "If I were writing your lines, I couldn't have come up with a better lead-in for me to say, 'Suppose I want to take off your clothes, lay you down on that bed and—'"

"This is where you'd have to write that I say, 'In your dreams, mister.'"

"I already did, in my dreams, sweetheart." His eyes held hers, and there was not a trace of mockery or laughter there now, only a deep, passionate hunger. "Last night I had the hottest, wildest dream and you were the star."

Color surged to her cheeks. Her thoughts seemed to scramble. She was having trouble making the rapid adjustment from lighthearted teasing to this intense urgency that made her tremble.

She watched, hypnotized, as Matthew kicked off his shoes, propped up the pillows and stretched out on the bed. "Come here," he commanded huskily.

Hannah stood rooted to the spot, her pulse pounding in her ears. "I can't go to bed with you, Matthew." Her voice was little more than a breathless whisper.

"You think it's too soon to make love? All right, I accept that." He held out his hand to her. "Can you sit here with me for a while?"

The tip of her tongue flicked between her parted lips and traced their shape. "And just talk?"

"We can talk about anything you want." His tone was as soft and smooth as silk. "Even the weather. I bet you have some great stories about Hurricane Hugo when it hit the Carolina coast."

"As a matter of fact, I do." It occurred to Hannah that if any other man on the face of the earth was lying on his bed, urging her to join him there for a chat, she would've already been out the door. But Matthew Granger was the man, and she was in no hurry to leave.

"I can't wait to hear them," Matthew drawled.

"First I want the books you promised me."

"You know where they are." Matthew pointed to his canvas bag lying in the corner of the room. "Help yourself." He had already removed the birth certificate. Anyone in Clover could search his bag and find nothing to reveal his secret.

Remembering her earlier furtive hunt, Hannah rather sheepishly unzipped his bag. Among the collection of paperbacks, she chose the three titles authored by Galen Eden. On the inside back cover of each was a picture of Matthew himself, unsmiling as he stared into the camera with intense black eyes.

"It really is you!" she exclaimed.

"Did you doubt me? I'm crushed."

"I didn't doubt you. It's just that I've never met anybody I know on the cover of a book. It's exciting."

"I was hoping it would have that effect on you."

"Seduction by book cover?" Hannah laughed. "Do you often find yourself fending off literary groupies?"

"Not after they've seen this photo." He cast a critical eye at the picture of himself. "I look like a vampire contemplating blood types."

"The picture doesn't do you justice," Hannah said tactfully. "You are much better-looking in person." She sat down on the edge of the bed, leafing through the three books. "Why do you have all those other writers' books with you?"

"I like to check out the competition when I have the time. Don't you visit other antique shops?"

She nodded her head, then stacked the three books on the small nightstand beside the bed. "Thank you for the books, Matthew."

"My pleasure, Hannah." He leaned toward her and slipped his hands under her arms. "Still scared?"

"I'm not scared of you," she confessed in a quiet voice.

"Good."

With one swift, deft movement, he lifted her across him so that she was lying, half on top of him and half beside him, on the middle of the bed.

Their eyes locked, and the impact was physical. Hannah basked in his dark gaze, her body feeling warm and fluid. She felt as if she were drifting in a sensuous dreamworld, and she loved it. Matthew twined his fingers through her hair, stroking the silky tresses. He arranged it around her head like a lustrous raven cloud.

"You are so beautiful," he said softly.

The words meant nothing to Hannah. It was his warmly romantic tone and the sexy way he was gazing at her that thrilled her.

"I can't believe we met just twenty-four hours ago," she murmured, languidly reaching up to caress his cheek with her hand. "I feel as if I've known you forever."

Certainly she had been waiting for him forever, Hannah realized with sudden clarity. Through countless dates and three engagements, she had been waiting for Matthew Granger. And now he was here, looking at her with hot dark eyes, bold with desire.

A soft explosion of sensual need made her feel warm and swollen and achy. A wild and wanton recklessness careened through her. She had waited and waited, for years she had waited, joking her way through the propositions, slapping away eager, sweaty hands, enduring kisses that bored her, slipping furtive glances at her wristwatch while waiting to go home to dream about the man who would awaken the voluptuous passion slumbering within her.

She'd finally found him! Hannah gazed at Matthew with shining gray eyes. His kisses stirred her in a way she'd never before experienced and she yearned for the touch of his hands. Going home to her lonely bed was unthinkable. She wanted to stay here with him, talking and laughing . . . and loving.

Hannah was dazed by the force of the emotions surging through her. Her presence here in his bedroom took on the mystical aura of inevitability. Their meeting and this night had been fated, she decided. Matthew had been destined to come to Clover, just as her destiny was to be waiting for him when he arrived.

Just one tiny niggling doubt remained. There was a question she had to ask him, and if his answer was right, she would know . . .

"Do you do this all the time, Matthew?" Hannah bit her lip, trying to blink back a sudden rush of emotional tears. She succeeded, just barely.

He kissed her palm. "I'm not sure what 'this' is."

Hannah quivered. "Giving copies of your books to women you've charmed into your bedroom. Inviting them to lie down and...talk."

"Good grief, is that what you think of me?" Matthew bolted upright, insulted by the charge. "I've had relationships, but not one-night stands. I'm not one of those sleazy guys who hops into bed with any woman who crosses my path. As for the books, I usually don't even carry copies around with me. The concept of handing them out as lures to impressionable young women strikes me as nothing less than reptilian. I only brought them here because—"

He broke off abruptly. How could be explain that he'd brought the copies to Clover because he'd had some stupid—and decidedly erroneous—notion that the man and woman who had created him might be interested in seeing their own son's creations? What had seemed plausible while packing for this trip now struck him as pathetic.

He felt like an idiot. Considering who his birth parents had turned out to be, the very idea was laughable. Being a Polk, his father probably couldn't read; being a Wyndham, his mother would shudder with distaste at his prole endeavors. In fact, both would probably recoil in shock and horror when he announced his existence.

Hannah stared at him. His answer was the one she wanted to hear, but the mysterious pain flickering in his eyes concerned her, intrigued her, too. She wondered what he was thinking but instinctively knew he wouldn't tell her. He had retreated behind an impenetrable wall of reserve, closing her out.

She didn't like this sudden emotional distance between them. She wanted to erase the private anguish that he wouldn't share, to see his onyx eyes gleaming with laughter again. Or flaring with passion.

Hannah made up her mind then and there. It was time. Tonight was the night. Impulsively she linked her arms around his neck and drew his head down to hers, touching her mouth to his, the pressure light but persuasive.

Matthew's hand cupped the back of her head but he didn't take over the kiss. He tried to evade it. "This isn't a good idea, honey. You're a sweet girl, and I've got to warn you that getting mixed up with me at this time in my life would be a big mistake."

His warm breath caressed her lips as he spoke, making them tingle. Hannah wriggled against him, trying to get closer to the enticing heat of his body. "You're a sweet man for warning me, but in case you haven't noticed, we're already mixed up."

"Point taken." He smiled in spite of himself. "Who could argue with that bit of—"

"I don't want to argue about anything." Hannah gazed deeply into his eyes. "Kiss me, Matthew," she whispered.

She'd made up her mind, and there was no stopping her. Why should they wait any longer? She'd been waiting for him all of her twenty-six years.

"Does this mean they'll be serving strawberries with snow at the festival this year?" Matthew asked lightly. He touched her cheek.

Hannah remembered their earlier conversation and smiled. "I didn't beg you to kiss me. I *ordered* you to."

Matthew was enthralled. He forgot that he couldn't allow himself the luxury of falling under Hannah Farley's intoxicating spell. How could he not take that beautiful, sultry mouth? He had been crazy to think he could resist her. Why had he even tried?

Opening his mouth over hers, he thrust his tongue deep inside. Hannah moaned, clutching at him and responding in kind to the urgent strokes of his tongue, to the rapacious demands of his lips.

His hand closed over her breast, gently kneading. Hannah encouraged him with a sigh of pleasure. His fingers drew her nipple into a taut nub that was visible through the shirred cotton of her dress. He deepened their kiss as she shoved the thin straps of her sundress over her shoulders, then yanked the bodice down to her waist. He quickly disposed of her pale violet strapless bra.

For a moment, his eyes feasted on her. Her breasts were full and round, the nipples a dusky rose, beaded and prominent. The sight sent sharp stabs of pure male hunger vibrating through him.

Hannah whimpered as his fingers found her sensitive nipples, his touch deft and whisper soft. It was as if there were an invisible wire attached from the tip of her nipple to the inner depth of her womb, and shock waves of pleasure ricocheted through her. She arched upward as his mouth closed over her breast and he began to suck seductively, rhythmically, until she was writhing and moaning and clinging to him, almost sobbing with pleasure. Then he took the other rosy peak between his lips and treated it to the same sensual ministrations.

"It feels so good," Hannah groaned in a breathless, sexy voice she hardly recognized as her own. She slipped her hands under his shirt and smoothed them over the muscled strength of his back. "You feel so good, Matthew," she added throatily, giving herself free reign to touch him, luxuriating in the sensuous exploration.

A deep, low growl rumbled from Matthew's throat. "You're so responsive, so passionate," he breathed. "My sweet, sexy, beautiful angel." Her fiery arousal heightened his own excitement. Had any woman ever wanted him with such pure feminine need?

His body pounded with desire as the fierce and fiery pressure built and throbbed within him. He felt as if his mind was rioting. The terrible pain and grief, the anger and the doubts of the past six months were displaced by this profound and elemental need. For Hannah and Hannah alone. Gone was the numbness and detachment that had enveloped and darkened his life. With Hannah, he felt vibrant and virile, filled with the wonder and pleasure and healing powers of love.

"Oh, Matthew." Hannah sighed his name. Just saying it filled her with tenderness. "I love you," she whispered, her voice so low she wasn't sure if he'd heard her or not.

She decided that it didn't matter if he had. She reveled in the words, the ones she'd been wanting to say to a man all her life. Just last night she had watched Ben and Abby and wondered wistfully how it would feel to love someone enough to want to give him everything, to hold nothing back and forge a future together.

Now she knew. Who would have dreamed that it would happen to her so fast, so unexpectedly? But Hannah did not question this marvelous twist of fate. She was in love at last, and her man was here, wanting her as much as she wanted him. He might not have yet uttered the words but she felt the force of his love pulsing through his body as he lifted her higher and harder against him.

Impulsively, Hannah wrapped her arms around Matthew and held him tight. The soft cloth of his shirt rubbed her naked breasts as their lips met once again. Her nipples were damp and excruciatingly sensitive, and the cloth was an irritant. She tugged his shirt from inside his waistband and pulled it up, baring his chest. She knew instinctively that the sweet, sensuous pain would be soothed by the wiry mat of male hair on his chest, and it was.

They continued their ardent play, kissing lightly, their lips teasing and nibbling each other's until neither could endure the sweet torture for another second. They simultaneously moaned their pleasure and relief when their mouths mated in the deeply intimate kiss they both craved.

It was wild and hot; it was exhilarating. And grew even more frantic and unrestrained. Kissing madly, they fumbled with their clothing, separating only momentarily to unbuckle his belt or pull off his shirt, unwilling for their lips to be apart for more than a breathless second or two.

Matthew slid his hands under the skirt of her dress, gliding along the smooth length of her thighs to cup the rounded curve of her derriere. Hannah gasped. When he put his hand between her legs and cupped her intimately, she arched her back, uttering a small sharp cry of need.

He was pleased by her uninhibited response to his touch. "Yes, sweetheart, I'll give you what you want." He caressed her, rubbing and stroking her through the violet silk of her panties.

Hannah shivered helplessly under his fingers as a shockingly pleasurable spiral of tension grew tighter and tighter inside her. Clutching at him, she slid her hands beneath the waistband of his dark cotton boxer shorts and tugged at them.

Matthew helped her divest himself of them and groaned with sheer pleasure as her slim fingers fastened around his smooth hard shaft.

Hannah was fascinated by its size and shape, by its pulsing strength, and by Matthew's reaction as she held him in her hand. Her feminine sensuality was as irresistible to him as his own masculine virility was to her. Theirs was a union, not a competition, between male and female.

Gently, Matthew drew her fingers away, chaining her wrists above her head with one strong hand. "Take it easy, baby." His voice was deep and low. "Let's make it last all night."

"But I want to touch you," Hannah breathed.

Her sexy, wide-eyed plea was almost enough to drive him over the edge. "There'll be time for that later, honey," he said raspily. "Right now, I want to enjoy you. Just close your eyes and let me please you."

Hannah moved sinuously under his hands. Her breath caught as he slipped his hand inside her panties. When he combed his fingers through the luxuriant thicket of dark curls, she whimpered his name. He swallowed the small cry as he kissed her again, wildly, ardently.

It was a relief when he pulled off her panties. Hannah lay before him, nude and aching, a slow blush suffusing her skin. Matthew gazed at her, his black eyes glowing with male admiration and desire. She felt wanton and shameless. She felt feminine and sensual and free.

With a slow, seductive smile, he opened her legs with his hand and put it where she most wanted him to.

Hannah closed her eyes and moaned. She wanted him to touch her, *needed* him there in a way she had never imagined. He caressed her with gentle pressure, exquisitely probing the secrets of her swollen, wet heat. Hannah felt delirious with pleasure. Shuddering with urgency, she twisted and turned under his masterful hand.

"I can't wait anymore, sweetie." Matthew growled sexily against her ear. "I need you . . . I want you so much."

He knelt up on the bed and reached for the small paper bag he'd brought from the drugstore. Moments later, he had sheathed himself while Hannah watched him with wide gray eyes.

"You—you bought that tonight?" She paused and took a deep breath. "Did you know that you—that we—"

Matthew smiled, his onyx eyes glowing in the soft lamplight. "Let's just say I was hoping. Really, *really* hoping. But ultimately I knew it would be your decision."

"And that you would abide by it?"

"Absolutely."

"My decision is still yes, Matthew," she said, her voice soft with passion and yearning.

His dark gaze locked with hers as he moved between her legs, his muscled thighs spreading hers open wide.

Hannah squeezed her eyes shut as he penetrated the satiny sheath of her womanhood. She was small and tight, and her body tensed, resisting him. She bit her lower lip hard to keep from crying out, yet she welcomed the intimacy despite the pain. His possession of her body bonded them in a primitive and natural and elemental way. She had been waiting for this joining, waiting for *him*.

"Relax, sweetheart," Matthew soothed. He was unable to hold back a moan of pleasure. "Hannah, love, we're perfect together."

His impassioned declaration thrilled her. And as her body slowly accommodated itself to him, the burning sharpness dissolved into a melting, liquid warmth.

A heartbeat later, he was deep inside her, hard and full. He began to move, slowly at first, then with increasing power and speed. When her body began to instinctively move in counterpoint to his rhythm, his control seemed to snap. This would be no virtuoso performance in which he calculated his every move, observing with satisfaction his partner's surrender, his power and control were never wavering.

Sheathed deep inside her, Matthew was consumed by the rapture that raged through his body like wildfire. It was too intense, too immense to be contained. The searing pleasure exploded into a shattering release, and he gave himself up to it.

And echoing in his head during those climactic moments were Hannah's soft, fervent words of love.

Seven

For several long moments afterward, Matthew lay on top of her, exhausted and spent, his body blissfully drained. The urge to fall into a satiated sleep seemed a natural ending to the explosive passion that had consumed them.

But he did not succumb to it. His mind, which had ceded control to the hungry urgency of his body, was slowly reclaiming command.

Lying beneath him, Hannah rubbed her cheek against the hollow of his shoulder, pressing her lips to his skin and tasting the salty sheen. Mindlessly traced random patterns on the smooth expanse of his back with her fingernails. Though Matthew was still inside her, her body was not relaxed and replete like his. She felt restless and edgy. An erotic ache of unsatisfied arousal throbbed deep in her abdomen, and her breasts felt swollen, the nipples ultrasensitive.

She squirmed under his weight, seeking something she could not identify. Wriggling against him seemed to help ease those sensually bedeviling symptoms. So did clenching her inner feminine muscles that were holding him within. She did it again. And again.

"Hannah, don't!" Matthew moaned. "I—I'll get hard again."

"And that's bad?" she asked huskily, running her hand through his dark hair.

"Not for me. But for you..." He fought against the taut heat rising again in his loins. "You're too tender to...take again. You're going to be sore..." The thought of inflicting pain upon her soft body instantly tamped the desire sparking within him.

And as self-awareness took precedence over the driving force of sexual need, he was shaken irrevocably out of his orgasmic bliss. He had been unable to stop, unable to control himself with her, even after he'd realized she was a virgin. The realization blindsided him.

Matthew gazed down at her. Her hair was tousled, her mouth moist and swollen from their kisses. He had been the first man to possess her; she had cried out that she loved him as he took her from virgin to lover. The possessive male pride that filled him was astonishing and appalling, too. He'd always considered himself a thoroughly modern male. Who would have guessed that this primitive machismo lurked within him?

Even more daunting was the memory of his performance. Oh, it had been fantastic for him. But what about her? Had he been too rough? He knew he'd been too fast. She hadn't climaxed; he'd been aware of that and berated himself for not satisfying her. But he'd been unable to wait, and believing her to be sexually experienced, he had thrust into her, expecting her to find ultimate ecstasy in the act.

A cave-dwelling Neanderthal had probably been a more sensitive lover than he'd been!

"Matthew, are you okay?" murmured Hannah, lightly brushing her lips along the firm line of his jaw.

"I should be the one asking you that question," he grated through his teeth. If he'd been in a hot sweat during their tumultuous mating, he was in a cold sweat now. "Are you...all right?"

He began to slowly, steadily withdraw his body from hers.

"Don't leave me," Hannah whispered and tightened her arms around him. She wanted to be held, to be cuddled, to share the wonder of this momentous event.

"Answer me, Hannah. Are you—" he gulped "—in any pain?"

What if she said yes? Should he offer to drive her to a hospital? He was completely unnerved. He'd never made love to a virgin before—not even when he'd been one himself. An older, more experienced college girl had initiated him into the pleasures of the flesh the summer after his senior year in high school. And she'd done a helluva better job with him than he had with Hannah, Matthew conceded grimly.

"I'm fine," Hannah said. It was true; physically she was fine. But his response to her, which was fast bordering on outright rejection after the most intimate act she'd ever shared with any man, was emotionally devastating.

Ashen-faced, Matthew completed his withdrawal and sat up, swinging his legs over the side of the bed. Hannah felt a thrill of sensation as their bodies separated, then an intolerable emptiness. Anxiety surged through her as she stared at Matthew, who seemed to be taking great care not to look at her.

"I know I'm new to this, but I'm fairly certain that it's not supposed to end like this," she said, attempting to sound breezy and flip.

Matthew wasn't fooled. He worried that she was perilously close to tears. Remorse and regret flooded him, for what he had done and for what he wasn't going to allow himself to do again.

"Why didn't you tell me this was your first time?" he asked gruffly.

Hannah raised herself to a sitting position. "You didn't ask."

"That's not a question a man would think to ask a woman your age, especially one with your—" He broke off abruptly.

"With my what?"

"Hannah, for heaven's sake, you were engaged three times!" His voice rose.

"So?" Her voice rose to match his. "What's your point?"

"I should think it's obvious. Those *three* men agreed to marry you without ever sleeping with you?"

"I told them I wanted to wait until I was married to make love." Hannah was defensive. "They respected my wishes. Is that so inconceivable to you?"

"Frankly, yes."

"So you ascribe to the test-drive principle? The one that goes—you wouldn't buy a car without test-driving it first, so therefore you wouldn't marry a woman unless you've slept with her?" She heaved a disgusted sigh. "My grandmother told me that old spiel was around in her day, when cars weren't all that common!''

Matthew said nothing, but his expression was grim.

Hannah watched him gather up his clothes and pull them on with ridiculous haste, assiduously avoiding any eye contact with her. ''Are you afraid I'll attack you if you're not fully dressed?'' she asked caustically as he buttoned his shirt all the way to the top and zipped up his jeans.

She resisted the overwhelming urge to grab the bedspread and pull it around her, covering her own nakedness. Instead, boldly and complete nude, she leaned back on her elbows, her legs crossed daintily at the ankles, and watched him gather up her own clothes. Her temper, already aflame, grew hotter with every passing second.

''You don't have to worry. I'm not burning with lust for your incomparable body,'' Hannah snapped.

''No?'' Matthew dropped her violet sundress and the matching bra and panties onto the bed. He was furious with himself, but Hannah's lack of guilt-induced weepiness was making him angry with her, too. She was not acting like the wounded little bird he'd wronged. He was prepared to make his humblest apologies to that pitiful young maiden, but Hannah was not following the script. Instead, she was deliberately antagonizing him.

''No!'' Hannah assured him.

Her absolute confirmation riled him further. ''You certainly were a few minutes ago.''

''That was *before* we had sex,'' Hannah said nastily. ''As far as I can tell, the experience isn't worth repeating.''

For a spit second, she wondered if she'd pushed him too far. His eyes glittered menacingly and the expression on his face was unmistakably savage. A shiver of fear ricocheted through her, and with it, tingles of excitement. She wanted him to retaliate, she realized. She'd intended to provoke him so he would lie down on the bed with her and prove her brash insult wrong.

But Matthew exerted his normal steely self-control. He hadn't forgiven himself for losing control with her tonight; he was not about to compound his sin and do it again. ''Get dressed,'' he said tightly.

He walked to the window and looked outside, giving her privacy to dress.

Hannah resented both his control and the privacy he afforded her. She wanted him to be driven wild with desire, to be unable to drag his eyes away from her—the way he'd been earlier tonight. She quickly slipped on her clothes, choking back the lump that had lodged in her throat. She must have been the world's worst lover if he couldn't even stand to look at her afterward.

Hot tears filled her eyes as she compared his current icy demeanor with his impassioned urgency such a short time ago. Obviously, he had wanted one thing from her, and one thing only. Now that he had gotten what he wanted—and hadn't been particularly pleased with her while getting it—he was eager to be rid of her.

And she was just as eager to get away from him! Stepping into her sandals, Hannah grabbed her purse and headed for the door.

"Why did you do it, Hannah?"

Matthew's voice stopped her in her tracks. She turned around and stared at him. He was still standing by the window but he was watching her. His face was closed, his dark eyes hooded.

"Why did I do it? Why did I go to bed with you?" Pride came to her rescue, displacing the hurt with a fierce, sustaining rage. "That's a good question, Matthew. I've been wondering why myself. If and when I come up with an answer, I'll let you know. Right now I'm chalking it up to an unfortunate episode of temporary insanity."

She turned the doorknob, partially opening the door.

"You said you loved me."

Matthew's words hit her like the proverbial ton of bricks. Actually, being walloped by bricks might be preferable, Hannah decided miserably. It wouldn't be as humiliating.

"I hope you didn't believe me," she countered coolly. "It's what I tell every man I'm tempted to go to bed with." She stepped into the hall and slammed the door behind her, so hard that the whole boardinghouse seemed to reverberate.

When she heard Matthew open the door, she took off at a run. Along the hall, down the stairs and out the door, she ran. She didn't turn to see if he was following her, but when she heard footsteps behind her, she quickened her speed.

Matthew caught up with her on the sidewalk before she reached the corner. He caught her by the arm, swinging her around to face him. "Don't ever try to outrun me, honey. I was on the track team in high school and in college and I still run to keep in shape.''

''Consider me uninterested and unimpressed. And stop manhandling me!''

She couldn't have hurled a more effective charge to get her way. He already felt like a brute and a cad. Matthew dropped her arm at once.

Hannah started walking briskly along the pavement, not looking at him, not speaking, either. Matthew walked at her side, easily keeping pace with her.

''Go away,'' she ordered at last. ''Leave me alone.''

''Not until I see you safely to your car.''

''The streets of Clover are safe enough for me to walk alone. I don't need your protection.''

Matthew drew a sharp breath. ''Hannah, I don't blame you for being angry with me. I took advantage of your—'' he paused and swallowed painfully ''—your innocence, and then I hurt you and didn't—''

''You've booked yourself on quite a guilt trip, haven't you?'' Hannah cut in hotly. ''Well, you can reroute yourself, Matthew. You didn't do any of the things you're so arrogantly claiming credit for. I went to bed with you because I wanted to. I'll take full responsibility for my own actions, thank you. I'm not some simple airhead who can be lured into doing something that I don't want to do.''

''Of course you're not, but I—''

''Oh, shut up and get over yourself!''

Within him, fury and frustration soared to flash point. ''You are the most hardheaded, maddening, impossible brat I've ever had the misfortune to meet! And if you think that I will continue to make allowances for your bad temper and continue to apologize for what happened tonight, lady, you are—''

''Apologize?'' Hannah was stung. He was sorry he'd made love to her? She felt as if he'd stabbed her in the heart. For a moment, she feared she would burst into tears—a most horrifying prospect. She decided then and there that she would rather be caned than let Matthew Granger see her crying over him!

At that crucial moment, a couple turned the corner on the opposite side of the street. Hannah recognized them at once. It was Emma Wynn, who managed the bookstore on Clover

Street, and the man Emma was currently dating, Kenneth Drake, the handsome golf pro at the country club.

Hannah rushed across the street to see them, grateful for their fortuitous appearance. They were a welcome refuge from Matthew Granger. The last thing she expected was for him to join them. But he did.

"Hello there." Matthew's voice sounded behind them.

Hannah whirled around to glare at him. "Stop following me!"

"I came over to say hello to my new friends," Matthew countered. He recognized them from last night. If only he could remember their names.

Emma and Kenneth greeted Matthew warmly, much to Hannah's annoyance. She was further aghast when Kenneth suggested that the four of them go somewhere for a drink.

And then an idea occurred to her. A very wicked idea, but she decided she was entirely justified. "Emma, have you ever heard of the author, Galen Eden?"

"Why, yes." Emma smiled and nodded her head. "His books sell very well, both in hardcover and paperback. We have all his books at the shop. They make good vacation reading, I'm told."

Matthew guessed where this was heading. "Hannah!" he growled in warning.

Hannah ignored him. "Well, I have a big surprise for you, Emma. Galen Eden is standing right here. You know him as Matthew Granger."

Emma's green eyes widened as she gaped at Matthew. "You're Galen Eden?"

"He most certainly is Galen Eden, up close and in person," Hannah answered for him. "Emma, wouldn't it be cool if you could set up some kind of autographing session at the bookshop, featuring the acclaimed Galen Eden himself? I bet it would draw both locals and tourists."

"God save us all from your salesmanship," muttered Matthew.

Emma smiled uncertainly. "I certainly wouldn't want to impose on Mr. Eden, uh, Mr. Granger."

But Kenneth Drake didn't seem to mind. "So you're a writer, Hmm?" His voice was eager. "I have so many golf stories that people are always telling me I should write a book."

Matthew stifled a sigh of resignation as Drake fired questions about the publishing business at him. There was black fire in his eyes when Hannah started purposely down the street.

"I have to run!" she called over her shoulder, leaving Matthew with a bemused Emma and an effusive Drake. "See y'all later."

In the case of Matthew Granger *much later,* she promised herself as she fairly flew to her car, which was parked behind her shop. Preferably never!

"I never want to see that man again, Grandmother," she told her grandmother when she arrived home. Her parents and Bay were out, and her grandmother was watching a futuristic action-adventure movie on the VCR. "Matthew Granger is a smooth operator who is—who isn't—" She was horrified to hear her voice catch on a sob.

"My dear, what has happened?" Lydia Farley pushed the pause button on the remote control and the action on the screen froze. "This afternoon you were eager to assist him in his research, I've already set up a meeting with Alexandra Wyndham for tomorrow. She's expecting the three of us for tea."

"The three of us? You, me and Matthew?" Hannah sank down onto the sofa. "Oh, no!"

"Yes. She was most accommodating, rearranging her schedule to oblige us. This is one of those rare times that our relationship with Bay is actually useful to us. Since Alex hopes to foist her daughter onto him, she is quite eager to please the Farleys. If she only knew . . ." Lydia shrugged, her expression amused.

"Well, as far as I'm concerned, Matthew Granger can make the visit alone, Grandmother! I refuse to speak to him again."

"Oh dear, I sense a lover's quarrel has occurred."

Hannah flinched at the word 'lover.' What a fool she'd made of herself with her very first one! She'd spent her entire adult life waiting for Mr. Right; she'd suffered the slings and arrows of would-be lovers who had accused her of being finicky or frigid or pathologically vain because she'd turned down their advances. And to what avail?

Only to bamboozle herself into thinking she was in love with that coldhearted snake, Matthew Granger, who'd merely been looking for one wild night in the sack. Who'd felt so burdened

by her virginity that he couldn't even fake a kinder, gentler reaction to her inexperience. He couldn't have made his displea-
sure with her any more obvious if he'd taken out an ad in the
daily newspaper.

"Hannah Kaye, are you crying?"

"No!" Hannah used the back of her hand to roughly wipe
away the few renegade tears that had escaped from her eyes.
"As if I'd ever cry over any man, especially not an odious
cheesehead like Matthew Granger!"

"An odious cheesehead?" her grandmother repeated. "He
must have behaved dreadfully since our conversation this afternoon to have earned such an . . . unflattering epithet." The
action on the screen began again, and Lydia hit the pause button, once more freezing the frame. "Would you like to join me,
dear? There is nothing like watching a handsome, bare-chested
hero fell his enemies by the score to take one's mind off one's
troubles."

Hannah glanced at Lydia's bare-chested hero on the screen
and decided that Matthew was superior in every way. Women
had undoubtedly been throwing themselves at him for years,
and now she'd joined that hapless legion! She had gone to bed
with him on their first date—if tonight could even be classified
as a date. The reason he'd taken her to dinner was because he'd
lost their bet! And then . . . Hannah cringed with shame.
"Grandmother, please, I can't go with you tomorrow."

Her grandmother arched her brows, once the same dark
color and shape as Hannah's. "My dear, you must. It would be
terribly rude to cancel on Alexandra after I practically demanded that she see us." She wheeled herself over to the sofa
where Hannah was curled up against the cushions. "Do you
want to tell me what happened between you and this Matthew
Granger?"

Hannah covered her hot cheeks with her hands. "I made
such a fool of myself tonight, Grandmother," she whispered
miserably.

"My dear child, this certainly isn't the first time you've made
a fool of yourself," her grandmother said sympathetically,
patting her arm. "Your brother is forever accusing you of
making fools of the entire family. You've always laughed it off
before. Why not this time?"

"Because this time it's serious, Grandmother. This time it
matters."

"Because you're in love with the man." Her grandmother nodded her understanding. "I always knew that when you finally fell in love, it would be very fast and intense, as it was for your grandfather and me. That makes for some rough patches in the beginning because you don't know each other well enough to avoid the inevitable misunderstandings that—"

"I am *not* in love with Matthew Granger, Grandmother!" Hannah interrupted, her face flaming with color.

"You are certainly not about to admit it, and why should you? You're infuriated with the odious cheesehead."

"Oh, Grandmother." Hannah laughed a little, in spite of herself.

"Go to bed, dear. You need a good night's sleep. You want to be in top form when you face Mr. Granger tomorrow." Her grandmother smiled slyly. "If it's any consolation to you, I'm certain that he's spending a perfectly miserable night, recounting your quarrel and wondering how to proceed with you tomorrow."

"I'm certain that he's not." Hannah stood and tossed back her long dark hair. "But frankly, Grandmother, I don't care what kind of a night Matthew Granger has. As for tomorrow, I have no intention of saying a word to him. Since you insist that we go to the Wyndhams with him, you can consider him *your* guest and *you* can talk to him."

Lydia Farley heaved a sigh. "You can be a bit of a brat at times, Hannah."

"So I've been told." Hannah leaned down and kissed the silky white hair on top of her grandmother's head. "But you've always liked me anyway."

Lydia Farley's prediction of Matthew's perfectly miserable night was entirely correct.

He recounted his every moment with Hannah—the excruciating pleasure of being buried deep inside her, her warmth and her passion, her sweet words of love ringing in his ears. And then, inevitably, came the aftermath in which he critically dissected everything he said, everything he didn't say, and what he should have done and said. He imagined different endings to their tryst, all of them better than the way things had turned out.

He berated himself; he tried to defend himself. He didn't sleep a wink until dawn, when he finally fell into a stuporous slumber, only to be awakened shortly thereafter by a cacophony of birds in the tree outside his window.

"Damn birds!" he muttered as he gulped his third cup of strong black coffee in Peg's Diner. "Nobody could sleep through that racket. It was like a hundred boom boxes blasting chirps into my room."

Peg, who had been extremely sympathetic to his first plight in the rain-drenched room, offered him no consolation this time. "The guests at the boardinghouse love those birds," she reproved him sternly, her usual smile replaced by a look of reprimand. "Why, the Porter sisters told me this morning that they look forward every year to hearing what they call the 'lovely concert at dawn.'"

Matthew scowled. "Well, this morning I was looking forward to a cat ending the recital. Aren't there any hungry ones in the neighborhood?"

Katie, standing behind the counter nearby, laughed, but Peg fixed him with a severe look. Matthew took the hint. No cat jokes, at least not involving the precious avian chorus.

He was in no hurry to return to his room, so he hung out in the diner for a long time, eating a leisurely breakfast and eventually winning his way back into Peg's good graces. She and Katie introduced him to some of the Clover natives who dropped by to eat and chat on this lazy, sunny Sunday morning.

He met the sheriff, Ford Maguire, and his sister, Lucy, Captain Wynn, Emma's father, and Mike Flint, another charterboat captain much younger than Wynn. Matthew was grilled about himself by red-haired Jeannie Potts, a twentysomething beautician who was a virtual mine of information about everything and everyone in Clover. She already knew he was Galen Eden and requested autographed copies of his books.

Matthew thought of the copies that Hannah had left behind when she'd fled his room, and another pang of remorse chilled him. To take his mind off her, he did a little grilling of his own, asking Jeannie about the Polks, not even bothering to cloak his interest. Jeannie didn't seem to find his interrogatory style suspicious or odd; it was the way she herself conversed. She confirmed what he'd already been told about his birth father's relatives. The Polks were trouble, always in it or causing it.

By noon, Matthew decided he had clocked enough time in the diner and headed outside to Clover Street. The shops were closed on Sundays, keeping the traditional hours rather than the seven-days-a-week commercial hours that were now the norm in the malls and other resort towns. He took a long walk through the town, passing Hannah's shop, Yesterdays, and pausing to look in the window. A large wooden Victorian-style dollhouse, dating back to the turn of the century and priced in the four-figure range, was the centerpiece display.

Matthew smiled, remembering how yesterday Hannah had attempted to sell the dollhouse to her steady stream of customers, who had all proclaimed the price too steep. Even a super-saleswoman like her hit the occasional snag. Perhaps he should make another bet, this time focusing on whether or not she could sell the dollhouse. His chances of winning seemed higher than hers this time.

And then his smile faded. Hannah hated him; there would be no more lighthearted bets. He kept waiting for Katie to give him the message that his meeting with Alexandra Wyndham was canceled because the Farleys were unable to make it. But that message never came, and armed with directions to the Farley house from Katie, he drove his van there, half expecting to be ejected from the premises.

Instead, he was graciously ushered inside by a kind-faced, white-haired lady in a motorized wheelchair, who introduced herself as Lydia Farley, Hannah's grandmother.

"Of course." Matthew grinned, liking her on sight. "You're the great friend of my grandparents."

"Wonderful people," Lydia enthused jovially. "My son and his wife are dreadfully disappointed they were unable to be here to meet you this afternoon, but they were already locked into other plans. They were eager to meet the grandson of my very rich, very prominent friends, the Grangers of Florida."

Hannah joined them, slipping quietly into the wide vestibule and hoping that her entrance would go unnoticed. For a moment it did as Matthew chatted easily with her grandmother, who seemed bent on charming him.

Hannah let her eyes rove over him for that single, unobserved moment. He was wearing a light gray suit, and she resisted the urge to snidely ask if he'd removed the Luger from the pocket. She was not speaking to him at all, she reminded herself, and her silence precluded making snide remarks, however tempting. His snowy white shirt was starched and immaculate and highlighted his dark complexion. She'd never seen him dressed like this. He looked nothing like the sinister cat burglar she'd first imagined him to be.

He looked entirely respectable, a well-bred gentleman, a successful writer. He also looked devastatingly sexy, so masculine and virile that her senses filled and she nearly whimpered aloud at the fierce surge of desire and love that swept through her. She wanted him. Hannah was appalled by her body's betrayal. And determined not to succumb to it all over again.

"Hello, Hannah." Matthew met her gaze, and she immediately looked away.

"I'm ready to leave when you are, Grandmother," she said, ignoring him.

"You look lovely, darling," her grandmother said, smiling her approval. "Doesn't she, Matthew?"

Matthew's eyes roamed over her hungrily, his body already standing firmly at attention. She was wearing a loose oatmeal-colored dress that resembled a short-sleeved man's jacket and hung nearly to her knees. On anyone else, the color and style would be nondescript at best, but Hannah managed to look as alluring and sexy as she had in that eye-popping silver minidress she had been wearing on the night they'd met.

"Hannah always looks sensational. Her height tends to vary, however," he added dryly. Her oatmeal-colored platform sandals were at least three inches high, making her shorter than the night they'd met but taller than yesterday.

She made no reply but shot him a haughty half smile.

"Hannah is sensitive about her height, Matthew dear," Lydia informed him. "She thinks she should be tall and thin like her older sisters, whose figures, I am sorry to say, resemble telephone poles. I have told Hannah repeatedly that there is nothing wrong with being petite and curvy, but she doesn't believe her old grandmother. Perhaps if you were to assure her?"

"Grandmother!" Hannah groaned. "I don't need or want Matthew's approval."

"Nevertheless, you have it, sweetheart," Matthew said sincerely.

Her grandmother beamed. Hannah scowled.

The trip to the Wyndhams was a trial that only Lydia enjoyed. She insisted that Matthew drive the three of them in her beloved '68 dove-gray Mercedes Pullman sedan, then sat in the long back seat with Hannah at her side. Matthew felt as if he were behind the wheel of an M-1 tank as he steered through the imposing gates of the grand Wyndham estate.

His nerves were frayed. Hannah hadn't said one word during the ride, though her grandmother gamely kept the conversation going. Matthew did his best to respond correctly, but his thoughts were centered on Hannah, who was driving him mad by acting as if he didn't exist.

The prospect of meeting his birth mother face-to-face was an additional strain. His birth certificate rested in the inside pocket of his suit jacket. He was so conscious of the document, he felt as if it were burning its imprint through his clothes into his skin.

A uniformed servant greeted them at the door and ushered them into a sunny, plant-filled room that Matthew guessed was supposed to be informal, but was in reality, more formal than any living room he'd ever set foot in. Lydia was the only one at ease, smiling and chatting while Matthew and Hannah sat on opposite love seats silent and still as stones.

And then a young woman appeared, wearing a starched Laura Ashley floral dress that looked miles too big for her tall, thin frame, and bright yellow flats with bows on them. She had a yellow bow in her hair, which was sandy brown in color and cut in a short, straight bob.

"Why, hello, Justine, my dear." Lydia held out her hand and smiled warmly at the girl, whose big blue eyes were anxious and uncertain.

"Mother will be joining you shortly. She asked me to—to keep you company." Justine looked distressed and ill-at-ease. "That is, I'm delighted to keep you company. I'm glad she asked me to. I would've come down to see you, even if she hadn't."

"We're happy to see you, Justine," Hannah reassured her. She felt a swift stab of guilt. "Uh, about that present Bay gave you yesterday..." She'd meant to hurt Bay's chances at Wyndhamhood, not to hurt Justine personally. Seeing how fragile the young woman appeared, Hannah worried that she might have done just that.

"First allow me to introduce you to Matthew Granger, Justine," Lydia said smoothly, smiling from one to the other. "Matthew, this is Justine Wyndham Marshall, Alexandra's daughter."

Matthew, who had been momentarily transfixed by the sight of Justine, sprang to his feet. The girl, who appeared much younger than her age, and looked vulnerable and skinny and scared of her own shadow, was his half sister. He'd grown up an only child, never dreaming that he had a sibling. But he had a little sister! A wave of emotion rolled over him as he took Justine's hand in his. If anyone had ever been in need of an older brother's protection, he decided it was Justine.

There was an instant connection between them, he could feel it. He held on to her hand, his onyx eyes staring intently into hers.

"Mother loved the mourning picture, Hannah," Justine said breathlessly, withdrawing her hand from Matthew's. She flushed under the piercing intensity of his gaze.

"What?" Hannah gasped.

"Back in the 1830s, there were two mourning pictures painted to commemorate two Wyndham children who died when they were three and seven years old. One of them actually has a lock of the little girl's hair attached to the painting. Mother has always been fascinated by them. She keeps them in a special little gallery upstairs, and over the years she has collected three others. Not of Wyndhams, of course, but other mourning pictures of lost children. She was positively thrilled with Bay's gift. She thinks he is one of the most perceptive, sensitive men she's ever met."

"*Our Bay?* Perceptive and sensitive?" Lydia was incredulous. "Oh, gracious!"

"I can't believe it!" Hannah was staggered. "The plan backfired." She began to pace the room in agitation. "Justine, I wanted to help you," she confessed. "I thought that picture would put your mother off—I mean, who gives a mourning picture to a young bride-to-be? It's a bizarre gift. But she liked it."

Justine stared at Hannah. "You don't want me to marry your brother?"

"Not unless you want to," Hannah said earnestly. "And I can't imagine that you do."

"Do you want to marry Bay Farley, Justine?" Matthew asked, meeting and holding his sister's gaze.

"No!" Justine cried, her blue eyes filling with tears. "But I have to. I have no choice. Mother says that I—"

Matthew put his arm around his sister. "Come with me, Justine." He walked her from the room, leaving a stunned Hannah and Lydia behind. By the time Hannah hurried to the threshold to peer down the hall, Matthew and Justine had disappeared from view.

And Alexandra Wyndham, slender and beautiful in a blue silk suit that matched her vivid blue eyes, was walking down the hall toward them. She smiled at Hannah and gave a friendly little wave.

Hannah turned to her grandmother in a panic. "Grandmother, Alexandra is coming and Matthew and Justine are gone!"

"Oh my, this is a bit awkward, isn't it?" Lydia was mildly dismayed.

"What are we going to do, Grandmother? What are we going to say when she asks where they are?" Hannah whispered.

"We will simply say that they stepped out of the room. Then we'll talk—the usual social chitchat. And if, heaven forbid, Matthew and Justine still haven't returned, we'll discuss mourning pictures. You must insist that Alexandra show you her collection. Ask her many, many questions about them, Hannah Kaye. And so shall I."

Eight

___

"I hardly know what to say," Alexandra Wyndham said, her soft, cultured tones unable to disguise her anger and growing fear. "This is so unlike Justine. To just . . . just take off with a stranger like this . . ." She set her teacup down in its saucer, the drink untouched.

Hannah's hand shook as she reached for her own cup of tea. Her mouth was so dry she needed something to soothe her parched lips and throat. She glanced surreptitiously at her watch. Matthew and Justine had been gone over an hour!

She and her grandmother had followed their agenda, chatting politely with Alexandra, catching up on the latest news and sharing a memory or two. When conversation faltered and awkwardness loomed, Hannah had launched into the mourning-pictures discussion. She'd pleaded to see Alexandra's collection and been taken upstairs to the tiny gallery where the pictures were carefully hung. The picture Bay had bought for Justine was already there, and Hannah mentally kicked herself for choosing such a successful gift.

Ordinarily, Hannah would have been enchanted to see rare old pictures of a bygone era; she would've been delighted with Alexandra's valuable collection of French and German antique dolls, which were also in the room. But her thoughts were too full of Matthew to fully appreciate the treasures.

She kept replaying the scene of Matthew greeting Justine in the parlor—the way he'd looked into the girl's eyes and taken her hand. Juxtaposed with it was the memory of the first time she'd met Matthew herself. His intense dark stare, the breathless way she'd responded to it, to him. Hadn't Justine displayed a chillingly similar reaction?

And then he'd hustled Justine out of the room—out of the house—and hadn't been seen since. Hannah felt distinctly queasy. Was this his standard operating procedure? Mesmerize a woman with those eyes and then whisk her off to bed? It had happened to her only last night! Was it happening to Justine right now?

Hannah took a gulp of hot tea, scalding her mouth. Perspiration beaded on her forehead and she reached for a napkin to fan herself. The memory of that map of Clover tucked in his copy of *The First Families of South Carolina* haunted her. She might've been off the mark by suspecting him as a thief, but suppose she had been right in assuming that he'd come to Clover with specific designs on the Wyndhams? On Justine! Perhaps he'd arrived in town knowing all about the sheltered young heiress. Being a bestselling author didn't exempt him from being a first-class rat, and his earnings, however generous, could not compare to the Wyndham fortune.

What if he had used her to meet the Wyndhams? What if she'd given him the opportunity to seduce innocent young Justine? It felt as if the fine hairs on the back of her neck were actually standing on end. Last night, on the eve of his mission, Matthew had casually taken her to bed because she'd made herself so pathetically available. And now...

"Grandmother, I feel sick." Hannah rose swiftly to her feet. "I have to go home right now."

"You do look a trifle peaked, darling," agreed Lydia. She turned to Alexandra, her manners commendably intact. "Such a lovely visit, Alex dear. We must do it again soon."

"Lydia, I don't know what's going on." Alexandra did not possess the older woman's unflappable aplomb. Her face was pale and her lips quivered as she spoke. "I am absolutely horrified about Justine disappearing with—with your friends' grandson, the writer. What must you think of her! Please don't mention this to Bay, at least not until we have a chance to sort things out. The engagement is practically set and—''

"You're worried about Bay finding out?" Hannah was thunderstruck. "You're worried about this insane engagement you've dreamed up when right now your daughter might be . . . being debauched by a—a—''

"A libertine," her grandmother supplied. "My granddaughter has made a telling point, Alexandra. Your priorities are skewed, and that, my dear, is putting it kindly.''

"We're getting out of here right now, Grandmother!" Hannah announced, so furious that she could barely form the words to speak. She grasped the handles of her grandmother's wheelchair, but Lydia was already in full throttle. Hannah had to run to keep up with her. And it wasn't easy, running in three-inch platform shoes.

Alexandra scurried after them. "Please don't go." She followed them through the hall to the front door. "I am sure this is simply a terrible misunderstanding. We mustn't act rashly. We can't allow our—''

She didn't have the chance to finish. The front door opened wide, and Matthew Granger and Justine Wyndham Marshall strolled inside laughing, their arms around each other.

Matthew's gaze met Hannah's. He dropped his arm from Justine's shoulders and held out both his hands to Hannah. "Come here, honey. I have some—''

"Merciful heavens, what a bounder!" exclaimed Lydia. "Young man, you should be ashamed of yourself! You are a disgrace to your dear grandparents.''

Matthew thought she was kidding. He and Justine exchanged glances and burst into another round of laughter.

"Now I feel ill," Alexandra murmured, leaning against the wall.

"As do I," Lydia agreed. "Hannah, my dear, there is an infectious agent on the premises and we must be on our way." Holding her head high, Lydia powered her chair onto the porch, accompanied by her granddaughter.

"Hannah, wait," Matthew called after her. His reunion with his little sister had him feeling on top of the world, but he was fast becoming earthbound. Something was very, very wrong. He couldn't let Hannah storm off without trying to explain what had just transpired between him and his newfound, long-lost sister.

But Hannah and her grandmother didn't wait. The wheelchair zoomed across the smooth concrete driveway to the big gray tank parked in front of a flower bed of begonias. Hannah stayed close to the chair, not looking back.

"Justine, go to your room immediately," Alexandra ordered, her eyes a cold arctic blue. "I shall deal with you when I can bear to look at you without wanting to—"

"She's too old to be sent to her room," Matthew snapped, as Justine shrank against him. He started after Hannah with Justine at his heels. "Hannah," he called again.

Hannah made the mistake of turning to see him hurrying toward her. Justine, whose thin face was positively glowing, was with him, still holding on to Matthew and clinging to him as if he was a lifeline. Or her new lover, perhaps her first lover?

Pain ripped through Hannah. Last night she had looked at Matthew through the clouded eyes of love. Now she had to watch poor Justine suffer the same symptoms, while still acutely infected herself. Hannah glowered at the human plague that was Matthew Granger.

"Grandmother, excuse me a moment. There's something I have to do," Hannah said, her voice eerily calm. "It's essential to the cure."

"By all means do it, child. You must cure what is ailing you," her grandmother agreed.

Hannah walked toward Matthew. He smiled his relief and slowed his pace.

"She looks awfully mad, Matthew," Justine whispered nervously.

"Don't worry. I can handle her," Matthew assured his sister. "We're going to work everything out."

He and Hannah stopped and stared at each other for a long, silent moment, just an arm's length apart.

"Hannah, I know that we've—" Matthew began.

"Not even the most talented spin doctor could come up with a plausible explanation, so don't even try," Hannah said coolly and took a step toward him. "But I do have a message to deliver to you." She swung back her hand and slapped his cheek with bone-jarring might.

Matthew staggered backward a few steps. Hers was no ladylike little slap, administered for dramatic effect. She'd walloped him with every ounce of strength she possessed. Stars danced before his eyes, which watered from the sheer force of the blow. There was a ringing in his ears. He leaned heavily on Justine, who could barely support his weight with her thin frame.

"Dammit, Hannah, I think you broke my jaw," he groaned.

"I hope I did! It's nothing less than you deserve, you gold-digging snake." Hannah restrained the urge to hit him again. He was looking a bit pale. Instead, she turned her attention to the pitiful young woman struggling to hold Matthew up. "Justine, I know my brother is obnoxious, but you've gone from the frying pan into the fire with this—this—"

"I believe the term you used was gold-digging snake," Matthew finished for her.

He was furious with her, disillusioned, too. On this monumental and emotional day in his life, he could have used some kindness, some understanding and support, but Hannah Kaye Farley had none to give him. "Well, if I'm a snake, you're an evil-tempered, heartless little shrew."

After everything he'd done, he actually had the nerve to insult her? Hannah was crushed. Never had she been so terribly wrong about anyone. She was certain it would be years before she trusted her own judgment again.

Hannah turned and ran back to her grandmother, who was avidly observing the proceedings from her place beside the car. "Bravo, my dear," Lydia commended her. "I do hope you're feeling better now."

Matthew and Justine watched them speed out of the driveway, Hannah looking small behind the wheel of the mighty vehicle. He touched his cheek, which was painfully throbbing. The skin was hot, and he knew her handprint must be visibly red.

"You're probably going to have a bruise, Matthew," Justine murmured anxiously. "And here comes Mother. Oh, her face! She looks like she would like to kill us both."

"Don't worry. I'll handle her."

A faint gleam of humor lit Justine's blue eyes. "That's what you said about Hannah, and she clobbered you."

"Hannah is a spoiled brat," growled Matthew.

"I like her," countered Justine. "She's the only person who has ever tried to thwart one of Mother's plans and I appreciate her efforts, even if the mourning picture did backfire." Her expression saddened. "But I think she hates us now. If only you could make her understand! But how can you do that when she won't listen or speak to you?''

"Justine! I order you to go into the house immediately!'' Alexandra approached them, her face a mask of rage.

Matthew opened his mouth to speak up in his sister's defense, but Justine beat him to the punch. Holding tightly to her brother's hand, she drew herself to her full height and said firmly, "I am never obeying any of your orders again, Mother. From now on, if you want me to do something, you can ask me in a civilized way and I'll consider it and make my own decision.''

"Don't you dare disobey me, you little tramp!'' Alexandra's voice rose shrilly.

"I'm not a tramp, and I won't let you call me one ever again,'' Justine said bravely. She glanced up at Matthew and he gave a silent nod. "*I'm* not the one who slept with a Polk, Mother! That was you! And I didn't have a baby when I was only sixteen years old. You did! And here he is, all grown up!'' She pointed to Matthew. "He's my half brother. And he's your son, Mother! The son you had with a Polk!''

Alexandra blanched. And then in a scene that Matthew would have found clichéd in a soap opera, his mother swayed forward, her knees buckling in a faint.

He was positive that the faint was staged, a histrionic ploy to gain sympathy and attention, but he dutifully stepped forward and caught his mother in his arms. She was very slender, and he compared her slight girlish frame to the figure of the woman who had raised him. His mom. He remembered how good it always felt to hug her, and grief spasmed through him. As Alexandra opened her eyes and stared into his, he silently thanked her for giving him to Eden Granger, his real mother in every sense of the word.

Alexandra straightened and pulled away from him. "Is it possible? Can you really be the child that I—that we . . . Oh, God. Jesse!''

Matthew reached into the pocket of his suit coat and removed the birth certificate he'd shown Justine earlier. Alexandra took it and examined it, her hands shaking. "I remember filling it out,'' she said, her voice faraway as if in a dream. "Signing it. I wanted to name the baby Jesse but the nurse suggested that I let the adoptive parents name him. She said it would be harder for me to detach myself from the child, harder to forget him if I associated a name with him." Her eyes filled with tears. "So I wrote Baby Boy in that space."

"His name is Matthew, Mother," Justine said. "Matthew Granger. He came here to meet us, not to interview us for a book commissioned by the historical society."

"Do the Farleys know?" Alexandra's voice faltered.

"No," Matthew said coldly. "I haven't told anyone your 'shameful secret', Alexandra. Nobody knows but you, Justine and me. And Jesse Polk, of course. Unless you didn't bother to inform him that he was a father?"

Alexandra stared at the birth certificate another long moment and then handed it back to Matthew. Her face was hard, her blue eyes twin chips of ice. "I don't know what to say. Do you want money? The family might be willing to offer you a modest settlement, but blackmail—"

"Matthew isn't here to blackmail us, Mother," Justine interrupted, bristling with indignation on her brother's behalf. "He's successful in his own right, he doesn't want money."

"You are so gullible, Justine," Alexandra said disparagingly.

"No, she isn't," Matthew countered. He stared at Alexandra, his onyx eyes cool. "I want to know about my father, Jesse Polk. That's why I'm here. For information. I don't want a penny of your money. I've heard plenty about the exalted Wyndhams but I want to know about my father. And now that I know I have a sister, I'm going to be a part of her life, whether it meets with your approval or not, Alexandra."

Alexandra covered her face with her hands, and tears spilled through her fingers. "You look like your father. You even sound like him. Jesse James Polk." She cried harder. "I was crazy about him from the moment I met him. Oh, I can remember it so well. We were both at the Clover Train Station. I was fifteen and he was seventeen and he came up to me and started talking, as bold as you please."

The three of them walked slowly back inside the house. Alexandra continued her story through dinner, which was served on the screened terrace at the back of the house. Matthew listened dispassionately. It was almost exactly as he'd imagined—the rather unoriginal tale of two teenagers on fire with their forbidden love, too-early-and-no-precautions sex resulting in a pregnancy that panicked them both.

"Jesse wanted me to run away with him," Alexandra recalled dreamily, picking at her roast lamb. "He hated being a Polk, and he hated being looked down on as a failure before he even had a chance to make something of his life. He'd graduated from high school and planned to join the army. I could go along as his wife, he said."

"And you couldn't see yourself as a sixteen-year-old army wife with a baby," Matthew said dryly. He glanced around at the well-appointed terrace, the servants discreetly coming and going, the beautiful lush grounds of the estate stretching before him. "It would have been quite a switch in life-styles, to put it mildly."

"I can't tell you how many times I've wondered if I made the right choice," Alexandra said tearfully. "Maybe I should have gone with Jesse. Maybe we would've been happy."

"Chances are it wouldn't have worked," Matthew consoled her. "Then *my* life would have been a disaster. I'm grateful that I was Galen and Eden Granger's son, Alexandra. You made the right decision to give me up. But what about Jesse? Is he still in Clover? Have you seen him since—"

"Jesse is dead," Alexandra said, her voice taut and bitter. "When I was sent off to the maternity home in Florida—my parents told everyone I was in a Swiss boarding school—he enlisted in the army. It was during the Vietnam war and he was killed in action."

"When?" Matthew felt a peculiar pang of loss for the young father he had never known.

"Jesse was killed near the end of his second tour of duty over there. He'd volunteered for both. It was a heroic death. The papers reported that he was awarded the Silver Star posthumously." Tears welled in Alexandra's eyes. "His name is on the wall of the Vietnam Veterans Memorial in Washington and he's buried in Arlington National Cemetery. I was glad about that. He wouldn't have wanted to be in the Polk plot here in town."

"It's so sad." Justine sniffed, wiping her teary eyes with her napkin. "He sounds brave and smart. I wish he would have been my father, too."

"Did you ever see him again, Alexandra?" Matthew asked.

"After...the birth, I was sent to that school in Switzerland and I didn't return to Clover until I was ready for college. I saw Jesse only one more time, over Christmas break when I was twenty and in college and he was back on leave. I told him he had a son whom I'd given up for adoption." Alexandra swallowed hard. "He was very angry with me, very cold. He told me I'd cheated him out of knowing his own son and that he would never forgive me for that. He said I was a self-centered, cowardly snob who was ruled by the opinion of others and he predicted that I would never be happy. Then he walked away. I never saw him again. He returned to Vietnam. He was only twenty-three years old when he died."

There was a somber silence.

"Jesse Polk was right," Justine said, finally breaking the silence. "You never have been happy, Mother."

"No." Alexandra shook her head. "I haven't."

"I used to think it was because I'm such a dud," Justine said wearily. "I knew I wasn't pretty or lively enough to be your daughter but I thought if I did everything you wanted, maybe you'd finally be happy. But it wasn't me at all, was it?"

"You're not a dud, little sister," Matthew said firmly. "But you're going to start living your life the way you want to." He reached over and took Alexandra's hand, squeezing it hard. His black eyes were sharp and intense. "That means she transfers out of the college she hates into the one she wants to attend. That means she doesn't get engaged to Bay Farley or anyone else until she's ready to, which won't be for a while. It also means she is going to dress the way she wants to, wear her hair the way she wants to, and stop atoning for the sins you think you committed by giving birth to me. From now on, if you try to control Justine, you'll have to go through me, and I am not someone you'd care to tangle with. Do you understand, Alexandra?"

Alexandra looked chastened. "I...might have been too controlling with Justine," she conceded. "I worried constantly that she would be wild like I was, that she would repeat my mistakes. She's always been withdrawn and quiet, but I was still afraid she might change at any minute."

"And your solution to these imagined problems was to marry her off to Bay Farley?" Matthew was openly scornful.

"I fail to see what is so terrible about that," Alexandra said defensively. "I don't know why Justine doesn't want to marry Bay. He's from a respectable, socially prominent family and he's attractive and charming and witty."

Matthew and Justine exchanged looks of patent disbelief.

"Alexandra, instead of trying to set him up with your unwilling daughter, why don't you take up with Bay yourself?" Matthew suggested sardonically. "Why worry about the affair causing a scandal? After all, what's a twenty-year age difference to someone who gave birth to Jesse Polk's illegitimate son?"

"Apart from the insult to me, young man, don't you dare disparage your father that way. He was a war hero, and he would've loved you." Alexandra leaned over and slapped his cheek, the same one that Hannah had smacked. Then she pushed back her chair with such force that it overturned. Ignoring it, she stalked grandly from the terrace.

"I admit I deserved that," Matthew muttered, rubbing his battered cheek.

"I think you might've deserved the slap from Hannah, too," Justine said thoughtfully as she righted the chair. "At least, from her point of view. You said you haven't told anybody that we're sister and brother, Matthew. So as far as Hannah knows, you came to my house, met me, and then went off with me. And when we came back we were laughing as if we had some sort of naughty secret between us."

"Are you implying that she thought you and I had some sort of...tryst?" Matthew scowled, annoyed. "That's ridiculous! Of all the stupid, paranoid, jealous—"

"Her grandmother thought so, too," Justine reminded him. "She called you a bounder and a disgrace. And an infectious agent, too, I believe."

"I intended to tell Hannah that you were my sister. She didn't give me a chance to explain anything. You saw her, Justine. She refused to speak to me and then she whacked me across the face and took off. She thoroughly distrusts me. Who needs a woman like that?" He stabbed his fork into a piece of raspberry mousse pie, mashing it.

"You're probably right," Justine agreed. "Who am I to give advice? I almost let myself get pushed into an engagement to that patronizing pill, Bay Farley! But Hannah is so different from him and from her prissy sisters and her parents, too. She's lively and fun and she doesn't let anybody push her around. My cousin—*our* cousin—Ridgley has a gigantic crush on her. He says that she must by dynamite in bed because she's had a million boyfriends and—"

"If I ever hear *our* cousin talk about her that way, I'll deck him," snarled Matthew. "Hannah doesn't sleep around."

He ought to know. Last night he'd become her first lover. And he'd let her walk away from him without letting her know how much the experience had meant to him. How much *she* meant to him. He hadn't let Hannah know much about him at all, he conceded, except for a few basic facts. But she'd made love with him anyway. She'd been engaged three times and hadn't been to bed with any of her fiancés but she had given herself to him after knowing him only a day. He pondered that.

"Maybe I've given her reason to distrust me," he murmured. "First last night, now today." He heaved a rueful groan. "I think I've made a mess of it, Justine."

"Then fix it!" Justine urged. "You can do it, Matthew. You made it possible for me to finally stand up to Mother, something I never thought I could do. You told me you could handle Hannah and work things out with her. Now prove it! You know you want to," she added ingenuously. "Admit it!"

Matthew did not admit it, but he allowed his sister to drive him over to the Farley residence, where he'd left his van. He was relieved to see it was still parked in their circular driveway. Hannah and her grandmother hadn't had it towed and impounded in a spree of vengeful fury.

Ten minutes later, he was walking along the Farleys' plushly carpeted second-story hallway. His pass of admission had been his original birth certificate, which he had shown to Hannah's grandmother. At first, she had eyed him like a cockroach that had surfaced in the soup, until he'd presented that shocking document, proclaiming him a Wyndham and a Polk and thus absolving him of his suspected sins on the basis of his mother's proven ones.

According to Lydia Farley, Hannah's bedroom was the fourth door on the left. Matthew counted the doors, his pulse beginning to pound in anticipation. Lydia had said she feared that Hannah was crying in her room, "her heart badly bruised." By him. The news filled him with both remorse and hope. He hadn't wanted to make Hannah cry, but if she was crying over him, it meant that she cared about him. That he could kiss away her tears and comfort her...

He didn't want to knock and spoil the surprise of his appearance—or give her the chance to tell him to get lost. So Matthew boldly opened the door and glanced at the bed, on which he expected to see a sobbing Hannah curled up and weeping over him.

She wasn't there. She was on the floor, wearing a white tank top and bright red running shorts and doing push-ups, while "Build Me Up, Buttercup" played on her compact disc player. Her hair was pulled high into a ponytail, which bounced as she did. He watched her for a moment—until she must have sensed his presence and quickly jumped to her feet.

"You!" Hannah exclaimed sharply. She did not look heart bruised, and she certainly did not seem pleased to see him.

"Now I see why your punch packed such power," drawled Matthew. "You work out."

"Get out of my house or I'll have you arrested for breaking and entering."

"Sorry, Wonder Woman, the charge won't stick. I was invited in and given directions to your room. By your grandmother, who thinks you're up here crying over me," he added.

"If Grandmother said that, she was being sarcastic. If you believed her, you're as stupid and gullible as you think I am."

"I don't think you're stupid and gullible, Hannah."

"If you didn't, you wouldn't be here, about to spin some tale that I have no intention of hearing, let alone believing."

Matthew heaved an exasperated sigh and sank onto her bed. "Your grandmother warned me it wouldn't be easy getting you to listen to me. It wasn't easy getting *her* to listen to me. But when I told her the truth, she believed me. And she encouraged me to come up here to see you, Hannah."

"I can't imagine what possible excuse you gave for your extended absence at the Wyndhams with—with poor, confused, pathetic Justine." Hannah grabbed his wrists and tried to pull him off the bed. "Get up! Get out of here! What did you tell Grandmother anyway? That you were abducted by a UFO and held captive by aliens? She might've bought that one—she actually believes in UFOs—but I don't!"

Matthew didn't budge, but his body was heating under her touch and her nearness, even though she was in the midst of a hostile attempt to dislodge him. "You'll probably find the UFO-alien story more believable than the one I'm about to tell you." He pulled his hands free and fished the birth certificate from his jacket pocket. "Read this," he insisted. "It's the real reason why I came to Clover."

"I don't care why you came to Clover. I just want you to leave."

His hands snaked out and he grabbed her around the waist and pulled her down onto his lap. "Just read it. If you would have had a little more time the night you searched my bag, you would have found it. I almost wish you had. It might've saved us a slew of misunderstandings along the way. You would've known from the start that I'm not a cat burglar or a jewel thief or a fortune-hunting rake."

Hannah's hands trembled as she took the paper from him. She was excruciatingly aware of the powerful muscles of his thighs under her, of the strength of his arms as he kept her firmly on his lap. Hot, sensual memories of last night washed over her—memories of his arms and legs holding her, entangling her own limbs as he joined his body with hers.

Heaven help her, she wanted it to happen again! What power he exerted over her, to make her feel this way! Aroused and alarmed, Hannah tried to master the sensual weakness sweeping through her. Fighting the need to surrender to him once again, she wriggled and struggled in an effort to break free. Matthew held her tighter, closer, and she felt the unmistakable evidence of his arousal pressing solidly against her.

"Quit squirming and read, unless you want to end up on your back right here and now," Matthew said gruffly.

"Don't flatter yourself, mister. Just because you got lucky last night doesn't mean that—" She lapsed into stunned silence. Her eyes had just connected with the names on the document, which was a birth certificate issued thirty-two years ago by the state of Florida.

The mother of the infant boy was Alexandra Wyndham. The father, *Jesse Polk?* A Wyndham and a Polk had mated and produced a child? From a Clover viewpoint, an alien abduction in a UFO did seem a bit more credible.

Her jaw dropped. She read it again. "This—this doesn't make any sense." She turned her head and met Matthew's deep dark gaze.

"This is my birth certificate, Hannah. Alexandra and Jesse are my parents. I was adopted by the Grangers from the maternity home where Alexandra stayed until I was born."

She sat very still and listened as he told her about Galen and Eden Granger's fatal car accident six months ago, when a pickup truck ran a stoplight at a busy intersection and plowed

head-on into the Granger's car. He told her about learning of
his adoption for the first time, about the sleazy but effective
private investigator who had unearthed the original birth certificate, which led him to Clover. He finished by describing his
confrontation today with his birth mother, Alexandra Wyndham, and his instant rapport and alliance with his young half
sister, Justine.

"Justine is your sister," Hannah breathed. She felt as if
fireworks were going off in her head. If she closed her eyes, she
could see them.

"Yes." He threaded his fingers through her ponytail and
tugged, drawing her head back until it rested against the hollow of his shoulder. "You needed proof, so here it is. I'm not
the gold-digging snake you accused me of being. But I don't
believe in holding a grudge, so I'm willing to accept your apology."

"I'm not going to apologize for what I thought or for hitting you, either!" Hannah was incensed. "You're as much to
blame as I am, maybe more! All the secrecy, all the lies and the
half truths! You've been playing games with everybody, ma-
nipulating us like pieces on a chessboard. Or characters in one
of your novels."

The pent-up tension of the day was taking its toll on her
temper. She'd been confused and miserable since last night, and
today's debacle at the Wyndhams' had only served to under-
score how helpless and out of her depth she felt with Matthew.
Hannah hated feeling this way. She had always prided herself
on being able to hold her own with anybody—until Matthew
laid that illusion to rest. A look, a touch, a few words from
him, and she was totally disarmed.

"Now you suddenly appear in my room with this piece of
paper and expect me to—to what, Matthew?" Hannah fumed.
"What do you expect me to do?" She jerked herself upright,
but his fingers were still tangled in her hair, and he pulled her
back against him.

He arched his dark brows. "Maybe I expect you to prove that
you're not an evil-tempered, heartless shrew. Can you do that,
little girl?"

Quicker than a snake could strike, he pushed her back on the
bed, lying down with her and anchoring her there by slipping
one muscled thigh between her legs. She placed her hands on

his chest, ostensibly to push him away, but ended up sliding them to his shoulders instead.

Their gazes met and locked.

"Probably the last thing in the world I want to do right now is fight with you," Matthew said softly.

"I can guess what you want to do." Hannah made a valiant effort to be stern. But at this moment her anger and astonishment were dissolving like soap bubbles in the air.

"Thank you for not launching a shocked harangue about the unlikely mating of a Wyndham and a Polk." Matthew nuzzled her neck with eager lips. "Things aren't always what they seem. Having met the Wyndham, I think I would've preferred the Polk."

A potent mixture of empathy and passion rendered her already-weakened defenses against him useless. "I can't imagine going through what you have for the past six months," she whispered. "The grief, the shock, the upheaval. It must have been a living hell, Matthew."

"There have been occasional respites. Even glimpses of heaven." He kissed her throat, then took her lobe between his teeth and worried it gently. "Last night with you was one of them. Right now is another."

She clenched and unclenched her fingers against the muscles of his shoulders. He felt so strong, so warm. His clean male scent filled her nostrils, and she inhaled deeply, closing her eyes as a dizzying surge of desire rushed through her. "About last night," she began shakily. "It wasn't exactly . . . what either of us thought it would be."

"Sweetheart, it was so much more than I thought it would be. I wanted you so badly. I can't remember wanting or needing any woman as much as I wanted and needed you last night. You were so honest and sensual and sweet. The most exciting, responsive woman I've ever known. I completely lost control with you, and that was a first for me. I've been intimate with women, but last night was the first time I felt such a strong emotional connection, too, and—"

"It was too much," Hannah concluded. "You weren't looking for emotional involvement last night. You were looking for good-time sex. Imagine your surprise when you found yourself in bed with a virgin!"

"I confess to being surprised," Matthew said tightly. "But I liked it, Hannah. I'm proud to be your first lover. Your only lover. Hell, I loved it! And I panicked. You're so beautiful, so sexy. I couldn't believe that you'd held back your passion for so long and then given it all to me. That's why I didn't say any of the things that I should have said to you, that I wanted to say. Before I had the chance to pull myself together and tell you, you took off.''

"I didn't feel like sticking around while you bemoaned the fact that I'd never slept with any of my ex-fiancés."

"I admit I was an insensitive ape." His mouth hovered over hers, then his lips touched hers as he spoke.

"Yes, you were. But I don't believe in holding a grudge, so I'm willing to accept your apology." She didn't expect one. She thought he'd come back with some wisecrack about apologizing to her after she'd begged his pardon for slugging him.

"I'm sorry," Matthew growled, and her eyes widened in surprise.

She touched his cheek, the one she'd smacked. Hannah winced. "I'm sorry, too, Matthew. For hitting you. I've never hit anybody in my life except for Bay when we were kids. And he hit back twice as hard."

Matthew smiled and covered her hand with his. "The siblings were rivals, huh?"

"More like mortal enemies."

"You're very passionate about everything, whether it's selling or dancing or hating ... or loving."

Hannah blushed. His dark eyes seemed to see inside her. She felt exposed and vulnerable, and the intensity of her feeling scared her. She understood more clearly those unnerving feelings that had driven Matthew to withdraw from her last night. Right now she very much wanted to retreat behind a protective cover herself.

"When I said I loved you last night, I—I didn't mean it," she said, averting her eyes to avoid his piercing stare. "It was the kind of thing I thought I ought to say under the circumstances. I've always pretended to be sexually sophisticated but no one knows better than you that I'm not."

"I promise not to hold you to any declarations of love made in the passionate heat of the moment," he said lightly. But his deep frown and the hard glitter in his eyes belied his casual air.

"Good. Because I couldn't possibly be in love with you. I hardly know you, Matthew."

"You don't have to keep explaining. I understand."

"I'm glad. Because I would hate for you to think that I—"

"Hannah, kindly shut up."

She slanted him a sultry, challenging glance. She was desperate, shivering with frustration and reluctant but raging need. "Maybe I feel like talking."

"Well, I definitely don't feel like listening." His mouth came down on hers, fierce and hard and demanding.

Nine

Instantly, Hannah raised her arms and linked them around his neck, arching herself into him as he kissed her, then kissing him back with a hot, wild urgency of her own.

His warm weight pinned her to the mattress; her breasts were nestled snugly against the hard plane of his chest. He pressed his thigh higher and harder against her, until she was straddling him. As he increased the rhythmic pressure, a sensuous, syrupy warmth suffused her.

"I owe you more than an apology, sweet baby." He slipped his hands under her tank top and caressed her through the cotton of her sports bra. "I owe you pleasure. A lot of pleasure. And I intend to deliver."

His words and the smoky sensuality in his eyes made Hannah quiver. And then his mouth took hers again, gently this time, his tongue teasing her, slipping between her teeth to taste her, then drawing back. She opened her mouth wider, to deepen the kiss, inviting the strong, full thrust of his tongue. Still he kept on teasing her until she was so desperate to have him that she slid her own tongue past his and kissed him hungrily, deeply, the way she wanted him to kiss her.

Matthew gave a low growl and took control, his mouth rough with passion as he kissed her so intimately and intoxicatingly that Hannah sighed and surrendered completely to his mastery.

He unclasped her bra and fondled the warm, bare flesh that spilled into his palms. His hands were exquisitely gentle at first, caressing her, tantalizing her until her nipples were tingling and taut, sensual proof of her heightened arousal.

His mouth brushed her breast lightly, tasting her skin, and she arched against him in a silent plea for more. She shuddered with pleasure as his tongue and teeth played first with one nipple, then the other.

While his mouth pleasured her, his hands were busy, too. He slid his fingers beneath the waistband of her shorts, beneath her high-cut cotton panties to cup her bare buttocks and settle her precisely where he wanted her, against the full thickness of his masculine arousal. His hips rocked her in slow, seductive circles. Hannah moaned as her body succumbed to the age-old erotic rhythm.

The fire between her legs grew and spread. He withdrew one hand to stroke the smooth length of her thigh, then extended the caress to her hip, her belly and back again. He lifted her leg over his hip, gliding his hand along her inner thigh, lightly kneading its silky softness. But he didn't touch the hot, melting core of her that throbbed and ached until she whimpered a soft plea.

"Is this what you want, sweet?" His fingers slipped between her legs, probing the hot wetness there.

"Please, Matthew." She could barely speak as his deft caresses made her arch and writhe against his hand.

"Yes, baby, I'll take care of you. I promise I'll please you."

He kissed her again, his tongue moving in her mouth with the same shatteringly intimate strokes of his fingers deep inside her. Hannah completely gave herself up his kiss, just as she surrendered to the sensual magic of his hand.

He seemed to know exactly what she wanted and how to make her want more. Higher and higher she soared, until the pleasure was so intense that the spiraling coil of tension deep within her suddenly unwound and exploded into a vibrant frenzy of release.

She loved it. Hannah caught her breath on a sob as the waves of ecstasy pulsed through her. She dug her fingers into his back and clung to him while the rapture slowly subsided, leaving her limp and weak and radiant in the warm afterglow.

He held her, stroking her hair, occasionally kissing her forehead, her cheek, until she opened her eyes.

He was watching her. Hannah blushed under the intense scrutiny of his gaze. She tried to think of something to say but she couldn't find her voice.

Matthew kissed her lips lingeringly, then disengaged himself from her to sit up. Lying flat on her back, too replete to move, Hannah watched him put the birth certificate, which had been pushed aside, into his jacket pocket. Then he removed the jacket and began to unloosen his tie.

Hannah was so sated, so languorous, that it took a few moments for his actions to fully register. He'd already taken off his jacket and tie and unbuttoned his shirt when it finally dawned on her.

He was getting undressed!

Hannah sat up. "Matthew?"

He shrugged out of his shirt and unbuckled his belt. "What is it, baby?" His fingers moved to the zipper of his gray trousers.

"Matthew, stop!"

He paused and looked at her, his black eyes glittering fiercely, possessively. Hannah's eyes darted to the thick bulge straining against that unzipped fly. His whole body was hot with passion, while her own had been deliciously satisfied.

A few moments ago, her mind had been fuzzy from the urgency of desire. Now she was thinking clearly. Very clearly.

"Matthew, no." She scrambled off the bed. "We can't."

He stared at her, his eyes glazed. "What?"

His voice was thick, his thought processes muddled. He felt as if he were becoming unglued. Never had he known such ferocious desire, not even last night, which had been the pinnacle until this moment.

His eyes swept over Hannah. He thought of her passionate response to him a few moments ago when she had cried out with ecstasy. He had given her much pleasure, just as he'd promised, and he wanted to give her more. And to share it with her this time.

"Matthew, we—we can't do this. My parents and Bay might come home, and my grandmother is—"

"You're right, you're right," Matthew agreed, pulling on his shirt. He didn't bother to button it. "We can't stay here." He draped his tie around his neck, and it hung there loose and unknotted as he grabbed his suit jacket and stood. "Come on, sweetie, let's go."

"Go where?"

"For a little ride." His smile was sexy and inviting. "My van is parked out front."

"Your van," Hannah repeated. With the big air mattress in the back. She was appalled by how much she wanted to go with him in that van, park in some secluded spot and then climb into the back and onto that air mattress with him.

She braced herself against the insidious melting desire that was already beginning to build within her as she gazed at him. His open shirt revealed the mat of wiry dark hair, and a body taut and strong. She raised her eyes and they focused compulsively on the firm, sensual lines of his lips.

A convulsive little shudder rippled through her as she remembered the moist warmth of his mouth on her breasts. If she went with him, he would do that to her again. And much more. He would touch her intimately with his strong, clever fingers....

Hannah gulped. Just saying no was not as easy as it was purported to be. But she persevered. "No, Matthew, I can't."

Matthew caught her arm. "I think I understand," he said huskily. "Last night wasn't all that great for you and you're in no hurry to experience that sort of...discomfort again." He began to stroke a path along her inner arm.

The sensuous motion of his fingers reminded her of the arousing patterns he'd traced on her inner thighs. Hannah shivered.

"Don't be afraid, baby. I won't hurt you," he soothed. "I promise that this time it will be what you—"

"Matthew, last night was an aberration. I was acting completely out of character when I went to your room and... and..."

"Made love with me," Matthew finished for her.

"We had sex, Matthew," Hannah countered flatly. "Love had nothing to do with it."

"Semantics," Matthew snapped. His grip on her arm tightened. "If I felt like playing word games, I'd be back at the boardinghouse with the Porter sisters and their Scrabble board.''

An unholy combination of frustration and fury surged through him. He hating hearing her dismiss last night as nothing but a sexual romp. It had been much more than that. His senses, numbed for so long, had come alive again. He'd experienced emotions and sensations he had never encountered before. He wanted it all again; he wanted her again. Over and over.

But she was telling him no.

"Is this your idea of revenge?" he demanded roughly. "I didn't satisfy you last night and tonight you're paying me back for it? Sending me away while I'm so hot and hard I can hardly stand?"

"That's a pretty good plan. Too bad I didn't come up with it myself." Hannah pulled her arm free. "But the truth is, I'm not punishing you, Matthew. I'm trying to do the right thing, and having sex with you tonight in your van doesn't strike me as right."

"But you want me!" His voice rose. "And I want you." His voice softened and turned cajoling. "It doesn't get any more right than that, baby. Hannah, sweetheart, we need each other."

"You're suggesting that we have sex because it's a physical urge that we should assuage? Kind of like scratching an itch? Or taking a drink of water to quench your thirst?"

Matthew did not like the turn this conversation had taken. "You don't have to make it sound so damned prosaic," he muttered.

"But that's all it is to you. And it isn't enough for me, Matthew. It never has been." She smiled wistfully. "What did you expect from a woman who's been engaged three times but still wanted to wait until—"

Matthew panicked. "I want you desperately, Hannah, but I won't marry you to get you into bed again!"

"Who asked you to?" Hannah was indignant. "Not that I'd marry you, even if you begged me."

"I wouldn't have to beg. If I even hinted at a proposal, we'd be engaged tonight."

"Your imagination is working overtime for you to come up with that bit of fiction!" Hannah flared. "Oh, no, Matthew, I absolutely will *not* put myself and my family through a fourth broken engagement."

"Baby, if you were engaged to me, you wouldn't dream of breaking it off. Because we wouldn't have one of those insipid, sexless, failed arrangements that you called an engagement. We'd have the real thing."

Hannah shivered a little with excitement. Being engaged to Matthew would be very different indeed from her previous engagements. Nothing involving Matthew would ever be insipid or sexless. That indescribable sense of rightness that she had felt the night they'd made love suffused her, and she gazed longingly at him. He was the right man for her but he hadn't realized it yet. Would he ever?

He began to button his shirt, though he left his tie undone.

Hannah watched as he donned his suit coat. "I guess you're leaving?" *She didn't want him to go!*

"I guess I am. And I'm leaving alone, apparently. Unless you've changed your mind?"

She shook her head. "I just can't, Matthew."

"You mean you won't." He opened the bedroom door and started down the hall.

Hannah followed, scurrying to catch up and walked alongside him. He gave her a questioning glance. "I'll see you to the door," she explained.

"The old family retainer has retired for the night?"

"The Farleys don't have an old family retainer. It's *your* kinfolk, the Wyndhams, who do," she noted. "Remember that nice old butler who let us into the mansion today? He's been with the Wyndhams forever."

"Don't call them my kinfolk."

"Why not? They are. You claimed the Polks. Why not the Wyndhams?"

They stood before the wide front door in the vestibule. "I don't plan to publicly claim either," Matthew grated through his teeth. "I'm not going to violate Alexandra's privacy. Aside from Alexandra, Justine and me, nobody knows the truth but you and your grandmother. I know I can trust her, but so far your track record with my secrets isn't too good."

Hannah flushed, remembering how she'd identified him as Galen Eden to Emma Wynn. "I shouldn't have told Emma. I promise I won't say a word to anybody about anything else. I swear I won't, Matthew."

"I'm holding you to that, little girl."

They stood staring at each other as the silence grew and stretched awkwardly between them.

"I guess I'll go check on my grandmother," Hannah said at last.

He wasn't going to make a move on her, Matthew vowed to himself. He wouldn't kiss her, wouldn't touch her. She was expecting him to, he could tell. But since she'd set herself up as the sex police, she was going to have to live by her own rules. If she wanted him around, she was going to have to do the pursuing. He'd done enough chasing after her. So far, he had exerted more effort trying to win her favor than he'd ever expended on any other woman. And to what avail? To be sent away, his insides tied in knots!

Oh, yes, the next move must definitely be hers.

Hannah inched closer to him. Didn't he know that a goodnight kiss was perfectly acceptable? She was standing so close to him that their bodies were almost touching. A thin piece of paper could barely be slipped between them. She tilted her head and raised her face invitingly. Her body language was unmistakable. *Surely he would kiss her now!*

He didn't. "Maybe I'll see you around Clover, little girl," he called over his shoulder as he strode from the house.

Hannah quickly closed the door. From the small hallway window, she watched him walk to the van and climb inside. She stood staring at the darkness outside long after the taillights of Matthew's van had disappeared from view.

Business was slow. The temperature had soared into the nineties, the air-conditioning in Yesterdays was not working to full capacity, and when she'd called for a repairman, Hannah had been told that no one could come to her shop until they'd finished maintenance work on all the individual units at the Clover Street Hotel. That could take days.

Hannah closed the shop early, shortly after four. No one seemed to want to browse in an antique shop in this heat. With the air-conditioning malfunctioning, it was like being trapped in a stifling old attic. She sat in a booth at Peg's Diner and sipped a tall glass of iced tea while trying to regain and maintain her composure. It wasn't easy. She hadn't seen or heard from Matthew in nearly a week. Every time the phone rang at home, she reached to answer it, but it was never Matthew on the line. Every time the door opened in Yesterdays, she looked up, her heart racing, but it was never Matthew who entered the shop.

She'd refused to have sex with him and he'd stayed away, re-affirming the wisdom of her decision. But feeling wise was little consolation for this misery, caused by his rejection.

Katie came over to the booth. "You look blue," she said quietly.

"I'm fine," Hannah insisted. "Just wilted from the heat."

Katie slid into the booth across from Hannah. There were only a few customers in the diner, and all were in the capable hands of Aunt Peg and the waitress. "Abby called this morning. Ben is out of town, and she wanted to know if you and I would like to go to the movies with her tonight."

"Going to the movies with the girls on Friday night," Hannah said glumly. She abandoned her pretense that nothing was wrong. Why pretend with Katie? "Just like in the sixth grade. Maybe we can go to the Sweet Shoppe for ice cream after the show. Goody."

Katie hid a smile. "Does that mean you don't want to come with Abby and me?"

"I'll come." Hannah sighed. "It'll be better than dating myself, which I've been doing all week."

"Dating yourself?" Katie was amused. "Does that mean you're spending evenings alone?"

Hannah nodded morosely. "My grandmother currently has a livelier social life than I do. She's been out almost every night this week."

"The Porter sisters, who are in their seventies, certainly have a busier social life than me, too," Katie commiserated. "Of course, most of my tenants do."

"Including your tenant, Matthew Granger?" Hannah hated herself for asking about him but the words slipped out before she could stop herself. "That is, if he's still in town." She tried to sound insouciant but her heart clenched at the thought that he might've left Clover forever, that she would never see him again. It was a grim possibility that had haunted her all week long.

"Matthew is still in room 206," Katie said. "I think he's dating his laptop computer. He spends all evening up in his room, and his light is still on when I go to bed. I wonder if he's working on a new novel."

Hannah sat up straight and stiff. "Who cares?"

Katie cast her a curious glance, but she was too tactful to subject her downcast friend to a barrage of questions about her seemingly broken romance. "I read one of his books," she said instead. "It was very good. I'm looking forward to reading the others."

"I haven't read anything he's written." Hannah glowered mutinously at the tabletop. "I hate to waste my time reading hack writers. Uh-oh!" Her eyes widened and she began to compulsively stir her iced tea. "It's the hack himself. Katie, pretend we're having a conversation!"

"That shouldn't be too hard to do," Katie said dryly. "I take it he's headed this way?"

Hannah nodded and conjured up a merry peal of laughter. She had completely switched from the gloomy specter she'd been only moments before into the vivacious and vibrant young woman who was admired by the whole town. Katie stared at her, somewhat awed by the instant transformation.

"And then I told Sean that he has to go to the Strawberry Festival. He simply can't miss it," Hannah was saying to Katie when Matthew slipped into the booth beside her. At first, Hannah appeared not to notice that he was sitting next to her, then she turned to face him coolly. "This happens to be a private conversation."

"About the Strawberry Festival?" Matthew grinned. "I hear it's going to be struck by a blizzard this year."

Katie looked puzzled. Hannah blushed scarlet. His blatant reference to their little joke on the night she had gone to his room with him, that momentous night when she had made love for the first time in her life, caught her completely off guard. He was very good at that, she thought crossly. Showing up when he was least expected and throwing her into a confusing conundrum.

"The acclaimed Clover Strawberry Festival is being held this Sunday, right?" Matthew said, an unholy gleam in his dark eyes. "Everybody in town says it's an event not to be missed. Will you go with me, Hannah?"

"No," Hannah replied coldly.

"What about tomorrow night?" he persisted. "Dinner at the restaurant of your choice?"

"No, thank you," Hannah said in the same glacial tones.

"How about tonight then?" He encircled her wrist with his fingers.

"I'm busy," she snapped.

"Abby and I will understand if you'd rather go out with Matthew tonight, Hannah," Katie offered quickly.

Matthew laughed.

Hannah restrained herself from kicking Katie under the table and settled for yanking her wrist from Matthew's grasp. "I'm not about to change my plans and dump my friends simply because a man shows up at the last minute," Hannah said loftily, glaring at Matthew.

He was undaunted. "Not *a* man, baby. *The* man."

"You're arrogant enough to actually believe that, aren't you?" Hannah seethed. She turned her full attention to Katie. "What time is the movie tonight, Katie? Do you want me to drive? I can pick Abby up first and then—"

"If there's a group going to the movies tonight, I'd like to come, too," Matthew interjected, also addressing Katie. "Is it all right with you if I invite myself along, Katie? I hope you don't have any ironclad rules about the tenants not socializing with the landlady?"

"Not a single one," Katie replied, her green eyes sparkling with laughter. "Abby said she would be glad to drive tonight, Hannah. She can pick up, uh, Matthew and me and then come out for you."

"I hope you don't intend to change your plans and dump your friends simply because a man is included at the last minute, Hannah," Matthew taunted.

Hannah drank the rest of her tea in one long swallow. "I wouldn't dream of it," she grated through her teeth.

Hannah was not surprised to be consigned to the back seat of Abby's car with Matthew. She'd expected it. Unfortunately, it was a compact car, and the two of them were crowded together in the minuscule back seat, their bodies touching because there wasn't enough space for them to sit far apart.

Abby played her CD at full volume and chatted with Katie in the front. For a few long minutes, silence reigned in the back. Hannah was the first to break it. She'd overreacted to Matthew's presence in the diner this afternoon, she decided, and sitting here in sulky silence, pretending she wasn't plastered up against him seemed ridiculous. He didn't seem to mind at all. In fact, he was wearing a pleased little smile that set her teeth on edge.

How best to annoy him? Hannah considered the ways. Her chatty socialite airhead persona seemed a surefire hit, and she launched into it, watching gleefully as his jaw tightened and his smile grew more forced and finally disappeared altogether. By the time they reached the movie theater, *he* was the one sitting in sulky silence.

There was a line at the ticket booth, and Hannah and Matthew stood in it together. Somehow they'd become separated from Abby and Katie, who were a few feet ahead of them.

"Will you kindly drop your Scarlett-O'Hara-on-acid routine?" he said at last, scowling at her. "It's migraine inducing."

"You're not having a good time?" Hannah smiled with satisfaction. "Ahh, too bad. But you're the one who muscled in on our Girls' Night Out."

"How else was I supposed to see you?" he growled. "You shot down everything else I suggested for the entire weekend."

She gaped at him. "Did you actually expect me to jump at the chance to go out with you just because you deigned to speak to me at the diner today? After not hearing a word from you for an entire week?"

The moment she uttered it, Hannah regretted her impulsive outburst. The vacuous flirt she was trying to play would never care so much.

"The phone works both ways, Hannah. You didn't call me either."

She laughed in disbelief. "You actually expected *me* to call *you?*"

"Well, yes, if you wanted to talk to me. Why not?"

Hannah held her head high. "I don't call men, they call me. And I especially don't call men who storm out of my house in a fit because I won't hop into the back of a van for a one-night stand!"

"Who said it would be only a one-night stand?" Matthew demanded testily.

"It was a natural assumption. You never gave me a reason to believe it would be anything more," Hannah fired back. "For all I knew, you intended to go back to Florida the next day.

You've never said how long you were planning to stay in Clover."

"That's because I don't know." His voice rose. "I still don't. I'll leave when I leave."

They both became aware that the people in line around them were listening avidly and making no pretense to hide it. Hannah blushed and lapsed into silence. Inevitably, somebody would report this conversation to Jeannie Potts at the Beauty Boutique. By tomorrow night, it would be all over town.

"Could we skip this movie and go someplace to talk?" Matthew growled. "I realize that the concept of privacy doesn't exist in Clover, but I don't care to conduct my personal life in front of a live audience."

"Well . . ." Hannah considered it.

"We're leaving!" Matthew grabbed her hand and pulled her out of the line. "Katie, Abby, later!" he called to the two friends, who watched him drag Hannah off, their faces wreathed in knowing smiles.

They walked to the beach, not touching or talking. They both took off their shoes and left them on the wooden steps leading to the beach, then walked barefoot through the warm, dry sand to the ocean's edge. Water lapped over their feet, and the wet sand oozed between their toes. The moon lit a brilliant pathway across the boundless expanse of ocean, which rippled with whitecaps.

"I met some of Jesse's family," Matthew said at last.

Hannah stopped and stared up at him. A gentle wave swirled around her ankles, then retreated out to sea. "Did you tell them who you were?"

He shook his head. "I told them I was researching a book on Vietnam vets and that I had heard of Jesse's death and the medal he'd won. I was directed to one of his nieces, Sharolyn Polk. She's about your age. Ever heard of her?"

Hannah shook her head. She'd gone to school with some of the Polks but couldn't remember their first names, if she'd ever known them at all.

"According to Sharolyn, Jesse's mother moved away from Clover and now lives in California. Nobody knows where his father is—he left town years ago and never bothered to keep in touch. Jesse's younger brother was killed in a motorcycle accident a few years after Jesse's death. His sister, Sharolyn's mother, died in a house fire eight years ago."

"How tragic! Jesse and his sister and brother all died violently and prematurely."

"Not an uncommon way for a Polk to go, apparently," Matthew said wryly. "According to Sharolyn, she and her sister are Jesse's only nieces and the closest next of kin left in Clover. They each have three kids apiece." He shrugged. "I ran into them. It seems a shame..." His voice trailed off. He started walking again, shoving his hands deep inside his pockets. "I saw the way they live, down there in 'Polkville,' and I appreciated the way I'd been raised and the people who raised me even more."

Hannah wasn't sure how to reply so she said nothing at all. They walked along the beach in a silence that grew less tense and more companionable.

"Sharolyn gave me Jesse's Silver Star," Matthew said after a while. "I guess I seemed so interested in it, that she offered it to me. 'For the book,' she said. I offered to pay her for it and she wouldn't take any money. She could've demanded any sum and I would've paid it, just to have something of my father's," he added.

Hannah's eyes misted. "She doesn't sound so bad, Matthew."

"She's not. She and her sister have had a tough life. Both are divorced from bums who rarely come across with child support. I'm going to give them money regularly, Hannah. They're my father's nieces and they need it to raise their kids."

"Are you going to tell them who you really are? That you're their cousin?"

"Maybe, someday. As for now, I'll concoct some tale about a fund for the nearest relatives of decorated Vietnam vets and let them believe the money is coming from there."

Hannah smiled. "Your undercover stories are becoming much better, certainly more believable than that first one of yours."

"It seems I've recovered from my imagination impairment."

"I should hope so. Researching the area's bugs for a textbook? That was truly pathetic."

"You won't let me forget that one, will you?" He reached out and hooked his arm around her waist, yanking her to his side. "Well, there are a few things I'm not going to let you forget, either. Such as this."

He pulled her into his arms and took her mouth with his. Her lips parted on impact and his tongue slipped between them into the moist warmth of her mouth, stroking in suggestive simulation.

She'd fought all week to keep her newly awakened needs at bay, but the feel of Matthew's body against hers and the hard possession of his mouth sent all the suppressed wild hunger sweeping hotly through her.

They clung together, kissing deeply, making up for all the time they'd been apart. Hannah moved sinuously in his arms, trying to get even closer, wanting more of him, all of him. She whimpered his name when his mouth left hers to nibble along the curve of her neck.

Her sweet sounds and yielding softness plunged Matthew deeper into sensual chaos. "I want you, baby," he whispered huskily. His hand closed possessively over her breast. It was round and firm and fit his hand perfectly. The nipple was peaked and hard against his palm. Matthew sucked in his breath. "Hannah, I've missed you so."

"No, you haven't," Hannah said sadly. "With you, it's out of sight, out of mind. If I hadn't been sitting in the booth when you came into the diner today, we wouldn't be here right now. You haven't given me a thought all week."

"Now that's where you're wrong," Matthew heaved a sigh and abruptly, unexpectedly, dropped his arms, releasing her. "I've been wanting and waiting to be with you all week long. The truth is that I can't stop thinking about you, Hannah. Every day, every night, I've wanted you with me."

Hannah folded her arms across her chest. "I was just a phone call away, Matthew."

"I was determined that the next move had to be yours. Of course, when I saw you in the diner this afternoon, that pledge was shot to hell. I came racing over and practically begged to tag along with you and your friends tonight." He did not look pleased.

"It didn't have to reach that point. If you'd have called me, we—"

"I hate wasting time talking on the phone." Matthew grimaced. "It's a necessary evil in business, I suppose, but otherwise . . ." He shrugged. "I don't call women. They call me if they want to keep in touch. That's the way it's always been."

"You've been very spoiled," Hannah said, frowning her disapproval. "And now we're at an impasse because I won't chase after a man who only wants me for sex."

"Would you chase after me if I wanted more than sex with you?"

"No. The man should pursue the woman. I learned that at my grandmother's knee."

"The man should pursue the woman until she traps him," Matthew amended. "I believe the term for that convoluted process is courtship. Is that what you want, Hannah? An old-fashioned courtship?"

"You make it sound as appealing as a case of the flu. Courtship is supposed to be fun and exciting."

"Well, I suppose that courting you would be infinitely preferable to being engaged to you. You probably treat your prospective suitors better than you treat your hapless fiancés. You certainly couldn't treat them any worse."

"You'll never know because you're too chicken to even try to court me!" She turned and started walking up the beach.

A gust of wind whipped the short skirt of her dress high around her thighs. Matthew gazed at her shapely bare legs and the enticing flash of snowy white bikini panties. He watched her push her skirt down and attempt to keep it there, battling the wind as she walked.

He had no doubt that she would keep on walking and that she would stay away from him. She wouldn't call him or arrange accidental meetings to see him. If he let her go, she would be gone. She'd proven her resolve this week, while he'd been waiting for her to weaken and come to him. She hadn't, and he had been lonely and frustrated, wanting to be with her.

Hannah believed that he wanted her only for sex. She couldn't have been more wrong. Of course he wanted her, but when he thought of her—which was constantly—sexual images were interspersed with so many others.

He liked being alone with her; he liked being in a crowd with her. She was good company—stimulating, funny and maddening by turn but always captivating. He could talk to her in a way he'd never been able to talk to a woman before.

And so much had occurred this past week to talk about. There were so many things he wanted to tell her. About his cousin, Sharolyn Polk, and her memories of her uncle Jesse, his birth father. About the lunches he'd had with Alexandra and

Justine at the Wyndham estate, strange and stilted encounters, initiated by Alexandra herself. He also hadn't told her that he had started his new book about the society-boy serial killer, and that it was going very well indeed.

He owed his creative resurgence to Hannah, Matthew acknowledged. It wasn't until they'd met that he'd been able to break free from the grip of angry desolation. What writer could afford to let his own personal muse slip away from him?

Feeling governed by some primal force far stronger than him, Matthew broke into a run. Moments later, he reached Hannah's side. "Nobody has ever called me chicken before." He caught her hand in his. She didn't pull it away but she didn't clasp her fingers around his in a mutual grasp, either. "I'm taking it as a challenge—which you intended it to be, of course."

"I intended it as an insult," Hannah stated coolly.

Matthew laughed. "You give as good as you get, don't you?"

"Always."

"Are you brave enough to take me on as a suitor?" His dark eyes glittered in the moonlight. "I won't be one of those saps who lets you walk all over him. If you think you can control me, think again, little girl."

"You're doing a terrible job of marketing yourself, Matthew," Hannah observed tartly. "You should be trying to convince me how very much I need you in my life, not how difficult you'll be once you're there."

"I defer to you when it comes to selling anything, angel face. You're the expert in convincing people that they simply must have something they never knew they wanted in the first place."

"So you're saying it's up to me to convince you that you simply must have me—on my terms and permanently."

"If you succeed, it'll be the sale of the century, babe."

"Does this mean you plan to stay in Clover for a while?"

"I guess it does."

"For how long?"

"Maybe that depends on you. Do you intend to make me want to stay?"

She nodded her head. "Yes."

"Why?"

Hannah experienced a rush of euphoria so heady that she felt momentarily breathless. And dizzy with delight. "As it happens, I don't want a sap who'll let me walk all over him. I want a man to want me enough that he won't let himself be pressured into some kind of insipid, sexless arrangement. And I don't want to control a man any more than I want a man to control me."

"Is that so?" He put his arms around her and pulled her close. "Then let's get started right now. Will you come to my room with me tonight?"

She stood on tiptoe and raised her lips to kiss him lightly. "No. We haven't known each other long enough, Matthew."

He brushed her lips with his. "We've already been lovers, Hannah. We know each other very well. Why go backward?"

"Because we took things way too fast, physically. Now we have to catch up on an emotional level."

"Who made up this timetable anyway?" grumbled Matthew. His hands smoothed over her back and cupped her buttocks through the soft material of her dress.

Hannah gulped for breath as a fierce stab of desire pierced her. It would be so easy to go back to his room, to lie down on his bed with him. Was she making a mistake, asking him to wait?

"Do you still want to catch that movie tonight?" he asked, nuzzling her. "There's a later show at ten o'clock."

Hannah trembled. He was willing to wait for her. Her heart seemed to swell. "I'd like to see the movie tonight, Matthew," she said softly.

"And then I'll drive you home."

"But we won't park and make use of that air mattress in the back of the van." She clung to him, savoring his male strength and warmth. "A first date ends with a good-night kiss at my front door."

"Once I get you into that van, you'll find yourself in a wrestling match, honey. I guarantee it."

"That'll be fun. Because I know you would never do anything to hurt me. Or make me do anything I don't want to do."

"I think I hate courtship already." Matthew abruptly scooped her up and walked through the shallow water, carrying her in his arms.

"I think we're off to a wonderful start, Matthew." Hannah linked her arms around his neck, snuggling against him. "And yes, I will go to dinner with you tomorrow and I'll go to the Strawberry Festival with you on Sunday."

"I'm invited to dinner with Alexandra and Justine on Monday night. Are you brave enough to face that ordeal, little girl?"

"I wouldn't miss it for the world. Do you want to come to an estate auction with me on Tuesday? My part-time assistant will run Yesterdays for me while I'm gone."

"An estate auction, huh? Normally I'd avoid that sort of thing but maybe I'll let you talk me into it."

"How gracious of you!" Her gray eyes were shining with humor and happiness. "I plan to leave around seven Tuesday morning. It's a two-hour drive to get there."

"I'll pick you up. The van will be useful in transporting the junk you'll buy—I mean, the antiques and collectibles," he corrected himself, grinning.

"You'll have to remove your air mattress to fit everything in," she warned.

"Don't worry. I'll put it back after the trip. On Wednesday, we'll be parked in the woods, and the air mattress will be very useful indeed."

"On Wednesdays I take my grandmother out to dinner and we play cards when we get home. We have a weekly date. Grandmother is a genuine card shark and she beats me at every game, no matter what it is. Do you want to join us?"

"What are you offering as an incentive?"

Hannah smiled a sultry, provocative smile. "The chance to get to know me better."

"I'm going to know you very, very well, Hannah Kaye. Count on it." His voice and his gaze were filled with promise and intent.

Hannah sighed with longing and anticipation. "I will," she whispered.

Ten

Hannah was delighted to see both Katie and Emma in the Beauty Boutique. It was a hot and sunny Thursday afternoon, and business had slowed to a crawl following the Fourth of July holiday weekend. All three young Clover businesswomen had taken advantage of the lull, and thus their rendezvous at the beauty parlor.

Katie was being shampooed while Jeannie Potts trimmed Emma's short, wavy dark hair. Hannah flitted from chair to chair, chatting with everybody while awaiting her turn with Jeannie.

"I have an interesting bit of news for you, Jeannie," Hannah teased brightly. "Sean Fitzgerald came into the shop this morning looking for a birthday gift for his mother, and he told me that Blaine Spencer was in Fitzgerald's Bar and Grill last night with Susan."

"Susan?" Emma echoed. "I thought Blaine and Judy were getting serious."

"So did Judy!" Jeannie's eyes held an eager glint. "I already heard about Susan's date with that cute Dr. Spencer. Judy did, too. She isn't happy about it, I can tell you that.

But Dr. Spencer just isn't ready to settle down with one woman yet."

"I should've known I couldn't outscoop you, Jeannie." Hannah pretended to be disappointed. "Nobody can."

"True," agreed Jeannie. "But while Sean was gossiping about Blaine and Susan, I bet he didn't say a word about his cousin's secret fling with her old flame. Hmm, maybe he doesn't know. It's still very much a secret." She didn't bother to reveal how she happened to know this deep dark secret. Jeannie's sources were as plentiful as they were impeccable.

"Which cousin?" Hannah asked. "There are lots of Fitzgeralds, Jeannie."

"I'm talking about a certain edgy redhead whose biological clock is ticking so loud she might end up mating with a male disaster zone," Jeannie confided.

There was only one red-haired Fitzgerald in the clan. "Maureen?" Hannah guessed.

"Of course Maureen," affirmed Jeannie. "Remember how crazy she was about that rat, Preston Sedgwick, from Charleston a few years back? He sweet-talked her into bed on their first date and they practically spent the rest of the year there. She was sure they'd get married but he went back to Charleston and took up with some society belle. Married her, too. Maureen was devastated," Jeannie added dramatically.

"Don't tell me that Maureen is seeing Preston Sedgwick again?" exclaimed Hannah. She did remember Maureen's unfortunate fling, now that Jeannie had refreshed her memory. To be sure, she didn't recall the details as well as Jeannie, but few ever did.

"I'm telling you exactly that, hon," Jeannie said firmly.

Her hair dripping wet and a towel draped around her shoulders, Katie left the shampoo chair and came to sit next to Emma. "What are you telling exactly, Jeannie?" Katie asked, smiling.

"Maureen is back in bed with that snake, Preston Sedgwick," Jeannie announced. She shook her head disapprovingly. "Apparently he's separated from his wife and looking for a little something on the side. Poor Maureen! It's the Smart Women, Stupid Choices Syndrome, you know."

"Sounds like a talk show in the making," Katie observed.

"Exactly," Jeannie agreed. "Maureen should watch them. You learn a lot."

"Why would Maureen want to take up with someone who treated her so badly in the past?" Hannah mused aloud.

"I've heard it said that no flame burns hotter than an old flame," Jeannie said, sighing.

Hannah laughed at that. "I think it's closer to the truth to say that no flame is as cold and dead as an old flame."

Katie was staring down at her nails, studying them with great care. "Do you think I should have a manicure today, Jeannie?" she asked suddenly.

Jeannie glanced at her nails. "Definitely, hon." Then she immediately resumed the debate. "We'll have to discount Hannah's theory on the old flame because she has such a hot *new* flame! What's up with that superhot, supercool Matt Granger, Han?"

Hannah's cheeks reddened. She didn't want to discuss Matthew here. Their relationship was too intense and too private for her to speak casually of him, especially to Jeannie, the Voice of Clover.

But when Jeannie asked a question, it was wise to provide an answer.

"He's been in Pensacola for a few days," Hannah said. "He had some personal business to take care of there." Matthew hadn't gone into detail, and she hadn't pressed him. She knew if he wanted her to know, he would tell her in his own good time.

"You must miss him like crazy!" Jeannie exclaimed. "You two have been practically inseparable since he dragged you out of that movie line and the two of you headed to the beach."

Sweet exciting memories floated through her mind. Matthew had been courting her, as she'd challenged him to do. And just as Jeannie had said, they'd been inseparable, together every day... except for the few days when Matthew had returned to Pensacola.

She missed him so much! The few days he'd been gone seemed ten times that long.

"When is Matthew coming back from Pensacola, Hannah?" Emma asked.

"I'm not sure," Hannah replied vaguely, trying to pretend that it didn't bother her that she didn't know when he would be back. It did bother her; she'd thought of little else. Matthew had said he was unsure how long he would be gone, and he hadn't called her from Pensacola. Not that she had actually expected him to.

She was now well acquainted with Matthew's aversion to the phone. When he'd said he didn't call women, they called him, she thought he was being flippant. But she'd learned that he didn't make calls to *anyone* if he could possibly avoid it. When he received a call, he grimaced and kept the conversation short and to the point. No, Matthew would never tie up the line for hours, conducting a romance by phone.

And now that she knew, she could accept that particular quirk of his. Her lips curved into a dreamy smile. She knew him so well. And she was deeply in love with him. If only she could be sure that he loved her, too! But Matthew hadn't said the words, and she kept herself from saying them again, as well. After telling him she loved him that first and only time they'd made love, she hadn't summoned the courage to say it again.

They hadn't made love since, not for Matthew's lack of trying. But Hannah continued to hold back. She hoped they weren't at cross-purposes, with him waiting to tell her that he loved her after they made love while she waited for him to say it before.

At best, it was stupid and frustrating; at worst, he really didn't love her and had no intention of ever telling her so. After all, he still hadn't told her when he planned to leave Clover permanently. *Unless he'd already done so.* Was his alleged business trip to Pensacola a convenient way to leave her behind, without all the inconveniences of a final, messy breakup and goodbye?

A chill rippled through her. No, Matthew would never do such a thing to her, she assured herself. But an icy particle of doubt refused to melt. Maureen Fitzgerald probably hadn't believed that the nefarious Preston Sedgwick would walk out on her, either!

"Well, I hope that Matt doesn't pull a Preston Sedgwick and show up three years later, expecting to take up where he left off," Jeannie said, chortling. "Just kidding, of course, Hannah. No guy would ever dump you!"

Hannah resisted the urge to knock on wood to magically undo the possible curse Jeannie might have evoked. It was unnerving enough that Jeannie had practically voiced her own thoughts aloud, but wasn't it tempting fate to categorically state that something would never—*could* never—happen? It certainly didn't ease Hannah's anxiety to recall that she'd slept with Matthew on their first date, just like the hapless Maureen had done with dreadful Preston!

"Hannah certainly wouldn't take him back if he did," Emma piped up. "I happen to agree completely with you, Hannah. What's finished should stay finished."

"Sometimes a certain man is just too hard to forget, I guess," Jeannie speculated. "Or maybe Maureen is just desperate. She's closing in on thirty and really wants to have kids. That requires a man, unless you want to go to some lab and—"

"Jeannie, please! Not the syringe-and-petri-dish alternative again," Hannah cut in, grimacing. "Let's talk hair color. What does Alexandra Wyndham use to get that gorgeous dark shade of hers?"

"I wouldn't know." Jeannie sniffed. "Alexandra Wyndham doesn't lower herself to come into the Beauty Boutique. Oh, no, only those ritzy hair places in Charleston are good enough for her. And speaking of the Wyndhams, Hannah, is it true that Justine dumped your brother, Bay?"

"Absolutely one hundred percent correct, Jeannie," Hannah said. She didn't add that Bay was still spending an inordinate amount of time at the Wyndham mansion. With Alexandra. For the first time ever, she could probably genuinely scoop Jeannie on a tantalizing bit of gossip, but she refrained.

Anyway, Jeannie had returned to her original subject, which seemed to fascinate her—Maureen Fitzgerald's incomprehensible fling with the man who'd done her wrong. "I bet Maureen is wishing she had *your* options, Emma," Jeannie said cheerfully, tilting Emma's head forward. "Hold it right there, hon. Yeah, like that. How's that sexy Michael anyway?"

"If you mean Michael Flint, I have no idea," Emma replied crisply.

Jeannie chuckled. "Come on, Emma. Don't clam up on us. We all know that hunk of a charter-boat captain is crazy about you."

Emma seemed a bit riled by Jeannie's persistence. Hannah could relate to that. "I'm sure Emma doesn't give Michael Flint a thought," Hannah said, coming to Emma's rescue. "She's too busy concentrating on Kenneth Drake."

"The golf pro at the country club," Jeannie said flatly. She was visibly disappointed. "So you're still seeing him, Emma?"

"Since you know everything that goes on in Clover, you *know* she is, Jeannie," Hannah said succinctly.

"Yeah, I know." Jeannie frowned thoughtfully. "But I always thought Emma and Michael would make such a darling couple. And they have so much in common—Emma's daddy is a charter-boat captain. Michael is a charter-boat captain. And when it comes to hot bods, that Drake guy isn't even in the same league as Michael, who is so tanned and blond and—"

"You never told us how Preston Sedgwick happened to be back in Clover, Jeannie," Hannah cut in. It was definitely time for a change in subject. Emma looked ready to scream if Michael Flint's name was mentioned one more time. "Did he come back specifically to see Maureen? And where is he staying? With that aunt of his, like the last time?"

Hannah was certain Jeannie would know all the answers to the questions. And she did, launching into a detailed account of the infamous Preston Sedgwick's return to Clover. The touchy subject of Michael Flint was dropped. Emma cast Hannah a look of thanks, grateful for the reprieve.

When Emma's hair was cut, she gave the chair to Hannah. "If you want to wait for me and then go to the diner for some iced tea, I'll only be a few minutes," Hannah said to her. "Jeannie is cutting my hair dry, and she's only taking off one-sixteenth of an inch all around. Right, Jeannie?"

"One-sixteenth of an inch?" Jeannie rolled her eyes. "Okay, hon, you got it."

"I'll wait for you, Hannah," Emma agreed.

"I'll be with you in a sec, Hannah," promised Jeannie. "I want to soak Katie's nails while she's waiting." They watched her busily set Katie's hands in a dish for the premanicure soak. "Omigod, Katie, with all the excitement about Maureen, I can't believe I almost forgot to tell you this!" Jeannie exclaimed suddenly. She clapped her hands to her cheeks, disconcerted by her own shocking lapse. "You'll never guess what I heard yesterday."

"I probably won't guess, so you'll just have to tell me, Jeannie," Katie said, smiling at the younger woman's enthusiasm.

"Luke Cassidy has a child! A little boy!" Jeannie's voice rang out. The words fairly echoed throughout the Beauty Boutique.

Katie seemed to freeze. But just for a moment. She quickly arranged her lips in her usual placid smile and murmured, "How nice. Oh, by the way, Jeannie, I wanted to ask you about that new conditioning shampoo I saw advertised in the drugstore."

"That awful stuff?" Jeannie squawked. "Don't you dare use it on your hair! It's like shampooing with glue!"

Jeannie launched into a long diatribe about the shampoo, against which she seemed to hold a personal grudge. There was no further mention of Luke Cassidy or his child.

But Hannah hadn't forgotten Katie's stricken look at the mention of the man's name. As they were leaving the beauty parlor, she murmured quietly to Emma, "Katie used to go with Luke Cassidy, remember?"

Emma nodded a little uncertainly. "He left town, didn't he? I don't think I've ever heard Katie mention his name since."

"Me, neither. And since he has a son, that definitely means there's another woman in his life." Hannah frowned. "I wonder what happened between Katie and Luke."

"Obviously, Jeannie doesn't know or we would've all been regaled with the full story," Emma commented wryly.

"Like the Maureen and Preston Sedgwick affair," added Hannah. They walked to Peg's Diner discussing the Smart Women, Stupid Choices Syndrome. "I hope I don't suffer from it," Hannah said edgily. She waited for Emma to reassure her that she must surely be immune.

Emma offered no such assurances. She bit her lip, looking preoccupied. "I hope I don't, either."

"Gracious, Hannah, you're as jumpy as a cat," her grandmother observed as Hannah prowled the room, pausing to glance out the window, pick up a framed picture, put it back, sit down and then stand up again to resume her pacing. "Did that phone call from Justine earlier upset you, my dear?"

Hannah chewed her lower lip. Justine had called shortly before dinner to ask if Hannah had heard anything from Matthew.

"Mother and I have been trying to call him for the past two days but we keep getting his answering machine," Justine had said plaintively. "We left messages but he hasn't returned our calls. When we called him today, some woman answered the phone and said he wasn't there. But if *she* was there, why wasn't he? What's going on, Hannah?"

A woman was there. Hannah swallowed hard, remembering the sickly, ominous feeling that gripped her when Justine had uttered those words. The feeling had never left, but continued to grow stronger all through the evening. It was now nearly ten o'clock and she felt ready to explode with nervous tension. Suppose Matthew had been there all along, listening to the phone ring and dispatching his female companion to answer it? And to claim he wasn't there.

"Justine wanted to get in touch with Matthew to tell him that the results of the blood work and DNA testing are back from the lab," Hannah said, hoping to divert herself as much as her grandmother from making speculations. "The tests show a 99.9 percent likelihood that Matthew and Alexandra are mother and son. That's considered a statistical certainty, both medically and legally."

"And what does Alexandra plan to do with the information?" her grandmother asked curiously. "Publicly and legally acknowledge him as her son?"

"Justine doesn't know. A lot will depend on what Matthew wants."

"I wonder what our Baylor will think?" Lydia grinned wickedly. "He's placed Alexandra on a pedestal, and I dare say that the news she has a son by a Polk will come as a great surprise to him."

"I think he'd rather have Alexandra in his bed than on a pedestal," Hannah said bluntly. "Maybe the news will inspire him to make a move in that direction."

"The situation become curiouser and curiouser." Lydia chuckled. "Just imagine if your dear brother should also become your stepfather-in-law! Why, it's something right out of a soap opera." Her grandmother was an avid fan of daytime drama on television. And an avowed romantic.

But tonight, Hannah's usually vivid imaginative streak didn't enable her to envision such a scenario. "That's assuming I marry Matthew and Bay marries Alexandra, Grandmother. What are the chances of that happening?"

"Bay and Alex? Doubtful. You and Matthew? I would bet the house on it, child."

Her grandmother was also an optimist. Hannah's shoulders slumped. She was not feeling at all optimistic. "Matthew's been gone for five days, Grandmother, and I haven't heard a word from him since he left. His own mother and sister can't reach him, either. For all we know, he's decided to put Clover and all of us behind him. Maybe he just wants to forget all about the Wyndhams and the Polks. And me," she added, gulping back a sob.

"Well, it is remiss of him not to call, but I'm sure he'll be back soon."

Hannah remembered the blissful days when her grandmother's reassurances were all she needed to believe that everything was going to be all right. Those days were long gone.

"I bet Maureen Fitzgerald's grandmother said the same thing to her the time that Preston Sedgwick blew town for good," she muttered. Of course, Preston had returned, separated from his wife, three years later to make Maureen the number one topic of gossip in Clover. Hannah shuddered. "I think I'll take a walk, Grandmother," she said, staring out the window once more. It was a still, moonless night with flashes of heat lightning occasionally illuminating the black sky.

"That's a good idea, dear. You're quite charged with pent-up energy this evening."

Hannah slipped on a pair of sandals and headed out the front door. Her grandmother called it energy, but Hannah knew it was anxiety and tension that were driving her.

She walked away from the house along an unpaved little lane leading into the woods. Though she normally didn't walk at night, she wasn't afraid. Her thoughts were too full of Matthew and the dreadful possibility of losing him to conjure up any fear of the dark.

She'd been walking about ten minutes when she heard the sound of a car engine. Her parents or Bay were probably pulling into the driveway at home after their respective evenings out. Hannah walked on.

Not long afterward, the glare of headlights lit up the woods far more more effectively than the increasingly frequent flashes of lightning. Hannah was startled out of her reverie. There was never any traffic along the lane. It was, for all practical purposes, a private road leading nowhere.

The sound of the engine grew nearer and nearer, while the headlights grew blinding. Hannah quickly left the small road to slip behind some trees alongside it.

She watched a van pull up and stop. Matthew got out. "I know you're hiding in there somewhere, little girl," he called. "Are you going to come out or are we going to play a round of hide-and-seek?"

Hannah stepped out into the lane, her heart thudding against her ribs. Matthew was standing beside his van, wearing the black jeans and T-shirt he'd had on the first night she'd met him and mistaken him for a cat burglar.

"You're back," she said, feeling absurdly shy. She wanted to run to him but she seemed to be rooted to the spot.

"Your grandmother told me you'd taken this path. Why in the hell are you running around the woods at this hour of the night?"

"I like to walk in the woods at night," she lied. "It's... peaceful."

"It's also stupid. And it's about to rain. Get into the van."

"It's not going to—" A crack of thunder interrupted her. It was followed by several cold, fat drops of rain.

"We're about two minutes shy of a deluge," Matthew predicted. He opened the back of the van and climbed in—onto the air mattress. He sat there, grinning at Hannah like a Cheshire cat burglar.

She stood staring at him. She was thrilled Matthew was back but furious that he had simply shown up without a word, and now expected her to give him a rousing welcome home.

"I have something in here for you," Matthew said, his voice both teasing and cajoling.

She felt warm all over. "I can guess what it is."

"Don't guess. Come here and find out."

There was another flash of lightning followed by a crack of thunder and then the rain began to fall. Hannah leapt inside the van.

"It was raining on the night we met," Matthew noted, staring out at the rain cascading through the trees. "Sort of symbolic, isn't it?" He closed the heavy doors. The back of the van was shadowy, the glow of the headlights providing the only illumination.

Hannah knelt on the air mattress, watching him. The surge of desire sweeping through her shook her to the marrow of her bones. "Symbolic of what?" Her voice was tremulous.

"Never mind. I'll tell you later." His dark eyes gleamed. "We're getting ahead of ourselves. First things first. And the first thing I want is to hear you tell me how happy you are to see me. Then I want you to prove it."

It took Hannah less than a second to decide that she wanted the same thing as he did. "I'm so glad to see you, Matthew," she said breathlessly before inching closer to him on her knees. She rested her hands lightly on his shoulders and touched her lips to his.

Matthew instantly pulled her against him, his hands strong and firm, his mouth opening over hers, hot and wet and seeking. He thrust his tongue into her mouth in a possessive, erotic demonstration of what he intended to do with his body.

Hannah responded with an equally erotic and possessive demonstration of what she intended to do with hers. She opened her mouth to him, welcoming him deep inside. She felt the thickness of his arousal against her and clung to him as he lowered her back on to the air mattress.

"This is the same dress you wore that night on the beach," Matthew breathed against her neck. He slid his hands under her dress, along the firm, bare length of her thighs. "The wind blew it up and I've been fantasizing about what I saw for weeks." He hooked his fingers under the waistband of her panties. "I wanted to do this...." And he deftly pulled them off.

His mouth caught hers in another deep, hungry kiss and she responded with all the love and longing she'd kept locked inside her. "I love you, Matthew," she confessed breathlessly. "I can't pretend that I don't anymore. I don't want to. I have to tell you even if you don't...love me."

"Of course I love you." He pushed the straps of her dress from her shoulders, then lowered the bodice to her waist, exposing her breasts. "I love everything about you. Everything." He kissed her breasts and she gasped with pleasure, crying out his name.

The dress seemed to slide off her body, leaving her warm and naked in his arms, lost in a sensual dream. She dared to place her hand over his steely arousal, which strained against the button fly on his jeans. His hand covered hers and their eyes met.

"I love you, Hannah," he said, his voice soft and intense. "Don't ever doubt it."

"Not even when you go away for five days and don't call even once to tell me if you're ever coming back?" She pressed her hand against him, her fingers kneading sensuously.

Matthew groaned with pleasure. "Haven't we been through this phone call routine before?"

Hannah smiled, and her smile was elemental and frankly feminine. "Maybe after tonight, I won't have to worry about the phone call strategy. Maybe I'll feel sure enough to call you since I'm not the one with the aversion to dial tones."

"I promise that after tonight you will be absolutely sure that I am well and truly—"

She slipped her bare thigh over his jeaned one. "Don't say trapped," she whispered.

He glided his hand along her silken flesh, to the soft folds of her heated wet center. "I wouldn't dream of it. I was going to say that I am well and truly in love with you."

They kissed and caressed with an urgent frenzy. Feeling dazed and delirious with need, she watched him strip off the rest of his clothes with an almost feline grace. He lay back down with her, and moments later was sheathed deep inside her.

He filled her hard and hot, and she arched beneath him, holding him deeply, tightly within her and reveling in his possession. They were a single entity, joined in body, mind and spirit.

"I love you, Matthew," Hannah cried as their passion burned and flared to flash point. Waves of pleasure radiated from deep within, finally bursting forth in a flood tide of rapture.

"You're mine, baby," Matthew growled just before he felt himself explode in ecstasy. "Always and forever."

They lay together for a long time afterward, naked and sated and warm, listening to the rain pound against the roof of the van.

"This was better than any fantasy I've ever had," Hannah said with a contented sigh, comfortably cuddled in his arms.

Matthew kissed her temple. "I'm glad, sweetheart." He arched his dark brows. "Hopefully you won't give me such a hard time when I want to do it again."

"Not a chance. I want to do it again, too." She tilted her head upward to gaze at him. "Matthew, you do understand why I wanted us to really get to know each other before we—I mean after we—"

"Don't go getting incoherent on me, little girl." He laughed softly. "I understand." He propped himself up on one elbow. "And now, I have something for you."

Hannah touched him intimately, her gray eyes playful. "Mmm, I thought you'd already given it to me."

"Behave yourself, Miss Farley. I've been planning this scene, and I won't have you messing it up." He removed her hand from its provocative hold. Seconds later, she watched him slide a diamond ring onto the fourth finger of her left hand.

Hannah's eyes widened. She glanced from the ring to Matthew's face and back again.

"It was my mother's engagement ring—my real mother, the one who raised me," he said softly. "I know she would've loved you, too." He took a deep breath. "Will you marry me, Hannah?"

"Oh, yes! Yes, Matthew!" Tears of joy trickled down her cheeks, and she tried to wipe them away while hugging Matthew at the same time.

He was holding her as if he would never let her go, grinning with loving pride as he kissed her forehead and her cheeks before finally taking her mouth in a long, lingering kiss filled with tenderness and passion and commitment.

The emotional intensity immediately heightened their desire all over again, and they came together once more in a shattering blaze of love and urgency, binding them to each other for all time.

Much later, after they dressed and faced the prospect of spending the night in two separate beds in two separate residences, they decided they couldn't bear to spend this very special night apart.

"I'll tell grandmother to tell my parents that I'm spending the night with Katie Jones," Hannah said as he steered the van through the rainy streets of Clover. She gazed down at the ring on her finger, then over at her darkly handsome fiancé.

Matthew grinned. "Grandmother, of course, will know the truth."

"Of course. And I'll tell her we're engaged. She'll be thrilled. You know how much she likes you."

"I know. How will the rest of the family take it?"

Hannah frowned a little. "They'll probably be scared to death to place an engagement announcement in the paper. Mother will warn me that another broken engagement will result in fatal Farley humiliation and Daddy will say—"

"We'll assure them that this engagement is *not* going to be broken," Matthew said firmly.

"It most certainly isn't." Hannah reached over and laid her hand on his thigh. "Because for the first time in my life I'm madly, wildly and totally in love with my fiancé. And this time, I'm engaged for all the right reasons."

"It's about time," Matthew growled. "Your track record is enough to want to make a man rush you immediately to the altar and to hell with this engagement business."

"I'll marry you any time, any place, Matthew. If you want to elope tonight, I'll be happy to."

They braked to a stop at a traffic light, and Matthew leaned over to kiss her. "I know, sweetie. But I want you to have the big white wedding your family has always wanted to give you. I want you to have all the stuff that goes on before the wedding, with all your friends."

"I think you mean an engagement party and a bridal shower."

"That's right." The light turned green, and Matthew stepped on the accelerator. "You know, I'm not the only brave one, risking an engagement to you," he said lightly. "You're pretty damn brave yourself, willing to marry a Polk. If I ever go public with my identity, you'll be branded right along with me."

"Should you ever go public with the news, I would be proud to be known as the wife of Jesse Polk's son."

"Don't forget, you'll also be the daughter-in-law of Alexandra Wyndham," he teased.

"The first time a Farley has ever snared a Wyndham in the past three centuries." Hannah smiled. "If we ever break that news, Bay will be inconsolable!"

They both laughed.

They were holding hands and talking when Katie met them at the door of the boardinghouse. She quickly ushered them into the living room. "I heard you outside," she said. "It's nice to have you back, Matthew." Her smile broadened. "And I can tell that Hannah is glad to see you."

"Katie, look!" Hannah impulsively held out her hand to show her the engagement ring.

Katie's face lit up. "You're engaged! How wonderful!" She gave first Hannah then Matthew a quick hug. "I'm so happy for you both. I feel almost like a matchmaker," she added, "since you met here in my boardinghouse."

"Where Miss Farley promptly decided I was up to no good," Matthew reminded them.

Hannah actually giggled. "What a night that was! In the middle of Abby and Ben's engagement party, you come roaring downstairs, furious because your room was getting rained on."

"Please don't remind me." Katie groaned. "I had the roof patched, but I'm still nervous that it isn't going to hold in a bad storm." As if on cue, lightning flashed and thunder roared and the rain began to fall harder. "I guess we might find out tonight."

"Katie, there's something I'd like to ask you," Hannah said eagerly. "And I hope you'll say yes. Will you please be one of my bridesmaids? I'm not sure when the wedding will be, probably late fall but definitely before Christmas. Will you, Katie? Please!"

Saying no to Hannah Farley was something most people had difficulty doing, and Katie was no exception. "I would love to be one of your bridesmaids, Hannah," she said graciously. "Thank you for asking me."

"I'm glad we have that taken care of," Matthew said. He wrapped his arm around Hannah's shoulders. "Let's go upstairs, little girl."

"Yes, darling," Hannah murmured and squealed a little when he scooped her up into his arms and carried her up the stairs.

Katie sank onto the sofa and stared into space. A tear rolled down her cheek, and she quickly brushed it away. But another seeped out, and then another.

Moments later, Hannah ran back into the room. "Katie, I hate to be a bother but I need a few—" She spied Katie's tears and broke off in midsentence. "Katie, what's wrong?" she cried, sitting down on the sofa beside her.

"Nothing." Katie tried to smile. It was a wavering, watery effort that pierced Hannah's heart.

"Katie . . . is it Luke?" she asked instinctively.

"Luke?"

"Luke Cassidy," Hannah clarified, though she realized that Katie knew exactly whom she meant. Her friend was stalling, rebuilding her quiet wall of reserve.

"That was over a long time ago, Hannah," Katie said quietly. "I certainly would never shed tears over him at this late date. I was just feeling a little... sentimental. What with you and Abby getting married, being a bridesmaid for the both of you, I guess I was being overemotional."

Hannah gazed at her in frank disbelief but did not challenge her. "Well, if you ever want to talk about Luke—"

"I don't," Katie assured her. "I won't." She stood. "Now what was it you needed?"

Hannah named a few personal items which Katie willingly supplied. Then she hurried back upstairs to room 206. Matthew was already in bed. "Lock the door and come here," he ordered sexily.

Hannah obeyed, seating herself on the edge of the bed. "I figured out what you meant when you said it was symbolic that it was raining tonight, just like it was on the night we met."

"You're a quick study, baby. I figured you would." He began to undress her.

"You came back from Pensacola tonight and you planned to ask me to marry you."

He kissed her. "A very quick study."

Nude, she slipped under the covers with him. "Who was the woman in Pensacola who told Justine that you weren't at home?" she asked, shivering with arousal as he touched her.

"Probably the real estate agent. I put my condo on the market while I was away and got everything in gear for my permanent move to Clover. I have something else for you in my suitcase but I'll give it to you tomorrow. It's that antique baby doll of my mother's. You can keep it or sell it in your shop—"

"As if I'd ever sell your mother's doll!" Hannah scolded. "It will have a place of honor in our house, and I won't let little Eden Lydia touch it. She'll have plenty of her own baby dolls to play with."

"Who is Eden Lydia?"

"Our daughter. That's what I want to name her—Eden Lydia Granger. And our son will be Jesse Galen. You can name our third child."

"Sounds like you've been giving the matter a lot of thought, Hannah Kaye. You were pretty damn sure of me, weren't you?"

"And you were *extremely* sure of me, to put your condo on the market and make arrangements to move to Clover without even bothering to call me for five days!"

"Yeah, I guess I was. Now kiss me."

"You want to make me prove that our engagement isn't an insipid, sexless arrangement, don't you?" Her gray eyes laughed up at him.

"Every single day of the week, little girl."

* * * * *

Turn the page for a sneak preview of

The Bridal Shower

by Elizabeth August,
the next book in the
ALWAYS A BRIDESMAID! series....

One

As she descended the stairs, Emma heard voices in the kitchen. Her father was at the back door pulling on his windbreaker in preparation for leaving while seated comfortably at the kitchen table was Mike Flint. That she'd been aware of his presence before she'd even come downstairs shook her. He caught her gaze as she entered the kitchen and she found herself noticing again how handsome he was. Immediately, she shoved that thought from her mind.

Peter regarded his daughter with interest. "Glad you're up. I was just on my way out." Approaching the table, he extended a hand to Mike. "Good luck, son. You'll need it." He glanced toward Emma and with a chuckle, waved goodbye and left.

Emma groaned. "He'd better not be trying any matchmaking."

"That sounds like a woman who's afraid she might weaken."

Emma turned to glare at Mike. "Don't count on it."

Challenge flickered in his eyes. "I could have sworn I saw you at the marina last night. Could it be that you were worried about me?"

"I just felt like taking a drive," Emma lied.

He cocked an eyebrow in disbelief. "In the middle of a storm?"

Her jaw firmed. "Yes, in the middle of a storm."

For a moment, he looked as if he was going to continue to argue his point, then his expression relaxed. He nodded as if her answer was exactly what he'd expected, then he rose from his seat and came toward her.

Reaching out he traced the line of her jaw with the tips of his fingers. "Just in case that was you last night and you were there because you were worried about me, thanks for the concern. I liked having someone waiting for me."

As she'd been afraid it would, his touch sent warm currents surging through her. Shakily, she admitted that the physical attraction she felt for him was strong. Then she recalled the panic she'd felt last night when the storm had built so suddenly. This was one attraction she would not give in to. She took a step back, breaking the contact.

"I'm sure there are several unattached women in town who would happily await your return." Something that felt like a jab of jealousy pierced her, but she forced herself to ignore it.

He frowned with impatience. "I've looked around for years, Emma. But like a magnet drawn to due north, my thoughts keep coming back to you. And I'd wager you've thought about me every once in a while." His expression dared her to deny this.

He reached out and cupped her face in his hands. Challenge again flashed in his eyes as his gaze bore into her. "Through the years, I'd swear I've seen you look my way more than once."

For the moment, all she could think about was the exciting feel of his work callused palms against her skin. Then she saw his face coming closer to hers and she knew he intended to kiss her. Terrified her body would betray her, she jerked free and backed away. "I might have looked but I have no intention of touching," she said shakily.

Her confession caused the blue of his eyes to darken with triumph. "We belong together, Emma. You know that."

Emma's defenses were dangerously weakening. Again she reminded herself of the fear that had caused her to drive to the marina last night, in spite of the raging storm.

"What I know is that I find you attractive. But it's merely a physical thing," she insisted.

His gaze narrowed and he took a step toward her. When she took a step back, he stopped and his impatient frown returned.

"You are the most single-minded woman I've ever known. Be careful you don't let that stubborn streak of yours cause you to settle for less than what you truly want in life," he cautioned. Heading for the door, he added over his shoulder, "I'll be seeing you."

His warning momentarily threatened her resolve, then her shoulders squared. "Not if I see you first," she muttered as the door closed behind him.

Don't miss THE BRIDAL SHOWER
*by Elizabeth August, available in June
from Silhouette Desire®.*

SILHOUETTE Desire®

COMING NEXT MONTH

NOBODY'S CHILD Ann Major

Children of Destiny

Cutter Lord had always secretly loved his brother's wife, Cheyenne, but her loyalties had been to her husband and son. Then her husband was murdered and her child kidnapped. Now Cutter had to rescue her son; after all, he was the boy's father...

JOURNEY'S END BJ James

The Black Watch

Merrill Santiago had retreated to Ty O'Hara's isolated ranch for some peace and quiet... Instead, the beautiful agent found Ty to be the most dangerous man she'd ever met because he threatened to tear down all her defences.

HOW TO WIN (BACK) A WIFE Lass Small

Tyler Fuller still loved his ex-wife, Kayla, and, having grown tired of spending the long, cold nights alone, he vowed to win her back. But Kayla wanted to take things slow...and Tyler was amazed to discover just how good slow could be...

THE BRIDAL SHOWER Elizabeth August

Always a Bridesmaid!

When Michael Flint learned that Emma Wynn was about to marry another man, he was determined to stop her. She'd turned down his proposal before, but Michael *would* get his 'yes' this time...

LONE STAR KIND OF MAN Peggy Moreland

Wives Wanted!

Years ago, Reggie Giles had loved Cody Fipes...and begged him to run away with her. But Cody had said no and gone off to seek his fortune. Now they're both back and Cody doesn't want to let Reggie go—ever again!

ANOTHER MAN'S BABY Judith McWilliams

Ginny Alton had agreed to impersonate her cousin and travel thousands of miles with her cousin's baby. On arrival, Ginny was met by Philip Lysander who decided to pretend to be the baby's father...and Ginny's lover...

On sale from 22nd May 1998

COMING NEXT MONTH FROM

SILHOUETTE®

Sensation
A thrilling mix of passion, adventure and drama

MIND OVER MARRIAGE Rebecca Daniels
LOVING MARIAH Beverly Bird
PRIME SUSPECT Maggie Price
BADLANDS BAD BOY Maggie Shayne

Intrigue
Danger, deception and desire

ANGEL WITH AN ATTITUDE Carly Bishop
FATHER AND CHILD Rebecca York
THE EYES OF DEREK ARCHER Vickie York
STORM WARNINGS Judi Lind

Special Edition
Satisfying romances packed with emotion

ALISSA'S MIRACLE Ginna Gray
THE MYSTERIOUS STRANGER Susan Mallery
THE KNIGHT, THE WAITRESS AND THE TODDLER Arlene James
THE PRINCESS GETS ENGAGED Tracy Sinclair
THE PATERNITY TEST Pamela Toth
JUST JESSIE Lisette Belisle

On sale from 22nd May 1998

DEBBIE MACOMBER

The Playboy and the Widow

A confirmed bachelor, Cliff Howard wasn't prepared to
trade in the fast lane for car pools. Diana Collins lived life
hiding behind motherhood and determined to play it
safe. They were both adept at playing their roles.
Until the playboy met the widow...

"Debbie Macomber's stories sparkle with love and laughter..."
—*New York Times* bestselling author, Jayne Ann Krentz

1-55166-080-6
AVAILABLE NOW IN PAPERBACK

Desire™ 15th Anniversary

FREE COMPETITION

C	A	K	E	S	Y	O	J	N	E
S	H	F	R	M	U	S	I	C	N
E	R	A	U	E	Y	T	R	A	P
S	C	E	M	N	S	S	O	D	A
S	O	A	M	P	M	E	B	A	R
E	L	D	S	A	A	U	O	N	T
K	D	I	A	K	E	G	R	C	Y
A	R	G	I	F	T	R	N	E	H
C	E	L	E	B	R	A	T	E	A
C	O	C	K	T	A	I	L	S	T

GUESTS
COCKTAILS
PARTY
PARTYHAT
MUSIC
CAKES

DANCE
CELEBRATE
CHAMP...

...d your entries to...
Anniversary Competition
FREEPOST
..., Surrey CR9 3WZ

...r over.
...service not
...4546, Dublin
...companies as a
...receive such offers,

mps MAILING PREFERENCE SERVICE

*See over for details
of how to enter.*